EIGHT BALL
STARSHIP FOR SALE
BOOK 6

M.R. FORBES

Published by Quirky Algorithms
Seattle, Washington

This novel is a work of fiction and a product of the author's imagination.
Any resemblance to actual persons or events is purely coincidental.

Copyright © 2022 by Quirky Algorithms
All rights reserved.

Cover illustration by Tom Edwards
Edited by Merrylee Lanehart

CHAPTER 1

The universe, as always, remained without mercy.

I wanted to die.

I didn't get what I wanted.

Time passed. My heart rate slowed. My muscles relaxed. The adrenaline flowed to a trickle. I remained awake the entire time, aware of my surroundings. Aware of my failure. The smell of death hung heavy in the air, Gia's torn up body resting less than a dozen feet away.

I still didn't want to move. Didn't want to live. We had failed. *I* had failed, and now everyone I cared about was so much worse off for it. I had never been so completely alone. Growing up, even without a father, there had always been someone around to lean on when things got hard. Mom, Matt, my siblings. There had never been a time where there was no one else for me to turn to. Even in Sedaya's prison, Keep had appeared out of the shadows to help me.

For the first time in my life, I had no wingman. No backup. I had only myself to rely on.

Blorb's words filled my head, reaching deep to pierce my soul.

"...he'll spend however long he has left alone, with nothing to occupy his mind beyond knowing that everyone he cares about in this galaxy is suffering more than he is."

Was the Aleal right? Would I spend the last days of my life curled in a fetal position on the floor, waiting for death? He had spoken those words to mock, taunt, and dishearten me. To cut me up with verbal barbs the same way he had ripped into Gia with physical blades.

To turn me into a puddle on the floor, the way I remained even now.

"...he'll spend however long he has left alone, with nothing to occupy his mind beyond knowing that everyone he cares about in this galaxy is suffering more than he is."

The words repeated, over and over, a growing chorus of self-defeating chanting in my subconscious. Except the words couldn't destroy me unless I let them. Sedaya, Sucaath, Blorb, whoever. None of them could destroy me unless I let them. Failure didn't come from losing the battle.

Failure came from giving up. Whatever doesn't kill you makes you stronger. Right?

I opened my eyes, miserable despair beginning to evaporate beneath the fire of my growing anger. Blorb's sentiments rippled through my mind again. The words were the same. The meaning, completely different. Instead of letting them push me down, I used them to motivate me to get the hell up.

A primal scream erupted from my mouth as I forced my body into motion, lifting my stomach off the deck and onto my hands and knees, and forcing myself to look at Gia. Deep cuts lacerated both cheeks. A hundred similar cuts slashed her arms, legs, and torso. A wave of nausea bit into me, along with an urge to drop back to the floor and rebury my head in the proverbial sand. I rejected the emotion, crying out a second time in anger, pain, frustration and determination.

I put my hand on the glass wall beside me, using it for balance and some leverage as I pulled myself to my feet. Legs still shaking but more stable than before, I didn't take my eyes off Gia. My last words to her had been filled with anger as I blamed her for betraying us, so confident she was the one who had given Sedaya our location.

I'd been so completely and utterly wrong.

Despite that, she had still come to the lab to save my life and had paid with hers. I owed it to her to do whatever I could to make sure her sacrifice wasn't in vain. Even if it didn't amount to anything, I owed it to her to keep fighting until my last breath.

Upright once more, I finally looked away from her, turning my gaze to the room behind me. The etcher sat next to the chair, its robotic arm slightly extended, frozen before activation. The side panel hung wide open, like the Tin Man from the Wizard of Oz, just waiting for a heart. Or in this case, more Gilded catalyst. Except I didn't have any more catalyst, Gilded or otherwise. The machine was useless to me.

Even so, I continued staring at it as I processed my situation. I was alone on a super secret base inside an asteroid in the middle of nowhere. I had to assume Blorb had taken the Star of Caprum from *Head Case* at the same time it sabotaged the guns. While the Royal Marines had installed a small backup power supply to transfer the ship from orbit to the ground, it probably wouldn't get me very far, and it definitely wouldn't get me into hyperspace. It might be enough to get me off the station and into open space where I could set off an emergency beacon. With any luck, someone would pick it up and stop by to check it out, even if only to see if there was any salvage they could claim or electro to be made. That had to be better than fulfilling Blorb's prophecy.

But it could take weeks for someone to pass anywhere

near this lightly-traveled section of space. And right now, I had days to spare at most. Sure, I would still be fighting, but only just barely.

It wasn't enough.

I leaned on the wall, using it to keep my balance as I made my way back to David's desk and sat down. The wires that had connected his laptop to the station's mainframe dangled off the edge of the desk. I followed them to the small outlet in the rear of the display, which remained active. Looking at the screen, my eyes narrowed in confusion. This was the pattern the etcher had been seconds away from cutting into my flesh. The *restore* sigil was there, majestic in its complex, dragon curve fractal. But while I had expected it to stand alone on the screen, contained within the hexagonal lines that composed the base activation algorithm, the version on screen was only a part of a larger geometric design.

Restore rested like a heart in the center of the overall pattern. The lines that branched out from it reminded me of veins, splitting and overlapping. The negative space between them allowed me to recognize additional embedded sigils. *Push*, of course. *Pull, absorb, negate, enhance*. Those were the easiest to recognize. But there were more I knew I had seen before in the slides of the Grimoire. Staring at the whole thing there had to be at least a dozen sigils in total, each line from *restore* an activation thread for multiple effects. In one place, the lines were so tightly overlapped I nearly missed the smallest sigil hidden among them. Leaning in and squinting, my mouth opened when I recognized the pattern.

Calmed-to-death.

At such a small size it wouldn't be powerful enough to work instantly, but just the fact that David had put it into his construct surprised me. Keep had warned him multiple times about offensive sigils, and every time David had promised he would never let them see the light of day. Obviously, he had lied. And with David in Sedaya's hands, Keep's worst fears were sure to come to pass. But maybe that was why David had included it in the construct. To give me the power to end his life if he was ever so compromised.

Or, with restore able to extend my life, maybe to give me the power to end it all. A power Keep's wife hadn't initially given to him.

Another small sigil appeared above *calmed-to-death.* A complex web of equation lines I wasn't sure was even a sigil at all, I had never seen it before. I was certain of that much. Either way, David never told me he planned to print an entire arsenal of symbols into my skin. Keep probably hadn't known either. I doubted he would have approved of the idea.

I leaned back in the seat and sighed. None of it mattered now. I didn't have any catalyst. The chunk of ore Bill and George had given me was the only reason I had come so close in the first place, and now the cupboard was dry.

Weeks to even have a chance at getting help and only days to live. The situation seemed impossible. Fresh despair pushed against the edge of my resolve. My gaze shifted from the display to Gia, partially obscured by the dentist chair. I couldn't give up, even if it was impossible.

There had to be a way.

I looked at the screen again, tracing the geometric construct once more. For whatever reason, something Druck, of all people, had said popped into my mind.

"We're getting quite a collection of that crap, aren't we?" he had said in relation to the sleeve I took from David's mother.

I got up so fast I had to brace myself as a wave of dizziness crashed over me. Waiting it out, I moved more deliberately out of the room, stepping gingerly over Gia on my way from the lab.

Maybe it wasn't the catalyst I wanted. Maybe it would kill me. But I had to try.

CHAPTER 2

A few days earlier, it had taken me fifteen minutes to walk from the lab to the hangar. Today, between rounds of dizziness, coughing, and general weakness, it took me nearly an hour. The simple journey felt epic by the time the inner bay doors slid open in front of me, revealing the eerily silent hangar and *Head Case* parked alone inside. My gaze immediately focused on where Admiral Lyke's ship had landed. The skid marks were still visible where they had disturbed layers of dust. The gun Lyke melted with sigiltech had hardened to the deck, and the rest of Team Hondo's guns remained scattered across the space. Taking it all in left my jaw clenched in fury, my resolve crystallized.

I hobbled across the gap between the hangar door and the ramp leading up into *Head Case*, and up into the ship to the elevator. I went to Deck Six first, needing only a minute to confirm the Star of Caprum was gone. It wouldn't have surprised me if Sedaya had *Dominator* built with a place for the power source already included. If he had, that space was undoubtedly occupied by the Star right now. Thanks to Alter's earlier lessons on ship maintenance, it only took me a few more minutes to also confirm the guns had indeed been sabotaged, the linkage undone between them and the primary battery.

My heart pumped a little bit harder when the elevator passed Deck Five. I knew Alter was dead, or absorbed, or however one Aleal consumed another, but I wasn't ready to move past denial just yet. Losing Gia was like being hit in the face by a brick. Accepting that Alter wasn't coming back was more like a cannonball. The thought of Matt as Sedaya's prisoner, being choked by the scarf or otherwise tortured for who-knew-how-long felt like a freight train rumbling down the tracks with me lashed to the rail. Not that Quasar, Druck, or Shaq in his hands was much better.

I didn't really worry about Keep. He had been on his own for a long time and could take care of himself.

Returning to Deck Two, I crossed to the armory as quickly as I could, the thoughts of my crew's fate filling me with a greater sense of urgency. "Levi, open the armory doors."

The doors slid open ahead of me, and I panicked as I stepped through. What if Blorb had taken all of the catalyst regalia we'd collected, too? The sleeve, the earrings, the rings. It could have tucked it all away in its body like a pack mule, smuggling it away to prevent its use. I only exhaled again after I opened the crate where we stowed the items, finding it all still there. I grabbed every last bit of it, stuffing the earrings and rings into my pockets and carrying the sleeve in my free hand. I picked out a sniper rifle there too, not bothering with ammo but using its extended length as a makeshift crutch, giving me a third leg to balance on. It helped speed up my movement through the station and I returned to the lab in half the time.

Entering the assembly room, I was surprised to immediately find myself inside the assembler, standing between the plates where the molecules would be recombined into new material. The machine was primitive compared to what we had on *Head Case*, but at the same time more advanced in its ability to create catalyst. A simple chute provided a feed for the raw materials, and I dumped everything in. Since it was already a finished product, I assumed everything it needed was already there, it just needed to be melted down.

Of course, this catalyst wasn't the same as Gilded catalyst. I couldn't just press a button and have it do the conversion. It took me some time to find the interface to the machine and then more time to gain access to the operating system. Fortunately, it ran on similar future Java to Asshole, making it easy for me to dig into the source code to see its recipes.

It was a good thing I didn't need to change the recipe.

The ingredient lists were composed of minerals and compounds with scientific names I could barely read, nevermind identify. All I had to do was tell the assembler to create the normal hemolytic catalyst in a liquid state. Even so, the changes took me nearly six hours, broken up by bouts of dizziness, coughing, and general fatigue, to complete. The fatigue left me napping on and off inside the machine, not that it mattered where I slept with no one here to complain.

The sense of purpose compounded my resolve, fueling the fires of my anger and determination. Looking back at how I had been ready to die after Blorb left with David, I only felt embarrassed by the pathetic show of weakness. Mom had taught me never to give up, and after everything that had already happened—from the Persophon Penal Station to Sedaya's dungeon—I should have known better. Maybe it was the worst hit I had ever taken, but it was still only one hit. I refused to be KO'd so easily.

I had to set a timer on the assembler and step out of the machine to wait for it to produce the newly formulated catalyst. I tasked it to make only an ounce of the stuff to start, just to make sure it came out as a liquid. Even with all the sigiltech stuff we had collected, its combined volume when melted down had come out only slightly more than the Gilded catalyst.

Even such a small amount needed nearly an hour to make. I used the time to set about the grisly task of removing Gia's body from the lab. It had already started to smell, making me gag every time I entered that section of the facility. Quasar had found a small morgue next to the station's sickbay, and I retrieved a body bag from there, laying it out ahead of Gia and slowly dragging her into it. I cried as I closed the zipper, her face vanishing beneath the thick material, along with the stench.

I wasn't strong enough to move her to the morgue, so I pulled the bag out to the atrium in the center of the lab and left it in one of the dead flowerbeds. It wasn't the end she deserved, especially considering her fame in the Spiral, but it was the best I could do at the moment.

Returning to the assembler, the outer display showed its countdown timer pinned to zero, the production of the recombined catalyst complete. Entering the machine, I found the small glass vial waiting on the bottom plate. A quick examination proved the process had worked. I wanted to feel elated by my success, but after what I had just spent the last hour doing, I was in no mood to celebrate. My smoldering fury rekindled into a five-alarm blaze. I dropped the liquid catalyst, vial and all, back into the assembler and reset the machine to make a full batch. Since it had to break down the prior material again, the timer ran close to two hours.

I left the machine, slumping against the door as soon as it closed and locked. Activities that wouldn't have registered as the least bit tiring a few weeks ago had left my body completely exhausted. The gentle vibration of its functioning helped ease some of my tension, quickly putting me back to sleep.

I awoke with a start, angry with myself when I saw the machine had finished. Every extra minute I wasted here was another minute Matt and the others were out there with Sedaya or his lackey Lyke doing who-knew-what to them. I pulled myself roughly to my feet and entered the assembler, scooping up the vial and practically running it back to the etcher, stopping to cough before circling the table to the mainframe interface. With no easy way to start the process and sit in the chair at the same time, I had to hope I could make it to the seat before the etcher started doing its thing.

Pulling off my shirt, my heart immediately began racing with anxious anticipation. Not being Gilded catalyst, there was an extremely strong chance the silver liquid metal I was about to use would either kill me or leave me horribly scarred, with the etched sigils completely inoperable. It was a risk I had to take. A risk I *wanted* to take. Even in the worst case, at least I could match my physical pain to what the others were either already going through or would soon be going through. At least I wouldn't die a coward's death or take the easy way out.

And if it actually worked?

Maybe I would live long enough to save them.

CHAPTER 3

I swallowed hard, trying to control my ragged, nervous breath as my finger hovered over the button that would start the etcher. I had already planned my route to the chair. Now I just needed to keep from getting dizzy on the way so I could make it into the seat before the clamps snapped closed and the machine started.

Cheating by taking a step forward, I reached back toward the keyboard, ready to initiate the process. I stifled a cough, took one last breath, and mashed the key down. The etcher's arm began moving while the vibrating hum of a pump pulled the catalyst up through a clear tube. I lunged forward, throwing myself into the chair. The ankle clamps caught my legs, but I was too slow to get my arms clamped down, leaving my upper body with freedom of movement.

I pressed myself back against the padding, wrapping my hands around the armrests and gripping them tightly. David already warned me how bad it could be if any of the sigil lines came out wrong. No matter how much it hurt, I had to remain absolutely still.

The robot arm swung forward in front of my face,

swiveling and bending from its many joints before lowering the rotating platter of tools sliding into position. The first one emitted a red grid across my upper body, which remained as a second blue grid joined it. They started out skewed from one another, slowly converging until they became a single, solid green. The grid shut off then, the platter spun to a second pair of tools.

The arm stopped moving, with the pair of tools aimed at my chest. I waited for it to do something, calming my breathing to keep from shifting the canvas too much. My arms and legs tensed in preparation of the pain to come. I was ready.

The etcher apparently wasn't. It remained static, hovering over me and leaving me wondering if something had broken. I couldn't see the display to know if an error message had popped up, but it wouldn't have surprised me. I waited to see if the machine would recover, maintaining my position on the chair even as my panic grew. I had considered that the machine might not work or that the makeshift catalyst would kill me on the spot. The idea that the etcher would break down immediately following initiation hadn't crossed my mind.

The universe didn't just fall short on mercy. It could be downright cruel.

Five minutes passed. Ten. I kept glancing over at the machine, looking for status lights or anything that might indicate the thing was totally broken down. I tried to spot the reflection of the display in the glass behind it, but I couldn't quite turn my head far enough to see with more than the edge of my peripheral vision. Additional glare made seeing the screen impossible.

Becoming more agitated, I leaned forward, ready to grab at the clamps around my ankles to pry them loose. My shoulder bumped the robot arm, knocking it back an inch or two. That seemed to break it out of whatever had jammed it up. The platter on the end started spinning again, the different joints rotating it into a new position. I quickly sat back, making it into position again just in time for the etcher to go back to work.

The tip of the etcher dove toward my chest as my hands wrapped around the armrests. A bright laser lashed out, sending an immediate flash of pain resonating through my body as it began slicing open my skin. A second tool sucked up the blood that surfaced from the cut while a needle pushed the catalyst into the wound as if it were pouring concrete.

I knew beforehand that it would hurt. I had badly underestimated how much.

I released an agonized scream, muscles flexing as I fought to remain in place when every instinct told me to bat the etcher away. My hands clenched the armrests, knuckles white while my neck muscles tensed to hold my head static. Starting at my pecs, the etcher worked in quick, precise motions—slicing, sucking, and filling—as it swept across my chest. Oddly enough, I wondered what it would mean if I gained weight, built muscle or took a wound to the chest. What would scar tissue or any other changes do to the sigil's mechanics?

The thought faded as a second burst of pain exploded through my nervous system. I cried out, still holding fast to the chair as the etcher continued making cuts, the laser scalpel shifting along my chest, the arm making constant, precise adjustments. I could almost imagine the pattern being drawn by the progression of the pain, starting with the containment lines that framed the construct and working its way inward.

I don't know how many more times I screamed after the first time, but the pain remained unbearable, especially as it was joined by a nearly irresistible need to cough. I didn't give in to it. I thought about Matt, from the first time we met in the hallway of the Section Eight apartment building all the way to Omega Station and beyond. I saw him captured by Sedaya, tortured and beaten, bloodied and in pain. I thought about Gia, from singing along to *Wherever I May Roam* to her lifeless body in the lab's dead and decayed garden. I thought about Teen Alter watching *That Darn Cat*, ended by one of her own kind when she was just starting to fully accept her own alien nature. I thought about Shaq, saving Matt and me from the catlike creature on Cestus Alpha to being caged and humiliated, and Quasar and Druck abandoned in the duke's dungeon. And then there was Keep, going from picking at my french fries at *McCrory's* to no doubt suffering the worst torture out of them all.

Those memories drove my anger and fueled my strength and resolve despite the terrible agony of the etching and absolute pain that came from needing to cough so badly but being unwilling to move a muscle. My mouth and throat dried up like parchment. My heart pounded. Every nerve ending was on fire. I kept my eyes clamped shut, mouth hanging open, even those memories beginning to blur as the seconds ticked by until I totally lost track of time. Through it all, the etcher continued its work, emotionless and unwavering, printing the construct David had created with the wrong type of catalyst, most likely putting me through this hell for nothing.

I don't know how much time went by. The pain made it impossible to track. One second, every single fiber of my being cried out at once. The next, there was sudden, inexplicable calm. The pain didn't fade. It vanished. The tension didn't ease. It relaxed. I opened my eyes, tilting my head just enough to look down at my chest. Thin lines of silver catalyst ran across my body, the skin immediately surrounding it bright red and still oozing blood. Tracing the discoloration downward, I saw the entire outline of the construct had been completed, the lines all linked by the complex dragon curve fractal cut into my sternum.

It glowed in soft, white light. That alone was amazing. Even more amazing was that the etcher had yet to finish the pattern. The arm continued sweeping across my body, cutting and injecting as it created the more delicate branches of additional sigils that stretched away from *restore*. Having that sigil complete and active had taken away the pain, working passively and immediately to repair the etcher's damage soon after it was created. I barely held back the tears of relief as I imagined it doing the same to the cancer, destroying the misprinted cells and replenishing my body with perfect, healthy replacements.

It was a better outcome than I had even hoped for. An outcome that went way beyond my wildest expectations. I could barely keep myself pinned to the chair because I wanted to get up and literally jump for joy.

Needless to say, the experience didn't last.

The *restore* sigil's glow blinked out, and when the pain returned, it came back with a vengeance, hitting me with double the intensity and setting me to writhing in the chair, arms and legs shaking in a sudden desperate effort to stay in the seat while the etcher continued its work. This time, the physical pain was joined by a massive headache and a deeper-rooted hurt I couldn't trace but that left me in tears. I knew without question that something had gone wrong with the catalyst, unsurprising but still disappointing and agonizing. And there was nothing I could do but ride it out and hope I emerged on the other side.

Alive.

More time passed. Seconds? Minutes? Hours? I had no idea. The etcher continued building the construct in my flesh, leaving behind a silver-lined magical circuit board across my entire upper torso that wouldn't carry any current. Every cut hurt more than the last, the cold burn of the process gaining in ferocity until it became completely overwhelming.

My vision darkened and blurred as the nightmare finally came to an end.

CHAPTER 4

Ringing in my ears was the first clue I was still alive. A high-pitched, steady scream, in the void of my subconscious, it sounded more like a high-school bell, alerting me that whatever class I was currently in had ended and I better get a move on to reach the next.

Eyes sliding open once more, it took me a few seconds to get my bearings. To remember not only where I was, but who I was. Benjamin Murdock. Cancer patient. Musician. Wannabe programmer and general geek. Starship captain. Archon. The last two descriptors resonated the most, the first rounding out the top three. Not only a cancer patient, but one that was knocking on death's door. But for whatever reason, death didn't seem to want to let me in.

I started pushing myself back to my hands and knees, in almost the same position I had been in right after Blorb had taken David away. The absence of Gia's body wasn't the only change from then to now. I managed to get off my stomach without feeling dizzy or sick. In fact, while I remained a little unsteady, my ease of motion and overall balance felt pretty good.

I could have stood straight up, but the realization that I was glowing brought me to a sudden stop. What the hell?

I didn't look down at my chest where the etcher had done its work. Instead, my eyes drifted to my left arm. The illumination seemed to be emanating from my veins, most visible where they were closest to the surface of my skin. Okay, so not all of me was glowing. Just my blood.

I swallowed a nervous lump in my throat turning my head to look at my other arm. Same thing. I didn't need David or Nurse Alter to tell me it was a side effect of the construct printed into my flesh, the non-standard catalyst I had used, and the strange mutation to my blood that was now making itself incredibly apparent. It was two parts creepy, one part cool, and what I really needed to know was if the bioluminescence was good, bad, or neutral. If it meant the *restore* sigil was doing what it should, then I could live with turning into a poor man's Doctor Manhattan.

I stood before glancing at my chest, rising easily on muscles filled with strength I hadn't experienced in weeks. So far, it seemed to be a good thing. The entire outer activation equation lines of the construct glowed with the same light blue energy as my blood. The dragon curve of the *restore* sigil pulsated with light, sending it out in bursts like a heartbeat pumping blood, renewing me as the energy rippled outward. It vanished where the veins went too deep for the light to emerge and reappeared where the veins surfaced. My extremities were the brightest.

Even so, I reserved my excitement, knowing the effect could be temporary. There was still a lot more that might go wrong. I could only imagine coming down with sigil sickness and ending up paralyzed, frozen in place while my new sigils kept me alive for a lot longer than I would ever want. The thought of spending weeks or even months lying motionless on the floor, my mind fully alert but my body refusing to move a single muscle terrified me. Only the memory of what I had just gone through to get to this point and the reason I had gone through it kept my nerves in check. Matt and the others were still out there somewhere, and they needed my help.

And for now, at least, I felt strong enough to help them.

I looked down the corridor to the sliding door at the end of the lab. Raising my hand, I whispered the focus word for *push*. A light tickle on my chest and an increase in the light reflected off the glass partition. The door parted, forced open by the action. Not too hard. Not too soft. I let it go after only a few seconds. The fear of potential repercussions convinced me to only use the power when I absolutely needed it, at least for now.

"You did it, David," I said out loud, picking my shirt up off the table and slipping it on as I headed for the exit. Pausing before I left the lab, I returned to the workstation and quickly closed out of the software, locking the terminal. Without the password. I couldn't get back in. I didn't need to, but on the off chance that Sucaath and Sedaya could return, I wasn't taking any chances.

Returning to the sliding door, I didn't force it open this time, letting it part of its own accord as I neared. The flash of a blaster greeted me as I stepped over the threshold, pain searing through my shoulder before I could react. Additional energy blasts followed, fired from the exit doorway on the other side of the atrium. I fell back into the lab, diving away from the door and behind the cover of the bulkhead as the door again slid closed.

Who the hell was shooting at me now?

A quick glance at my shoulder revealed a hole through my shirt, my arm deeply singed, with blood oozing from the scorched skin. It hurt like crazy, but in comparison to the pain of the etcher, it was hardly painful at all. I noticed too that the glow of my blood faded away soon after reaching the surface, leaving the escaping plasma a more normal red.

Footsteps outside the door told me that my attackers didn't plan to wait forever for me to again emerge. I got back to my feet, staying pressed against the bulkhead, ready to act against whoever came through as the lab doors parted a third time.

A small metal ball rolled through the opening, its momentum carrying it toward the back of the lab. Somehow, it triangulated my position and changed course, suddenly coming right at me. I didn't think, only reacted, raising my hands. "Glutiam," I said, my skin tingling ahead of the ball's detonation.

The explosion should have blasted me to pieces. Instead, *absorb* gathered all the fire and fury, including the shrapnel, in an invisible cage surrounding my hands. As I collected the last of the energy, I stared at fiery balls, one in each hand, feeling more like a wizard than ever. Eat your heart out, Gandalf.

Rather than wait for my attackers to sweep into the room, thinking I had died in the explosion, I stepped out into the open doorway and whispered, "disperge," as soldier clad in dark green armor and tactical helmets, swept into the opposite doorway. The balls of energy and shrapnel shot toward them, forcing them to skid to a halt when they saw what was headed their way. Flames and smoke filled the corridor, the blast knocking them flat before they could duck for cover.

"Wow," I said softly, amazed with what I had just done. I didn't stop there, rushing across the dead garden toward the downed fighters. The corridor they were in was the only way out of the lab. The last thing I wanted was to be pinned down.

The door to the assembler opened as I reached the middle of the atrium. Another fighter, this one in lighter green armor, opened fire with a plasma rifle. I swung toward the shooter, *push* creating a barrier the bolts couldn't penetrate. It didn't dissuade the fighter from continuing to shoot, each of the rounds hitting the invisible wall a few feet ahead of me, instead of hitting me right between the eyes.

I ducked down as I ended the *push*, the next few blasts passing overhead. A second *push* sent the shooter tumbling backward, returning him to the assembler. Far enough back for the doors to close in front of them. Unfortunately, by the time that fighter was neutralized, two from the original group were back on their feet. A second energy blast hit me in the thigh before I could *pull* the guns from their hands and *push* them both aside.

Grimacing with pain, I straightened up and made a run for it. I didn't care about the station. I didn't need it anymore. I had to get to *Head Case* and get the hell away from whoever was attacking me. Not Sedaya, I was pretty sure of that much. It had to be Sucaath. Nobody else knew we were here.

I almost laughed at myself. It seemed like every interested party in the galaxy knew we were here. Maybe Lyke had decided to tip off General Nattic. Or perhaps Blorb had called it in as Empress Li'an, sending the Royal Guard running. But the Royal Marines wore white and gold or blue and silver, didn't they? Not forest green.

Did it even matter at this point?

I reached the two fighters just as they were recovering. One of them tried to tackle me, but I *pushed* him back again, pinning him to the bulkhead. The other one managed to grab my shirt. The existing hole from the blaster hit, letting it tear easily away. I could swear I heard the soldier gasp when he saw my glowing sigiltech construct. The distraction allowed me to *push* him away as well, clearing a path and allowing me to break past him.

I was almost to the blast door at the lab's entrance when a plasma bolt hit me in the back, knocking me forward onto my knees. This one hurt more than all the others, and I winced,, casting a look back over my shoulder. The fighter in the lighter green armor, obviously a woman, stood in the atrium, weapon leveled at me, about to fire again.

"Speculo," I whispered, holding my hand out toward her. The plasma bolt zapped across the corridor, testing my confidence in the reflection as it came within centimeters of hitting me before bouncing back the way it had come. The fighter took the round in the chest as she tried to spin away, her armor absorbing the blow.

I stumbled forward, through the blast doors and into the corridor that split at the lab. I turned in the direction of the control room, the pain in my back almost unbearable. How quickly might the *restore* sigil fix the damage? *Could* it fix the damage? Keep had never mentioned that as anything his sigil took care of for him. Normally a passive mark, what if I made it active?

"Restituo," I said, imagining the wounds I had taken quickly closing over, the damage reversing. The dragon curve on my chest glowed more brightly, a delicious warmth spreading from it. Glancing at my shoulder, I watched the burned skin flake off as new skin quickly took its place, while at the same time, the pain in my back started to fade.

It was working!

I shouted with triumph, punching the air as I healed the wounds I had taken, feeling almost godlike in my new abilities. As long as I could get off the station and back to civilization, I was going to find Sedaya and Blorb and kick both of their asses. I was going to find Matt and the others, and rescue David. I was completely unstop—

My breath caught in my throat as a sudden chill replaced the warmth, my body instantly turning cold. My legs refused to move, all of the energy fleeing me at once. I only realized the light in my veins had flamed out as I fell forward onto my face. Unable to get my two-ton arms up in time, my head hit the deck full force.

I blacked out like a burned out light bulb.

CHAPTER 5

Believe it or not, I awoke in sickbay. Again. At least this time, it was the one on Omega Station and not the one on *Head Case*. But it was still a sickbay.

Not surprisingly, my hands and feet were shackled to the bed, held fast by thick electromagnetic cuffs that I didn't think I could pull off even with the sigils on my chest. Not that using sigiltech was even an option. As my eyes opened, the pressure of a rifle muzzle against my temple intensified. The guard keeping watch over me wasn't taking any chances.

"Hello," I said, looking up at the armored fighter. His dark green, hard-shell armor was scuffed, dented, and scorched—the last bit of damage taken when I *dispersed* the bomb blast into the corridor. I couldn't see his face through the opaque helmet of his visor, but I imagined him scowling in response to my greeting.

I didn't see any reason not to be friendly. Considering my captors hadn't killed me and had actually brought me to sickbay to maybe make sure I was okay, I figured they couldn't be all bad. I was pretty sure they weren't with Team Suck Ass, and almost as sure they weren't Royal

Guards, though there was a chance they were some Special Forces unit or something. The way I saw it, the only chance I had to get out of yet another fine mess I'd gotten myself into was to hopefully get on their good side.

"Who are you guys?" I asked when the guard didn't offer a reply. "This base is supposed to be super secret, but it's like the worst kept secret in the Spiral."

He didn't move a muscle, keeping the deadly end of his rifle against my head. My body was covered with a sheet, but I could still see the glow of the sigils through it, including on my arms. I think I understood what had happened to me. My bloodstream had become a battery of sorts, and in fighting my way out while healing my wounds, I had used up my available charge. An embarrassing, painful, and potentially disastrous lesson.

"You aren't with Sedaya, though, right?" I continued, even though I had yet to get anything out of the guy. He probably had orders not to speak to me, and to alert whoever was in charge as soon as I was awake. I hadn't heard him contact anyone, but I knew the full tactical systems of modern Spiral combat armor had various methods of internal communication. "You can ease off the pressure on my temple. I'm pretty sure the plasma bolt will be just as deadly from an inch away as it is jammed into my skull."

He still didn't move.

"I figure you aren't with Sedaya or I'd either be dead or on my way to one of his ships to be tortured again. And you probably aren't with Sucaath, except I don't really know what his followers are like. I just assume since he's in cahoots with Sedaya he's an asshat too and also would probably be preparing to torture me. Are you with the Royal Guard? Because if you are, I've got some pretty crazy news for General Nattic that he definitely won't believe. Unfortunately."

Still nothing.

"Is your boss at least on the way down here?" I asked. "I'd like to speak to somebody who might actually..." The door to the room opened. The fighter in the lighter green armor, the one who had shot me in the back, stood behind it. "I should have known."

I'd already had more than a split-second to look at my latest arch-nemesis, her armor lighter and more shapely than the heavy brick the other guy wore. She stepped into the room with an air of authority, stopping at the end of the bed. "Who are you?" she asked, her voice exemplifying that same authority.

"Benjamin Murdock," I replied. "Captain of the starship *Head Case*. She's parked out in the hangar." I paused. "How did you get in here? The door controls are locked down."

"Were locked down," she replied. "Someone unlocked them for us."

"That's not possible. I'm the only one here."

"The body bag in the old garden suggests otherwise." Maybe Gia had unbuttoned everything before she died? She had been in the control room when I blamed her for something she never did. "I know your ship. And you. Wanted for murder, an escapee from Persephon Penal Station. And also enough of a thorn in Duke Sedaya's side that he put out a twenty million electro bounty on you, which has since been rescinded."

"That all sounds about right," I said.

"What are you doing here?"

"It's a long story. What are you doing here?"

"We've been monitoring this place for a long time. Waiting to see who might make a play for it. We knew there was action when we lost contact with our drones."

"Your drones? Quasar said they were Royal Guard models."

"We plundered them from a surplus warehouse some time ago."

"Plundered? Meaning you aren't with the Guard."

"No, we aren't with the guard."

"Space pirates?"

"Do I look like a pirate to you?"

"I don't know. Do you have a peg leg under that armor? An eye patch? Anyway, you missed all of the action. Maybe if you had come sooner, Sedaya wouldn't have made off with my crew."

"You're telling me you didn't kill the woman in the body bag?"

"She was my friend, working with me and my crew," I replied, fighting not to get emotional. "Look, if you're not a pirate and you're interested in what's happening here, maybe you can help me? I'm actually one of the good guys."

She responded by unclasping her helmet and lifting it away from her head. The face underneath was older than mine, heart-shaped and kinder than I expected. Her purple eyes surprised me, as did the scar on her cheek that marred an otherwise ethereal look.

"No eye patch," I remarked with a smile.

She motioned with her head, and the guard backed his rifle away from my temple, lowering the muzzle to the ground. Still not speaking, she picked up a slab at the end of the bed and looked it over.

"Do you know why you're still alive?" she asked without glancing at me.

"Because you're curious why my blood is like a Hue light?"

"I am curious about that," she admitted, holding up the slab. "Which is why we ran a full battery of blood tests and diagnostics on you. But that's not it. You're still alive because even though we shot you multiple times and tried to blow you up, you didn't kill any of us. And from what I know of sigiltech, you could have done so pretty easily."

She already knew about sigiltech? After this station, that had to be the second worst kept secret in the Spiral. "I took a chance that you weren't with Sedaya or Sucaath. That's all. And to be honest, I didn't actively try to not hurt you when I released the energy of the bomb into the corridor."

"You also didn't actively try to hurt us. You tossed us around a bit, but mostly just tried to run."

"And you shot me in the back in appreciation for my effort. Or lack thereof."

"Have you looked in a mirror lately? You're not the kind of person I would feel comfortable allowing to run freely around the galaxy. Especially considering your rap sheet."

"My rap sheet is bullshit," I replied. "A misunderstanding piled on top of a lie because Duke Sedaya hates my guts."

She smiled then, slightly crooked thanks to the scar. "I'll tell you a secret, Benjamin. Duke Sedaya hates my guts too."

"That seems to be a common thread with the people who don't try to kill me," I said. "Can I ask you another personal question? Who are you?"

"I'm not ready to tell you that," she answered.

"What *are* you ready to tell me?"

"What are you doing here, Ben? How do you know about Omega Station?"

"I have the exact same questions for you."

"That's understandable. But since you're the one chained to the bed, I insist that you go first."

"How can I argue with that?"

"You can't."

"I'll answer in reverse order. I know about the station through a friend. We came here to use the lab equipment to print the central sigil on my chest. It's called *restore*. We were hoping it would cure my cancer."

Her eyes narrowed. "That's it? You came here to cure an illness?"

"A fatal illness," I replied. "And yeah, pretty much."

She waved the slab again. "Then you'll probably be happy to know that it worked. According to our tests, outside of the mutation in your blood you're in perfect health."

I wanted to be happy, and maybe if Matt and the others were here and I wasn't shackled to a bed, I would have whooped and danced with excitement. Instead, I settled for a nod. "I can feel that, but it's nice to have confirmation. What about the mutation in my blood?"

"You seem to be storing chaos energy."

"Chaos energy?"

"That's what I'm going with because I don't really know how else to describe it. All I can tell you is that physically, there don't seem to be any ill effects. In fact, the benefits seem to be mostly positive."

"I feel that too, but again it's nice to have confirmation."

"The catalyst in your skin isn't meant to be in your skin," she said.

"I know. I had Gilded catalyst, but it turned out my alien crewmate wasn't the alien crewmate I thought she was but an evil alien who calls itself Blorb."

"Blorb?" the guard beside me questioned. It was the first time he had spoken.

"Ridiculous, right?" I agreed. "He destroyed Alter and took her place, ratted me out to Sedaya, and stole the catalyst along with my crew, one of whom rediscovered the tech part of sigiltech. He made this *restore* sigil. He can make others, and not all of them are warm and fuzzy."

"Someone learned how to make new sigils?" she asked, obviously concerned.

"That's what I said. Yeah. Blorb left me here to die. He didn't plan for me to improvise like this. I took a chance melting standard hemolytic catalyst and etching it. Fortunately, it seems to have worked, but I'm not convinced it'll hold out for the long haul."

"There's nothing in our test results to suggest it won't. You probably already know that standard catalyst can't channel as much chaos energy as Gilded."

"I do know that. And when I drained the chaos energy from my blood, I fell flat on my face. Literally. I had kind of hoped to come out of this a little more powerful so I could take on Sedaya's Gilded. I'm not sure that's going to be possible. Especially…" I shook my hands in the restraints. "…if you're planning to keep me prisoner."

"I haven't decided what to do with you yet. If the bounties were still active it would be pretty tempting to claim the electro. I could do a lot with that kind of funding."

"I bet you could. It's your turn. Why are you here?"

"Because of the drones."

"Right. I mean why were you here to place the drones outside in the first place?"

"I was looking for someone."

"In a top secret Sashkur research facility? I assume you don't like this someone very much, since your drones tried to blast us when we came in."

"You cost me a lot of money destroying them."

"Sorry, not sorry."

"But you are right. I've been hunting the man who betrayed me for over twenty years. Practically since I was a child. It took more time, effort, and electro than I can even measure to trace him back to this place. And the things I learned along the way." She shook her head. "There's a whole other history of the Manticore Spiral a lot of very powerful people don't want anyone to know."

"You're referring to the Sigiltech War." It wasn't a question.

"And its aftermath. The truth is out there if you're persistent enough, but most people lack the motivation or the will to dig that deep."

"Why should they? It's ancient history."

"Is it? Then why is your blood glowing?"

"Good point. It was supposed to be ancient history. But you aren't the only one motivated enough to uncover it. Maybe your intent is less maniacal than Sedaya's. Maybe it isn't. I know I'm a good guy, but what about you?"

"I'm no fan of the Empress, if that's what you mean," she replied. "But I hate Duke Sedaya even more. He nearly took everything from me."

"And you're aware he intends to steal the throne? Scratch that. He already has."

"What do you mean?"

"Blorb is from an alien race called the Aleal. They're not spacefaring. They're actually pretty harmless left on their own. But Sedaya found their planet and took a few. He turned them into assassins. My friend, Alter, had a change of heart and got out from under Sedaya. Blorb seems to enjoy what it does a little too much. Anyway, they can steal people's essence, their persona, by killing and eating some part of their brains or something. Once they do that, they can become nearly perfect replicas of that person. Blorb killed the Empress."

The woman's face went from a soft brown to a pale white. "What?"

"Yeah. The Empress isn't the Empress. She's Sedaya's pet assassin. He's been calling the shots in the Hegemony for some unknown amount of time." I paused. "Come to think of it, I'm willing to bet Prince Hiro's kidnapping is related. In fact, what if it wasn't a kidnapping at all?"

"What are you talking about?"

"What if the prince figured out that his real mom was dead and an imposter had taken her place? Maybe Sedaya arranged to get him out of there before he could tell anyone. General Nattic, for example. Maybe the Blue Burn was all for show."

The woman paused, looking thoughtful. "Why not just kill Prince Hiro too?"

"Maybe Sedaya figured his abduction would make for a good distraction while he maneuvers more of his resources into place? I don't know, it's just a theory I cooked up right now. But it kind of works."

"Yes, it does." She bit her lip, still considering the situation. "I'm no fan of the Empress, but I strongly prefer the Li'an line to remain in power over Sedaya."

"Then maybe you should let me go?" I said. "Or better yet, help me track down my crew so we can find a way to stop him."

"You said a friend told you about this station," she replied. "Not many people know of its existence."

"I'd argue the accuracy of that statement."

"What's your friend's name?"

"I don't see how that's—"

"What's his name!" she shouted, pulled a pistol from her hip and pointing it at my face.

"And here I thought we might be friends," I said, staring down the barrel.

"Tell me," she seethed.

"Card," I replied. "Orban Card."

She lowered the gun, shaking her head and laughing sardonically. "Orban Card. Don't you mean Avelus Keep?"

"You know about that too?"

"Yes. But it was a good try. What were you doing with him?"

"I just told you. We were trying to stop Sedaya from gaining control of the Hegemony."

"Why? What did Avelus hope to get out of it?"

"Originally, he wanted to stop Sedaya from gaining more power. To bring him down and make up for his failure on Caprum. Once we found out what Sedaya knew about sigiltech, it became about a lot more than just trying to clear his conscience."

"You're lying. Avelus Keep doesn't have a conscience. Do you know how many innocent people he's killed? Caprum was no mistake. He left me to die."

My heartrate kicked up ten notches as I stared into the woman's furious purple eyes. "Geez. You're Duchess Dryka."

CHAPTER 6

"I am," Dryka replied. "Duchess Jacinda Dryka, rightful heir to the Dryka territories and ruler of Caprum, exiled long ago when the man I trusted with my life abandoned me. Any friend of Avelus Keep is no friend of mine."

She scowled at me, turning on her heel to leave.

"Wait!" I shouted. "Please!"

She paused and looked back at me over her shoulder.

"I don't know everything that happened between you and Keep. Maybe he totally lied to me and he really was responsible for what happened and for you almost getting killed. According to him he was almost killed that night too, and he's been searching for you ever since so he can help you get your throne back. He sold me the starship out in the hangar with the Star of Caprum in it to keep it away from Sedaya. He chose me because he thought I could help him take out the duke and find you."

"I found you," she said, "looking for him. So I could confront him and put an end to his sorry life."

"I get that. And whether it's a misunderstanding or not I get that you're upset. But in case you weren't listening just now Duchess, we've got a lot bigger problems to solve. Forget Keep even exists. I need your help."

She continued glaring at me. "And who was there to help me, when my planet was stolen from me because I, as a child, refused to marry an adult? When I barely escaped Caprum with my life and spent the next ten years scraping and clawing my way forward from nothing? Who helped me in those first months when I was cold, tired, and hungry, begging on the streets? Who helped me when I wound up on an illegal pleasure cruiser, forced to give up the treasure I wanted only to give freely to a man of my choosing? I don't owe Avelus Keep or the Hegemony anything."

"No, you don't. I'm sorry for what you went through. I'm not asking you to get involved. All I'm asking for is a lift back to a planet where I can get my ship repaired, so I can go after my friends. All I'm asking for is a chance to help them, like somebody should have helped you. It's not much of a chance, but I have to try. If you can't do that, at least let me out of these shackles."

Her face softened as her fury faded a little. "It's not fair for me to blame you if he lied to you about his past or his motives," she said. "You could have killed my people, but you didn't. For that alone, I'll honor your request." She removed the glove from her right hand, revealing a sigiltech ring. With a whisper, she used it to release the cuffs on my arms and legs, setting me free.

"You're an archon, too," I said, slowly sitting up.

"Hardly." She turned the ring toward me. "I can do just enough to be mildly dangerous with it." She sighed. "Avelus gave me this ring. He never told me it was anything special. It was his pledge to protect me. I don't really want to hate him, Ben. I want to believe he's a good man, that maybe he made a terrible mistake. But the more I've learned about him, the harder that's become."

"I can't pretend to understand everything you've been through. All I can tell you is the Keep I know has saved my life a few times already. That's not to say he can't be a little shady sometimes, but overall I do believe he has the Hegemony's, and your, best interests at heart."

"I hope you're right."

We stared at one another, sharing a moment of calm. "So what happens now?" I asked.

"Since you've confirmed Avelus won't be returning to the station, I suppose it's time for us to leave. You said you needed a place to have your ship repaired. Do you have electro?"

"About twelve million."

Her eyebrow went up. "That's a lot."

I shrugged. "I ran a high-level dex job with Enigma. She let me have the entire take."

"Enigma? You aren't talking about your Aleal friend Alter, are you?"

I nodded. Since she was gone, it didn't matter who I told about her identity. "Yeah. She was Enigma. She killed innocent people too, for Sedaya. But she had given up that life by the time we met. And she regretted ever having done it. If Keep is guilty of the things you say, maybe he regrets it too."

"Maybe. But regret isn't always enough to make up for the past. Anyway, if you have electro, I know where you can spend it without resurfacing on Sedaya's radar. I was heading that way myself."

"So what are you now? Not a space pirate. Soldier of fortune?"

She smiled. "Not quite. Let's just say there are a lot of people out there that want my territory back under my rule."

"Rebellion then?"

"Bingo."

I laughed. "That sounds familiar. How long will it take to get there? Sedaya's already promised my crew pain, and I know he'll make good on it."

"A week in hyperspace. A week or two to effect repairs, depending on what you need. If Sedaya promised your crew pain, I have an idea where he might deliver them. I can get my people on it. If I'm right, another two weeks of travel after that."

"A month?" I said, shaking my head. "That's too long."

"Considering the actual distances involved, that's not bad at all."

"Tell that to my friends. This place we're going, would I be able to purchase another starship there? I don't need anything big. That would let me shave off the repair time."

"I can't make any promises. Black markets are tricky that way."

"Yeah. I understand." I pulled off the sheet and slid from the bed to the deck. Dryka's eyes fixed on the construct, mesmerized by the pulsing light. I didn't blame her. It was pretty amazing.

"Can I touch it?" she asked, reaching forward with her bare hand. She paused a few inches away, waiting for my answer.

"I guess so," I replied.

A jolt of electricity went through me the moment her fingertips hit the sigils. She felt it too, yanking her hand away as her sigiltech ring glowed brightly in response to the contact. She laughed. "I guess we have good chemistry."

"If the goal is to make a bomb, maybe," I replied.

"I have some other matters to attend to before we wrap things up here," Dryka said. "Justus, make sure the others know Benjamin is a free man, and an ally. Ben, we'll be skids up in two hours."

"Copy that," I replied. Dryka put her helmet back on as she turned to leave the room. "Duchess, wait."

"What is it now?" she asked, glancing back at me again.

"Do you have a doctor on your crew that I can borrow?"

"Justus is the closest thing I've got. He has emergency field treatment training. That's why he's the one guarding you. He's been keeping an eye on your vitals and such at the same time. What do you need?"

"It's kind of a long story, but it could help both of us moving forward."

She nodded. "Justus, help Ben with whatever he needs, as long as it isn't harmful to us."

"Of course, Your Grace," he replied.

"Two hours," she repeated before leaving the room.

CHAPTER 7

"What is it you need?" Justus asked as I pulled on the simple black t-shirt he provided to me. A snug fit, the pulsing of the *restore* sigil became visible through the material when it reached the height of its output.

"The woman in the body bag," I replied. "She had a neural link. I was hoping we might be able to salvage it."

The idea itself was more than a little dark and not really something I wanted put into action, but Gia had spent a lot of time tracking down Prince Hiro over the last few weeks. I knew she had narrowed her search to a handful of potential providers for the blueburn, details that were no doubt either stored directly on the link's embedded memory or accessible through her personal network. The way I saw it, cutting her skull open to take the link was my best chance at avenging her death. I figured she would appreciate that.

"We took her down to the station's morgue," Justus said. "Why didn't you?"

"I didn't have the strength. You attacked me right after I operated on myself." I touched my hand to the center of my chest. "A few more minutes and you would have found me unconscious." I glanced at him. "Throwing a bomb at me was a bit much, wasn't it?"

"I suggested to Her Grace that we should blast the asteroid to rubble," he replied. "You're fortunate she wanted to confront you in person."

"Because she thought I was Keep?"

"Affirmative. We watched the lab door open and close, which was strange. And then you stepped out with your glowing veins. That's not something you see every day, or the kind of threat you question before you start shooting. In that scenario, the risk of taking out a friendly is worth saving the entire unit from an enemy. Nothing personal. So far, I'm glad we didn't kill you."

"And I'm glad I didn't kill you," I replied with a smile. "What do you think? Can the neural link be salvaged?"

"It's a possibility, but I need to do a closer examination to confirm."

I motioned to the door. "Shall we?"

Justus and I left sickbay. The morgue was only a short distance away, a small space that could only handle a single corpse at a time. Surrounded in sterile steel, a bare table for autopsies rested in the center of the room. A small freezer sat behind it with cabinets on either side. Justus pulled open the slide-out drawer. Gia's body waited inside, a light cloth covering her nudity. A light tug on a tab at the bottom of the drawer delivered her from the freezer to the table with minimal effort.

I swallowed hard, already chilled by what I had asked Justus to do. I reminded myself that Gia would have wanted it this way.

Justus finally removed his helmet, revealing a kinder, more handsome face than I had expected from his otherwise gruff voice. He removed his combat gloves next, freeing up his hands for more delicate work. "I'd rather not do this kind of stuff in my business suit," he said, placing helmet and gloves on the floor. "But I didn't bring a change of clothes."

"It's still nice for me to put a face to the name," I said. "Good to meet you, Justus."

"Likewise," he said softly, reverent toward the situation. He motioned toward Gia. "You two were close?"

"She was a friend, and a member of my crew. She died trying to save my life. I think I probably feel closer to her now than I did when she was still alive because of that."

"I know the feeling. My former CO gave his life to save the whole unit during a strike on one of Sedaya's arms compounds. He was a hardass leader, which was fine. But also a hardass outside his duties, which rubbed a lot of people the wrong way, including me. But ever since he died to save me and the others, I can't bring myself to say a single bad word about him."

He smiled, reaching for the sheet over Gia and delicately pulling it back, folding it gently at the top of her chest to maintain her dignity. He had cleaned her wounds before putting her in the freezer, giving me a clearer indication of the depth of Blorb's lacerations.

"This wasn't done with a knife," he said, looking at the cuts too.

"No. The alien, Blorb, in his natural form, has tentacles with sharp barbs. Although I don't know if the barbs are natural or if he formed them to do this. He seemed to have better control over his shape than Alter ever did hers."

"He must have really hated her to go so deep."

"I think he just enjoyed it," I answered, the thought unsettling my stomach.

His eyes shifted to her face, more recognizable even with the cuts now that it wasn't covered in blood. Seeing her like this was harder to deal with than I had thought. I turned away, exhaling sharply, trying to quell the nausea.

"Are you okay?" Justus asked.

"I'm not a soldier like you," I replied. "I'm just a kid from Earth who bought a starship. I thought it was a joke at first. And then, I thought it would be this great adventure." I looked at Gia again. "It's not fun anymore. At all. People I care about are dying, or being tortured, or who-knows-what else."

Justus' eyes met mine. "I feel you, Ben. War is hard. It sucks. But just think about how gratifying it'll be to kill the thing that did this. To rescue your friends if that's what you aim to do."

"That's all I'm trying to think about. Now that my cancer is gone, that's the only thing driving me."

"Hold onto that as tight as you can. That's what'll carry you through the hard parts." He looked down at Gia again. "Her face looks so familiar to me. Like I've seen her somewhere before."

"Yeah, a lot of people think she looks like the lollipop superstar, Gia."

He stared at her for a few more seconds. "Damn. You're right. She *does* look like Gia. I love her music. Did she sing like Gia too?"

"Pretty close," I replied. It wasn't just the crew that had lost someone in Gia. Millions of individuals across the Spiral would be devastated when they learned she had died. That could take a while. She had most of her planet's functions running on autopilot, and had voiced some troubles to explain away her absence from the public eye.

"Do you know what model link she had? It'll help me pinpoint where to cut so I don't have to defile her body any more than necessary."

"I don't," I answered. "All I know is she said it was top of the line."

"You must pay well."

"She said she bought it with an inheritance from her folks," I lied.

"Probably stolen then. Though even black market tech like that would cost." Justus turned to the cabinets, rifling through them to find a few tools and laying them out on a small sterile stand next to the table.

"What I don't understand," I said as he activated a laser scalpel and leaned over Gia's head, "is why Keep spent twenty years looking for the duchess and couldn't find her if she was out here fomenting rebellion. Not in the beginning maybe, when she was still a kid, but later on."

"Unfortunately, what Her Grace calls a rebellion, Sedaya thinks of as random hits on relatively minor outposts at the edge of his territories. We're only a few hundred strong, with a half dozen half-beaten up ships, a handful of mechs, and a lot of determination. We're too small for Sedaya to care or know exactly who's responsible. Besides, Her Grace isn't taking any public credit."

"At least you're trying. Yet, I can't help but wonder why she isn't getting her name out there to bring more people to the cause."

He shrugged. "In the Dryka territories at least, most people see Sedaya's rule as inevitable. There's no will to fight."

"So why do you fight?"

"My name is Justus. I guess I feel compelled to stay true to it." He leaned in closer to Gia, using the scalpel to cut open her forehead. I had always assumed the link was in the back of her neck near her spine. Apparently not. He put the scalpel down and picked up a small saw, powering it on. The blade spun too fast to see the teeth. "You may want to back up a step or two if you don't want dust from her skull on you."

I stepped back and turned my head away as he brought the saw against bone, slowly cutting a channel in it. I only looked again once he put the tool down. "I'm sorry," I said to Gia's corpse. A necessary evil, but I still hated it.

"My crew and I, we're fighting Sedaya too. So is Keep. But we're way behind the eight-ball."

"I don't know what that means."

"He's a few steps ahead of us. The Duchess said she knows where he might have taken my crew. Do you know where she's talking about?"

He nodded. "Melchior. It's within Sedaya's territory. A barely habitable cesspool that happens to be one of the primary sources of iridium in the Spiral. Sedaya could have robots recovering the element. But forced labor is cheaper and more durable than machines in that atmosphere."

"So you think he sent them to a chain gang? A prison work program?"

"I think he sent them to Hell. And getting them out won't be easy, but looking at you…maybe you can do it. You did escape from Perspehon, after all."

"There was a lot of luck involved in that."

"So maybe you'll get lucky again."

He used a pair of small tongs and the scalpel to spread open Gia's brain before reaching in with a tweezer he held expertly between the last two fingers on his left hand. Feeling around in the gray matter, he pinched the tweezers closed and pulled out a pill-shaped gold device with a pair of leads hanging out of the back.

Justus whistled in awe. "You weren't kidding about top of the line. I've only seen this model on the hypernet. You can't even find a price for one of these. They won't even talk to you unless they're sure you can afford it. And no way this came off a black market." He looked at her face, and then at me, his eyes accusing. "Gia hasn't done a live performance in nearly two months after never missing a show in almost ten years." His hand slid toward his sidearm. "I have a hard time believing she would abandon her entire life to voluntarily hang out with a wanted fugitive."

"You know I could have you pinned to the wall before you even started to draw that blaster, right?" I said. "But I won't. Pull it if it makes you feel better. I admit, that's Gia. The real Gia. But no matter how impossible it may seem, she was here voluntarily. We were working together to bring down Sedaya. Blorb murdered her parents." I sighed wearily, eyes welling. "And then he murdered her." The words dripped off my tongue like venom.

Justus stared at me, hand remaining halfway to his gun. He nodded then, using the same hand to lift the sheet back over Gia's head. "This is a tragedy for the entire Spiral."

"The first of many to come if I don't act fast enough," I replied.

"I can't make any promises, but I'll talk to Her Grace. Maybe I can convince her to give greater consideration to your needs."

"Thank you," I said. "I appreciate that. Are you and her together, then?"

"Not like that," he replied. "Unrequited love, I'm afraid. But we are good friends. She'll listen to me." He used a cloth to sanitize the neural link and held it out to me. "This belongs to you, though you won't be able to do much with it unless you have access to it through a connected network and know the password to access it."

"What if I don't know the password?" I asked,

"You'll get three tries before it's bricked. Guess wisely."

"Not what I wanted to hear, but understandable. Thank you for helping me recover it."

"You're welcome." He looked at Gia again, shaking his head. "Such a shame."

CHAPTER 8

Justus and I split up after leaving the morgue, but not before I had him promise to send a couple of other rebels to load Gia's body onto *Head Case*. I wasn't sure what to do with her yet. Sending her out of the airlock was one option. Trying to get her back to her planet, another. I knew I didn't want to abandon her on the station. She deserved a better sendoff than that.

Justus headed back into the station, to wherever Dryka had gone to finish whatever she had left to do on the base. She said she had come hoping to find Keep here, so it seemed strange for her to linger. I didn't worry about her picking anything out of the station's mainframe. Everything sensitive had been erased a long time ago, and I had logged out of the etcher, putting it out of reach as well. I realized as I made my way toward the hangar that I had left the slab with the Grimoire sitting on the workstation. Fortunately, that too was biometrically protected. If Dryka wanted a look at the contents, she would need my face. And I would give it to her. The Grimoire didn't matter anymore. Blorb hadn't even bothered to take the slab when he took David.

It wouldn't take much more than literally twisting his arm to get him to make whatever types of sigils Sedaya wanted.

David had saved my life, but now that I had the benefit of hindsight I realized I probably should have let Keep kill him. This was the exact eventuality he had hoped to prevent. I would still be on my deathbed, but at least the larger universe would be safe.

Or would it?

Capturing David didn't change Sedaya's ultimate goal. It simply adjusted his plans for how to attain it. Even without David, Blorb would likely have still killed Alter and infiltrated the crew to get the Grimoire and the Star of Caprum. Maybe it would have even killed everyone rather than taking prisoners. At least this way, there was still a chance I could get to it first.

The doors to the hangar parted ahead of me. A handful of Dryka's rebels were already in the cavernous space, loitering near the ramp into *Head Case*. Glancing at the crates stacked nearby, I didn't wait for them to speak before pointing and shaking my head. "That's mine," I barked.

They had somehow found a way to bypass Levi and get into the armory, wasting no time offloading what seemed like most of our equipment.

One of the armored rebels stepped toward me, momentarily ignored as my gaze shifted to the other starship parked in the hangar. Large and boxy, it seemed to have started life as only the middle section, which was visibly older and more scuffed and worn than the added appendages. It had a pair of huge thruster nacelles on either side, connected to the main fuselage by thick, rigid pipes. Gun batteries were mounted on top of the nacelles and centrally on both top and bottom of the hull, which didn't have an obvious flight deck. No doubt the ship's controls were embedded in the center of the vessel.

"Excuse me," the rebel repeated, finally getting my attention. "And you are?"

"Ben," I replied. "Justus should have told you about me? And that you shouldn't be touching any of my stuff?"

"You mean the equipment?" he asked, pointing to the crates.

"Yeah, that. And anything else you stole from my ship."

"I'm sorry, sir. According to our records, this ship is unregistered and captained by a wanted fugitive. According to Hegemony law, that makes it and any of its contents permissible for salvage claim."

"The Duchess told me the bounties have all been lifted."

"The third-party bounties," he replied. "But you can't stop being a fugitive of the Hegemony that easily. Which means your ship is still up for grabs."

"Bullshit," I snapped. "You have no right to take a single item off my ship. I'm not your captive here, and neither is *Head Case*."

"I'm afraid that's not how it works. We're not breaking any laws by staking a claim to this equipment. Really, you should be thankful Her Grace is only laying claim to your surplus weaponry. She could commandeer the entire vessel if it was her will."

I stared at the rebel, unable to see his face past the opaque visor of his helmet. "You're telling me Dryka ordered you to break into my armory and steal my equipment?"

"*Her Grace*," the man replied, emphasizing the title, "ordered us to take anything we determined to be valuable to our cause. We need this ordnance a lot more than you do. How many guns can one man carry, anyway?"

I gritted my teeth. "There's not going to be one person on this ship after I get my crew back. I'll need that equipment." I closed my hand into a fist. "Either you put it all back on board or I will."

He noticed my fist, the veins on the back of it glowing brightly. Slightly unnerved by it, he moved back a step. "Sir, I'm only following orders from Her Grace. If you have a problem with us following perfectly legal protocol with regard to an unregistered and abandoned starship, you can—"

"Abandoned?" I snapped. "I'm standing right here. How is that abandoned?"

"You can take it up with Her Grace," he repeated.

I could have pushed the crates back up the ramp and at least into the hangar with minimal effort. Glancing at the other rebels nearby, I noticed they had all put their hands on their sidearms, ready in case I started a fight. Dryka had trusted me enough to let me go because I hadn't hurt any of her people. It wouldn't help my cause to change that now.

"Okay," I said, opening my fist and exhaling sharply. "I will. Where is she?"

He didn't answer right away. I heard his voice as a barely audible whisper as he asked Dryka for her location. "She's in the command center," he said. "She'll be here soon if you want to wait."

I considered waiting, but part of me was still curious what she was doing with the station. "I'll go to her. Don't touch anything else."

"Yes, sir," he replied condescendingly.

I left the hangar, grateful for the return of my strength as I walked briskly through the station to the command center, still annoyed by the violation of my ship. I never thought I would need to set the security system to keep *Head Case* unmolested out here.

A pair of guards were stationed outside of the command center, only the duchess and an unarmed man inside the small space. She leaned over his shoulder while he worked.

"Dryka," I said, trying to walk right past the guards.

They moved in front of the open door, blocking my path. She glanced back at me but didn't order them to step aside. "We need to talk."

She hesitated before motioning with her hand. The two guards moved aside, letting me in as she turned to face me. Removing her helmet again, she placed it on the workstation. "I don't expect you to address me as Your Grace, but I would appreciate Duchess, or Jacinda, or even Jackie or Jaycee if you need to be completely informal."

"How about Dutch?" I asked.

"No," she replied.

We both smiled in response to the exchange, which surprised me. "Duchess, we need to talk about my equipment."

"Don't you mean *my* equipment? The laws are very clear regarding ownership and claims on illicit materials."

I glanced at the other guy, who hadn't even glanced back when I called the duchess' name. He had the terminal open to what looked like life support settings. "What is he doing?"

"What Avelus should have done a long time ago. We're overloading the reactor to turn this place into space dust."

"Why? You've probably already discovered there's nothing useful here."

"Nothing obvious. What I'm worried about are the things we can't find, but maybe someone else can." She reached past her apparent nerd and picked up the slab. "I think this is yours, by the way. You left it in the lab."

"Are you sure you don't want to claim it too?" I asked.

She shrugged and tucked it under her arm with a smile. "Since you offered."

"You can't take my guns."

"I can and I did," she answered. "I'm sorry, Ben." She held out the slab again. This time I accepted it. "It's not that

I want to claim anything from your ship. But your armory was nearly as well stocked as some of Sedaya's outposts. We've paid for those arms with lives, and all we had to do here was cut through the door."

"But it's my stuff."

"Not anymore, it isn't. I need that equipment to fight Sedaya. The only reason I'm not claiming your ship is because it's...well...*underwhelming*."

"What?" I said. "*Head Case* is awesome."

"Maybe for pleasure or as a light freighter or smuggler. Ben, she's severely underpowered. At full charge that battery is marginally better than a starhopper. And right now you can't even hyperspace out of this system."

"Oh, I get it. Yeah, Blorb stole the power source. You know, the Star of Caprum?"

Her face turned to stone, her eyes practically popping out of their sockets. "You had my Star on your ship?"

"Yeah. It's actually *my* Star. Keep sold it to me."

"A dubious claim at best. It wasn't his to sell."

"I'm willing to bet there's some Hegemony law that says property that's unclaimed by its owner for over twenty years is fair game. Even Sedaya accepted the ownership as legal."

She grimaced. "Well it doesn't matter, because you just said Blorb took it."

"It matters because it's probably mounted in Sedaya's sigiltech battleship, *Dominator*, right now. Powering the sigils."

Her face twisted a little more, her scar making it especially ghoulish. "He has a sigiltech ship?"

"He would have had a lot more sigiltech ships, but we blew up the space dock where he was building them. Just that one got away. You're welcome."

"Why didn't you mention any of this an hour ago?"

"I told you Sedaya killed the Empress. You didn't seem to care that much about her."

"There's a big difference between *I snuck an alien assassin into the palace to kill the Empress* and *I'm building sigiltech warships to seize the Hegemony by force.*"

"I don't know if he'll actually need to use force. But when he eventually does, he'll have a fleet that can stand up to anything. That doesn't change the fact that the Empress' murder barely phased you."

"The Empress was very close to letting Sedaya marry a ten year-old me. She also didn't lift a finger to stop him from subverting my nobles and allowing him to steal my dukedom out from under me. I'm not exactly her biggest fan. Anyway, I thought if I helped you fix your ship you would take care of that part. Exposing Sedaya would give me the opening I need to launch a larger-scale assault against him while he's distracted."

"You missed the part where I can't exactly expose Sedaya because the Empress is an alien shapeshifter who works for him. Even if I rescued my crew and we killed Blorb, we would be blamed for murdering the Empress. And considering we're already persona non grata with the Royal Guard, that wouldn't go over too well."

She stared at me in silence, obviously considering the situation.

"Your Grace," the nerd said. "I've set everything up to create the overload."

"Thank you, Nevin," she replied. "Initiate the sequence."

"Yes, Your Grace." He turned back to the console.

"You would need to find Prince Hiro," she said. "If he knows the Empress isn't really the Empress—"

"—he can legitimize whatever we do to handle it," I finished. "I know. I'm working on that too. But like I said before, I can use all the help I can get. And helping me is helping yourself. So is not taking my guns."

"You have more guns than you need. Even with a full crew."

"You can never have too many guns, Duchess. I'm sure you know that."

She smiled. "I do. Which is why I'm keeping yours."

"I thought—"

"Consider it payment for getting you off this station before it explodes," she said. "I would say that's a fair trade."

"Fine," I agreed, relenting. "What about helping me rescue my crew and Prince Hiro?"

"I need to think about that."

"What's there to think about?"

"I can't help you directly with that without the risk of exposing my true identity."

"So what?"

"If we fail then I'll wind up joining your crew in the iridium mines."

"Instead of what? Playing at rebellion with your ragtag group of freedom fighters? This is the best chance to take down Duke Sedaya you're ever going to get. How much can you want your planets back if you aren't willing to take the risk?"

"You don't know anything about me or what I'm trying to do," she snapped defensively. "I told you, I'll think about it."

"Do you know whose body is in the morgue, Duchess?" I growled, angered by her reluctance. "Gia. *The* Gia. The most popular singer in the Spiral. A woman who owned an independent planet and had more electro than I can even conceive. She risked everything she had to fight against Sedaya because he had her parents killed. Now she's dead, and I know without a doubt she wouldn't have it any other way because she actually took action instead of just talking about it. She lived on her terms, and she died that way. What about you? You can have the guns, for all the good they'll do you."

I didn't wait for her response before spinning around and storming away from the command center.

CHAPTER 9

I didn't slow at all when I returned to the hangar, storming past the rebels assembled near the front of *Head Case*, up the ramp and into the ship. I scaled the steps to the elevator, teeth clenched, hands curled into fists. I still couldn't believe that after everything I revealed to Duchess Dryka, she had told me she needed to think about helping me. It was almost enough to convince me she was actually another Blorb in Duchess clothing. What kind of rebellion turned down an opportunity to cause massive damage to the opposition?

I already knew the answer. A rebellion being run by fear over fury. At this point, I had enough fury for me and them both.

"Captain!"

The man's shout stopped me from boarding the elevator as the doors slid open. I turned around and walked over to the railing to look down at him. The same soldier who had confiscated my stuff. He stepped aside as the other members of his unit carried the equipment back up the ramp into the hangar.

"I told Dryka she can have it," I said. "I don't want it back because she feels guilty."

"I can't speak to that, Captain. All I can tell you is that she ordered me to return your equipment."

"Are you going to fix the door you cut open too?" I asked.

"We can, if you'll allow us to stay on board. We have less than an hour before this place blows. The detonation's going to unsettle the field around it too, so we need to be well clear by then."

"As long as the duchess still plans to tow me somewhere I can install a more reliable power source, you and your team are welcome aboard. What's your name?"

"Kathkamalhotep," he replied, laughing under his helmet. "Everyone just calls me Kat."

"Gee, I can't see why," I said.

"Look, my parents claimed asylum on Caprum during the Scourge. They tried so hard to get away from unrest only to wind up in the middle of another period of chaos. They didn't have the strength left to fight against Sedaya when he seized control. But I did, and still do." He pointed to each member of his unit as they scaled the steps toward me, each hefting one of the weapons crates over their shoulders, using the enhanced strength of their armor. "We're all in this with you. That's Ki, Stearns, Narayan, and O'Neill."

"Captain." Ki, the petite female leading the group, nodded her affirmation. Stearns was her polar opposite, large and broad. Narayan fell somewhere in between, while O'Neill, the other female in the group, had a shorter, stockier build. Muscle, not fat.

"Are you in logistics?" I asked Kat.

"In Her Grace's army, we all do whatever we can," Stearns replied for him.

"You must have really made an impression on Her Grace," O'Neill said. "She's never returned salvage before.

Guns and ammo, no less. We have such a great need for them."

"Yeah, well. I might too where I'm going," I replied. The elevator doors remained open, and the soldiers boarded. I remained behind to wait for Kat while they carried my equipment back to the armory. "Tell the Duchess she can keep the rest," I said. "Fifty-fifty. I think that's fair." It wasn't really as far as I was concerned, but despite my frustration with her reluctance to act, I didn't want to get too far on her bad side just yet. I still needed her to deliver me somewhere beneficial.

Kat paused to speak into his comms before continuing up the steps to join me on the overhang. "Her Grace thanks you for your willingness to compromise. She accepts the remaining equipment."

"Great," I replied. "That's the end of it then. How long did you say we have until we need to be out of here?"

"Forty minutes now, give or take."

"Ben!" I looked over the railing again, recognizing Justus by his size and the wear and tear on his armor. He had a pair of fighters behind him, guiding the floating gurney with Gia's corpse on it. Seeing her again created a pit in my chest. "Where do you want her?" he asked.

I didn't really know where to keep her. I just didn't want her stuck in the station, especially since it was going to blow up. But how could I hold on to her corpse for weeks? *Head Case* didn't have a freezer.

"I'm open to suggestions," I replied.

"Tradition within most navies is to eject the dead from an airlock while in hyperspace," Kat said. "Let the rift turn them to dust to become one with the universe."

"Most navies aren't putting the most famous singer in the galaxy to permanent rest," Justus replied.

"What do you mean?"

"That's Gia under the sheet," I explained.

"Gia? You mean the Lollipop Queen?"

"Yeah. One and the same."

Kat reached up and tore off his helmet, tears already running down his cheeks. He was a handsome man, with a darker complexion, square jaw, and thick eyebrows and hair. "Please tell me you're joking. I love Gia." He did the weird twerking move, which looked even more creepy coming from a male soldier. "Everything's Cotton Candy is my favorite song."

"I'm sorry, Kat," I said. "She was trying to help us stop Sedaya from pushing the entire Spiral into war. She knew the risk."

"I can't believe it. I never knew she was so brave." Kat looked to Justus. "Why aren't we doing anything?"

Even with his helmet on, I could tell by Justus' body language that he didn't have a good answer. He shifted uncomfortably, saved when Dryka appeared on the ramp into *Head Case*, helmet tucked under her arm.

"We are," she replied, loudly enough for me to hear. "Thank you, Ben, for reminding me why I started fighting in the first place. I've become too complacent over the last few years, settling for nicks and scrapes when I should have gone for the jugular. Kat's unit is the best I have. They're yours for as long as you need them. So is Justus."

"Your Grace?" Justus said, confused.

"I wish I could come with you," she continued. "But I have to send a warning to the nobles I can trust that things aren't as they seem. Ben, I'll tow you close to the nearest trading post that caters to your kind of clientele. After that, I'll see about raising as much of a fleet as I can to stand against a sigiltech ship. From what I've discovered, without an equivalent ship to match we'll need quite a few."

I shook my head. "It won't matter. Sedaya's lackey is posing as the Empress. He has full control of the Royal

Navy through Blorb. I don't think there are enough ships in the Spiral to stand up to both."

"No, there aren't. That's why you need to find Prince Hiro. When you do, if I can help you in any way, I will. Until then, I think it's better for both of us if I remain in the shadows, working behind the scenes."

"But you're in?" I asked.

"I'm in," she replied. "Justus has all of the codes to the backchannels we use for private communications. He can help you get in touch with me whenever you need."

"Your Grace," Justus said. "I should remain behind with you."

"No. There's still some question about Ben's health, especially with the mutations in his blood. He may need a doctor, and you're the closest thing we have. Besides, you're the best I have to give."

"Yes, Your Grace."

"Also, I can take Gia's body with me, and have her preserved and prepared for a proper burial, if you'll trust me with her."

I glanced at Justus, who nodded. "Okay, you can bring her with you."

"I have one other request, Ben," Dryka added.

"What's that?"

"If you do manage to rescue Avelus, please don't mention me to him. I still want to confront him myself, on my own terms."

I nodded. If I did manage to get Keep back, having him deal with the duchess was the least of my, or his, concerns. "No problem."

"We'll be under way shortly." She shifted her attention to Justus. "Keep me apprised of your progress."

"Yes, Your Grace," he said, bowing his head as a show of respect.

She turned back around, regarding me critically. "Good luck, Ben."

"You too, Duchess," I replied.

She motioned to the two fighters handling the gurney, and they all left *Head Case* with Gia.

"I wanted Sedaya dead before," Kat said. "For killing Gia, I want him to suffer first."

I put my hand on his armored shoulder. "Let's see what we can do about that."

"Aye, Captain," he replied.

CHAPTER 10

It felt strange to be on the flight deck alone. Even during the times when Alter hadn't been in the co-pilot seat beside me, there had always been someone on the sofa behind me. Shaq most often, curled up on the armrest with his claws dug into the fabric just in case we had to make any sudden maneuvers. The scratches had become numerous enough that some of the foam stuffing poked out of the small rips. Matt had joined me here quite a bit as well. Keep a little less, Gia a few times. Druck, once or twice at most.

My hands danced in the air in front of me, working the augmented reality menus hanging between me and the forward transparency. I had started with a full system diagnostic, which had quickly eaten through half of the time remaining before we needed to launch. Dryka had made the mistaken assumption that *Head Case* was already spaceworthy when she ordered her tech to begin the overload process. Fortunately, she wasn't wrong. While power levels were way too low to even think about hyperspace, the ship did have enough juice to leave the station and navigate through the asteroid field, so long as we took the shortest path out. There was even enough in reserve to allow the shields to take a few hits if it came to that. The ion cannons were out of the question, so I was glad we wouldn't need them.

A chirp brought my attention to the comms. A hail from the only ship in the vicinity, parked in the hangar behind me.

"Head Case, this is *Radiance.* Do you copy?" Dryka said.

I accepted the comm link. "I copy."

"What's your status, Ben?"

"System check is good. All systems are go. Power levels aren't great, but it should be enough to get us where we need to be, wherever that is."

"Ultimately, you're headed to Windfall Station," she replied. "It's a semi-independent space station orbiting a red dwarf about three days in hyperspace from here, in the Crenshaw Duchy. Unaffiliated beyond the taxes and operating surcharges the owner, Rafael Washazaki pays for the privilege of remaining open to all, no questions asked. Windfall is Duchess Crenshaw's dirty little non-secret. A major source of revenue to help support her lavish lifestyle."

"And they won't have a problem with me being a fugitive? Or the ship being targeted by the Royal Guard?"

"Not with the amount of electro you said you have in your account. Money talks louder than the Empress on Windfall."

"What about someone trying to confiscate everything?" I asked.

"That's why you have Kat and his unit. They'll guard the ship while you're docked. We're ready to depart when you are, Ben."

I glanced over at the empty co-pilot seat, a fresh crater forming in my chest. It was way too late to be able to help Alter, but this was still far from over. I would do whatever I could to make Sedaya and Blorb regret leaving me for dead instead of killing me outright. "I'm ready."

"In that case, we're opening the hangar bay doors now," she said.

I lifted my head. The augmented reality let me see through the decks above the flight deck to the outside of the ship, where the large blast doors over the top of the hangar began to slowly slide apart.

"I'm sending you the rendezvous coordinates," Dryka continued. "We'll meet there to connect *Head Case* to *Radiance* so we can enter hyperspace together. It's on you to navigate through the asteroid field to get there."

"Copy that," I replied. "I handled the asteroids and the defenses you set up here when I could barely hold my head up, so it shouldn't be a problem."

"No, I don't expect it will be," she agreed, a hint of admiration sneaking into her voice.

"How did you find out about this place, anyway?" I asked. "And about sigiltech? It's all supposed to be a secret."

"The truth is out there if you know where to look and what to search for. And all it takes is one breadcrumb to lead anyone into the wormhole who's interested enough. For me, it started with the sigil ring."

The bay doors opened enough for us to be able to pass through. *Radiance* lifted off first, needing only a slight burst of thrust from the vectoring nozzles on the hull to push up toward the opening.

"It makes me wonder," I said, watching the ship go, "if maybe Keep gave you that ring on purpose, hoping that maybe it would lead you to him one day."

"I doubt that," Dryka replied.

"That's because you're still thinking about it as someone who believes they were abandoned. But what if Keep's absence is the only reason you survived? He went through a lot of trouble to protect the Star of Caprum, and to make sure it only came into possession of someone he thought would do the right thing with it. He's spent years looking for you without success. But you used the ring to almost find him. The timing was just a little off."

Radiance cleared the hangar, drifting out into the asteroid field before she responded. "I'm open to the idea that you may be right. I truly do hope that's the case. But I would still want to hear that from Keep's lips, unprompted."

"Yeah, I would too," I agreed. I pulled back on the stick, the computer translating the maneuver to wanting to climb without thrust, triggering the vectoring thrusters and pushing *Head Case* up along a similar track to the one *Radiance* had taken.

"We'll reconnect at the rendezvous," Dryka said. "*Radiance* out."

The comm link disconnected. The door to the flight deck slid open. I glanced back as Justus entered. He had shucked the hard shell of his combat armor, remaining in the wetsuit-like protective underlayer.

"A sofa?" he said, surprised by the seating arrangement as he reached the front of the flight deck. "Not exactly up to spec."

"It's probably more comfy than spec," I replied.

"Maybe. Do you mind if I grab the co-pilot seat?"

"Be my guest," I replied.

"Aye, Captain," he said, claiming the seat as *Head Case* reached the top of the hangar. He grabbed the helmet on the back of the seat and pulled it on.

"Are you a pilot?" I asked.

"Not at all," he replied. "I did a training course during my brief time in the Caprum Defense Force. It's better if I don't touch anything."

I smiled as I activated the ship's comms. "Attention all

hands. We're about twenty seconds from entering the asteroid belt. It could get a little bumpy. Appropriate safety measures are advised."

The flight deck door slid open again. Kat and O'Neill entered. They too had removed the outer layer of their armor.

"A couch?" Kat said, approaching the front of the deck.

"That's what I said," Justus replied.

"It has seatbelts," I argued in defense of the arrangement. "Better use them."

The two rebels hurried to the sofa and quickly strapped themselves in as we cleared the hangar doors and floated into the asteroid field. Reaching for the throttle, I juiced the mains, easing *Head Case* forward as the sensor grid began populating. *Radiance* had a decent head start on us, but I decided I would close the gap by the time we reached the coordinates the duchess had sent over.

The grid in the center console finished rendering. I pushed the throttle forward, opening the mains with enough force to gently shove us back into our seats. *Head Case* took off, headed right for a large asteroid spinning across the forward transparency.

"Uh, Captain?" Justus said, already nervous about my flying. He just didn't know me yet.

"Do you like rollercoasters?" I asked, glancing over at him.

"What's a rollercoaster?" he replied.

I smiled, happy to be underway. Happy to be alive. I didn't want to be greedy. I would settle for surviving long enough to rescue Matt and the others and put Sedaya and Blorb out of power. That didn't seem like too much to ask.

"What's a rollercoaster?" My grin stretched wider. "You're about to find out."

CHAPTER 11

I didn't just catch up to *Radiance* on the way to the rendezvous point. I beat them there, despite taking a wider path through the asteroids in order to avoid a potential collision with them. I wasn't trying to show up the other starship's pilot, whether it was Duchess Dryka or someone else. I did it to show myself I was well enough to do it. On the way in, I needed Alt…Blorb's help whenever I became too dizzy or had to cough.

"You okay back there?" I asked, glancing at Kat and O'Neill on the sofa. Justus had already turned green, keeping his head down and eyes closed so he didn't have to watch any more close calls. The other two rebels looked equally shaken, though they hadn't averted their gazes.

"Yeah," Kat said softly. "We're…fine."

"Where did you learn to fly a starship like that?" O'Neill asked.

"Video games," I replied. "Probably too many of them."

"And this is what a rollercoaster feels like?" Justus asked.

"Without coming face-to-face with an asteroid large

enough to crush us into oblivion from time to time, yeah," I replied. "I was never worried."

"That makes one of us," Kat said.

"Sorry. I wasn't trying to show off. I just needed to know I could handle the stresses before we're in a situation where it isn't optional."

"This is your ship, Captain," Justus said. "You set the mood. Fly the way you fly."

A chirp alerted me to Dryka's incoming hail.

"Nice flying, Ben," she said. "But then, I expected as much. Kill your velocity so you can maneuver into position to link up with *Radiance*."

"Copy that," I replied, spinning *Head Case* around so we were again facing the asteroids. I fired the mains, slow and steady, watching our speed drop as *Radiance* appeared from around the last asteroid in the belt. Dryka's ship slowed, altering course to make its approach. Two of her people already stood on top of the central hull, ready to connect the electromagnet that would link up the two ships.

"Nice and easy," Dryka said as *Head Case* came to a full stop and I cut all thrust.

Radiance needed five minutes to cut the small gap between us in half. Ten more to again cut it in half. Slowing to a near crawl, it was nearly an hour before the other ship came to a full stop just beneath us.

"We're in position," Dryka said. "Connecting the link now."

The two spacewalkers jumped from the top of *Radiance* holding onto the tether as they drifted the ten meters to reach us. Latching onto the hull with maglocked gloves, they quickly activated the electromagnet at the end of the cable. Its wide, flat head clamped onto *Head Case's* chin. A red LED on the head switched to green, and the spacewalkers each raised a thumb, confirming the lock. They pushed off the hull, releasing the maglock and floating back to *Radiance*, completing the entire process inside of five minutes.

"Link complete," Dryka announced. "You're just along for the ride now."

"Copy that."

"Initializing hyperspace drive."

I looked out through the forward transparency. *Head Case* was tethered backward to *Radiance*, giving me a permanent view of the ship's ion trails as the main thrusters fired, accelerating ahead through space. A sudden panic crashed into me when I saw the first ripple of distortion from the hyperspace drive creating the deformation of spacetime around us. For a moment, my mind convinced me this was all just another elaborate setup and Dryka was about to deliver me directly to Sedaya. Or maybe Sucaath. Either way, a momentary lapse in calm led me to think I had just made a terrible mistake by trusting the duchess. Four days to Windfall Station? Or four days to Melchior?

Not to rescue Matt and the others. To join them.

Of course, the idea was ridiculous, and as the spacetime distortion continued forming around both ships, I was able to begin reasoning the fear away. If Sedaya wanted me, Blorb could have taken me at the same time it took David. If he wanted me dead and Dryka was secretly working with him, she could have killed me while I was paralyzed and unconscious. And there was nothing left in my possession the duke could possibly want. He already had the Star. He already had access to new, deadly sigils. He had already left me to die.

"Captain, are you okay?" Justus asked, noticing my distress. I didn't take my eyes off the transparency until the stars stretched and vanished, leaving both *Radiance* and *Head Case* surrounded by emptiness.

"Yeah," I finally replied, looking over at him and exhaling the breath I hadn't realized I was holding. "I'm fine. I just had this panic attack that I let you lead me into another trap. I know that sounds ridiculous. I'm over it now."

"It doesn't sound ridiculous," Justus said. "You've been through a lot, Ben. It's only natural for you to be in a heightened state of alert. Hopefully, these next few days can help rebalance you a little. Give your mind a chance to come out of survival mode. Maybe even have a little fun. I saw the lounge the first time I came on board. Do you play piano or guitar?"

"I can play both," I replied, the change in topics immediately helping me calm a little. "But I prefer guitar. Do you play?"

"I know a few chords," he answered. "Maybe we can jam on the way to Windfall."

"Jam?" I snapped, throwing Justus a seething look. "I don't want to jam. I don't want to have fun. I just want to get my crew back."

"Sorry, Captain." he raised his hands in conciliation. "I get it. You're worried about your people. I didn't mean to minimize their predicament and the danger they're in."

"Hyperspace entry completed," Dryka announced before I could apologize to Justus for biting his head off. I hadn't realized how on edge I actually was, now that we were away from Omega Station. I regretted not having the chance to see the place explode, to put some kind of closure on what had transpired there. "Settle in and relax, Ben. Estimated time to drop is ninety-two hours, sixteen minutes."

"Copy that. Thank you for getting me out of there."

"You're welcome. Thank you in advance for what you're about to do to Sedaya."

"You're welcome in advance," I replied. "If you want to talk about anything, you know where to find me for the next few days."

"Nothing like a captive audience," she answered. "Same here. *Radiance* out."

The comm link disconnected. I sat back in my seat and stared into the black for a few seconds before locking *Head Case* in idle, removing my helmet, and standing up. Seeing I planned to leave the flight deck, Justus, Kat, and O'Neill all stood as well.

"Justus," I said. "I'm sorry for—"

"Nah, forget it," he replied, waving off the apology. "You've been through a lot. I can't even start to imagine what it feels like to be you right now."

"You mean the neon blood?"

He laughed. "Yeah, well, that too. But I mean almost dying of cancer and having your entire crew either killed or abducted."

"It feels like I have an elephant standing on my chest," I said. "But considering that yesterday I was sure I would die alone on that station, it's a major improvement." I exhaled some more of my tension. "Anyway, I'm going to start working on getting into that neural link you recovered for me. You're welcome to make use of all of *Head Case's* amenities for the duration of your time on board. I'll lock down anywhere I don't want you to go, primarily Deck Five. Also, please stay out of the Captain's Suite."

"If it's okay with you, we'll set up our racks in the hangar," Kat said. "You're going to need your individual quarters for when we get your crew back."

I smiled. "I like the way you think."

"Aye, Captain," he replied.

"Carry on then," I said. "Dismissed."

Each of them bowed their heads, turned and left the flight deck. Once they were gone, I retrieved Gia's neural link from my pocket and held it up to get a good look at it. The leads wouldn't give me access to the link. They were to provide electricity to the device, which had previously come from excess current generated by Gia's brain. I couldn't give it a like source without implanting it in my gray matter, but I didn't think such a drastic step would be necessary. All I needed to power the device was a small electrical charge.

And I knew exactly where to get it.

CHAPTER 12

I spent an hour getting cleaned up—shower, shave, and change of clothes—before taking the neural link, *Head Case's* larger control slab, and a bottle of Coke up to Deck Six. Seeing myself completely naked for the first time since the etcher had imprinted the construct on me had left me a little shaken. I knew my blood glowed now. Considering it was keeping me alive, I was mostly okay with that. Even so, looking in the mirror, I couldn't help feeling like a freak. Sure, I could cover most of the glowy parts with clothes, maybe grow a beard, but I couldn't cover everything, everywhere, all the time. Sooner or later, someone would get a glimpse.

Besides, trying so hard to hide it would only make me feel more out of place. I reminded myself that there were all kinds of aliens in the Spiral, from bipedal catlike species to giant bugs to blue squirrels, all of which were accepted within society. And that ultimately, it didn't matter what anybody else thought about the way I looked. Like Popeye the Sailor, I was what I was.

I had originally put on a long-sleeved hoodie and sweatpants. Deciding to embrace my discomfort and accept what

I had become, I approached the workbench Miklos and Archie had set up having changed into a basic navy tank and shorts, the glow of my blood enough to allow me to navigate the deck before the motion-activated lights came on. In fact, I was pretty sure the volume of so-called chaos energy stored in my blood was increasing over time, building back as I recovered from the etching and my body had more time to heal. It left me wondering if Dryka's forces had ambushed me at my weakest, and if so, what would I be able to do at my strongest? Would I be able to hold my own against a Gilded like Admiral Lyke, even with the wrong catalyst etched into my skin?

With four days to play with, I figured I would have time to test my might before we reached Windfall station. While Keep had always said it was too dangerous for me to mess with sigiltech on the ship, that was before near-suffocation had helped me learn control. While in the beginning I could only throw the full-force of my energy into an action, now I could dial the volume up or down on the fly, something Keep had said other archons, Gilded or not, couldn't do without restarting the action. It was a subtle but important divergence from the norm, one that could give me a leg up on the competition and maybe help close the gap between my maximum available effort and the enemy's.

All of that was for another time. Right now, my interest was in gaining access to Gia's neural link. All of the data she had collected on Prince Hiro's abduction was there, and I needed it.

The first step was to restore power to the device, which was why I had come up to Deck Six. Standing in front of Miklos' workbench, I couldn't help feeling a tinge of remorse for both him and Archie. The Acheon's actions at the space dock had been drastic, but I understood them even better now than I did at the time. The grief, the anger, the frustration. The overwhelming desire to do something about it. To make the person responsible pay. All of those things were like a cyclone inside me, driving me forward while at the same time threatening to overwhelm all sense of reason. If I had a candy bomb, using it on *Dominator* or *Eviscerator* would be incredibly satisfying, even if I died in the process. But it also wouldn't be the smartest move. It wouldn't help Matt or stop Sedaya from solidifying his control over the Hegemony.

I looked over the assorted debris scattered across the workbench. Pieces of wire, screws, circuit boards, tools, and devices in various states of completion covered the table, with only a small bare space in the center. I put the neural link down there, eying the other detritus more closely, pushing some of it aside to see what was underneath as I conducted my search. I wasn't an electronics tech by any means, and I had learned just enough from Alter to be dangerous. My biggest fear was that I would overload the neural link and fry the electronics inside, rendering the device useless. That's why I scoured the work area, moving the junk around until I finally found what I had come up here for.

"Eureka!" I shouted, the exhortation echoing in the room. I'd always wanted to say that, and it seemed like as good a time as any. I held up one of the small discs Miklos had designed to launch what amounted to a denial-of-service attack against a powered door controller. Used as intended, the disc could release the lock on almost any mechanical door. In this case, I didn't need the circuit board inside the disc or the software Miklos had written from scratch to make it do what it did, though it occurred to me I could have used the device back on the cargo hauler to open the hangar bay doors. Waiting for Gia to do it from the bridge had nearly put me face to face with an entire unit of guards. Not that it mattered now. That episode was ancient history.

The memory remained fresh though, in large part because Admiral Lyke had restrained my crew on Omega Station in almost the same manner Commander Kray had done it there. It was almost as if they had both studied the scenario in the same manual or taken the same evil Gilded archon class.

All I needed from the disc was the battery, located at the base of the device beneath its simple metal cover. I found a pair of magnifier goggles half-buried under a pile of electronics near the back of the workbench. Miklos hadn't been the neatest or most organized of people. Sliding the goggles on, I used a tiny screwdriver to pry the cover off the disc. Flipping it over exposed the battery. Pausing there, I unlocked the slab and entered *Head Case's* network settings, looking for the neural link. Of course, it wasn't in the list. Not yet.

I placed the link next to the disc. With a pair of tweezers, I pulled the leads out of the device and pressed them to the battery. Nothing happened. The link didn't power up, probably because there was no actual current running through that part of the battery. I needed to touch the leads to the conductive plate. Since I wasn't sure if the battery was soldered to the main board, I worked to slip the leads between the two layers, hoping to siphon enough juice to power up the neural link.

It took a lot of patience to get the minuscule metal plates where I wanted them. It left me hunched over the workbench, my back muscles cramping, a line of sweat popping out across my forehead. Pushing it the last millimeter into place, I straightened up and turned my attention to the slab I'd propped against a stack of debris beside the cleared space.

"Come on, you can do it," I said, waiting for the link to appear in the device list. I wasn't even sure if what I was doing had any chance of working. Maybe I should have waited to have someone on Windfall Station take a look at it. For one thing, I didn't think I could spare the time. For another, I didn't want anyone to find out I had Gia's neural link. Too many uncomfortable questions would surely follow. Even so, if this didn't work I wouldn't have any other choice.

The list of addresses connected to the network shifted down slightly. NL64-EXTREME appeared at the top. That had to be it.

"Eureka!" I shouted again, louder this time, pumping my fist in victory. "Yes!"

I left the neural link on the workbench and reached for the slab, careful not to bump or jog it in any way that might end in losing the connection. I tapped on NL-EXTREME to get the network details before opening a terminal and attempting to connect to the neural link's address. I fully expect a prompt for a password I didn't know. With only three guesses, I would need to be very deliberate about what I entered. I definitely hadn't given much thought to what the device's password might be. If Alter were still here, she would probably have some great insight.

But she wasn't here and never would be again.

A chill ran through my body, and I nearly fell off the stool. With everything that had happened from the moment Admiral Lyke arrived on Omega Station, I never had a chance to really process that truth before now. It hit me like a black hole, the elephant pressure on my chest becoming a sudden crushing sensation in my heart. I lowered my face into my hand, my elbow braced on the workbench, my mind conjuring images of Alter in her many personas as I fought back tears. I would never see any of them—*her*—ever again.

And then it hit me. When Blorb did whatever it did to her, it had captured all of her personas as well. Could that mean that maybe Alter was still in there somewhere? A part of Blorb?

More importantly, was it possible to pull her back out?

The idea felt more like wishful thinking than anything logical or reasonable, but it was enough to stop my mourning dead in its tracks. When Sedaya captured me, Alter continued to believe I would make it back. She hadn't given up on me. I wouldn't give up on her either, at least not until I knew for sure she couldn't be saved.

I rubbed at my suddenly tired eyes, a potential password popping into my head. Just like Aretha Franklin had said. R-E-S-P-E-C-T. It was one of Gia's favorite words, and if there was any chance at all she might have wanted me to be able to gain access one day, it would be the most likely choice.

I reached for the slab, eyes returning to the terminal, expecting a flashing cursor next to the password prompt. I flinched when I realized the neural link hadn't requested authentication. It had gone directly into the root, completely unsecured.

"What the..." I mouthed, quickly entering a command to display any other available commands and confirming the device was unlocked. I could hardly believe Gia hadn't set a password. The neural link ran the same base OS as *Head Case*, albeit with a slightly different flavor. Even so, I was able to easily poke around in the filesystem.

The file named 'BEN-README' was impossible to miss.

I could hardly believe she had left me a message inside her neural link. I opened the file, revealing a large epistle.

Ben, I'm sorry. I know you know now that I didn't betray you. I never would. This probably sounds hokey but you're actually one of the best friends I've ever had, even if I didn't get to know all that much about you or spend as much time with you as I would have liked. But coming from where I come from, having someone who always treated me like a person and not something special because of my fame or wealth has always been so refreshing and I'm incredibly grateful to you for that. It means more to me than you'll ever know.

I'm sorry for the lack of formatting but I'm dictating this while I'm lying on the floor of the lab. My body's cut open in so many places, I'm woozy and hot and cold. I have blood in my eyes and in my throat and mouth, and I can barely breathe. I don't want you to feel guilty for blaming me for giving up our location. And if you do, I forgive you. I know it sure seemed that way and if you hadn't, I probably wouldn't have figured out Alter was an imposter. But I was too late, and damn it, I shouldn't have gone for the head. I should have known better. And now I'm here on the floor, with you unconscious a few feet away. I'm doing my best to leave you this message when I can't talk or move. All I can do is lie here knowing I'm going to die. I didn't expect it to be like this. To come so quickly and so unexpectedly, but I guess that's how death is.

I hope you get a chance to read this. I hope you come to and that you find a way to survive. I don't know if you will but I believe in you and I'd rather talk to you while I die than just stare at the ceiling feeling so totally alone the way you will be in a few minutes.

If you do read this, it's because I removed the password protection to make it easier for you to get in. If you aren't Ben, screw you! Since I'm sure I'm dead the absolute best thing you can do for me is to keep living, to rescue the others, and find Sedaya and Blorb and kick their asses for me. May they rot in hell. I left you everything I found on the companies that had the tools and resources to build the components of the starship that took Hiro in a folder named forben. Since I'm sure I'm dead by now the absolute best thing you can do for me is to keep living, to rescue the others.

I'm going to assume you'll succeed because I know if there's a way to do that, you'll find it. That way I can rest in peace believing the Spiral won't fall into the hands of those murdering pricks. I've left you something else too but you'll have to wait a bit for it because it's harder to trace. And no, I didn't arrange everything while I was lying here dying. I figured this could happen after the candy bomb and planned accordingly. Don't worry about my planet. If Blorb is the Empress, I can pretty much guarantee he's going to take it back. That was always the plan I think which is why that assassin came for me. It sucks there's nothing I can really do about it, but I did have some contingencies so it'll still be a while before anyone knows that I'm actually dead or even missing. I know you have no idea what I'm talking about but you'll probably see evidence of it soon enough.

My vision's starting to blur, Ben, and I'm getting so cold, but I don't see darkness here only light and it's so damn cotton candy. Wow wow wow wow wow wow wo......

The text ended abruptly. I read it four times to make sure I didn't miss anything. Then I put the slab back on the workbench and lowered my head into my hand again. I never would have considered myself Gia's best friend. That she thought I was, whatever her reasons, meant more to me than I could understand. It was enough to bring me to tears. For her. For Alter. For Miklos and Archie. For the Empress and her son and everyone else whose lives Sedaya had ruined.

Thankful to be alive and glad to have Deck Six to myself, with time alone to mourn, I let out all of the emotion churning inside me. When the tears ended, I wiped my eyes clear, lifted my head and stared at Gia's neural link.

I had work to do.

CHAPTER 13

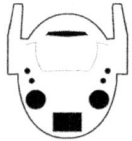

"Hey, Captain," Ki said as I entered the kitchen. She and O'Neill were at the table, finishing off a couple of beers.

"You look tired, Cap," O'Neill added, glancing back at me.

"I just spent the last six hours staring at a screen," I replied. I'd left everything set up on Deck Six, not wanting to do anything to risk disconnecting the power from the neural link or losing access. I had what I needed from the device, at least for now. The names and locations of the four companies Gia had identified as potential suppliers for the blueburn's structural frame. "Now I'm tired and hangry." I walked over to Asshole, opening the cabinet to get a plate.

"Hangry?" Ki asked.

"In a bad mood because you're so hungry equals hangry," I explained. "It's Earth slang."

"That's right. Justus told us you're from Earth. There aren't many Earthians in the Spiral."

"I thought Matt and I were the *only* Earthians in the Spiral. Well, maybe some of Sucaath's goons have made the transit, too."

"Sucaath?" O'Neill said. "Who's that?"

"I'm not completely sure. All I know is that he's aware of sigiltech and has been helping Sedaya gain access to them. I guess he's like the Emperor to Darth Vader. Or Sauron to Saruman. That kind of thing. But I could be completely wrong."

"I'm sorry, Cap," Ki said. "I have no idea what you just said."

I smiled. "Right. Because you aren't from Earth. Sorry. He's like Sedaya's mentor or something along that line. He was helping the duke complete the Grimoire, and in exchange, Sedaya was supposed to provide him with trained Gilded."

"Nope, I still have no idea what you're talking about. The only thing I understood from that sentence was *Sedaya bad*."

"That's probably enough for now," I admitted. "Do you know of other Earthians here?"

She tapped her chin, thinking about it before laughing. "Actually, now that I think about it, no. You're definitely the only one I've ever met. But honestly, if I didn't know you were from Earth I'd have no idea. We look the same."

"Your ancestors from the colony ship came from my future," I said. "And evolution doesn't happen that fast."

"So weird, isn't it?" O'Neill said. "Technically, you're like three thousand years older than us."

"It's definitely a little strange to try to get your mind around," I agreed. "I try not to think about what it would mean if Sedaya were to get what he wants and make a move on Earth. What if he won and seized the planet before the colony ship ever left?"

"Time only moves in one direction," Justus explained, entering the kitchen. "Time travel within the same timeline is impossible. But a wormhole or time distortion could theoretically drop you into an alternate dimension. A different timeline. In which case, even if Sedaya blew up Earth, the colony ship still arrived because it came from a timeline where Sedaya doesn't exist. Of course, that doesn't help your Earth." Done bullshitting, Justus turned his attention on Ki and O'Neill. "Playtime's over. Kat's looking for you two."

"Already?" Ki complained. "I thought we might get some R and R this transit."

"I'm afraid not."

"I wouldn't have had beer if I knew we were going to be training," O'Neill said. "Damn." She and Ki stood up.

"I'll clean up the bottles," I said.

"Thanks, Captain," Ki replied. "We'll see you around." They left the room, headed for the elevator.

"Asshole, I'll have half an eighteen inch pizza, pepperoni and extra cheese, well done."

"Oh, Bennie, you're makin' my mouth water," Asshole replied. "Comin' right up."

"And you can do beer in bottles now?"

"Whaddaya mean now? I've always been able to do bottles over here."

"So why do I keep putting cups in?"

"Why are you askin' me? I'm just the assembler. Half a pizza and a bottle of Schlitz comin' right up."

"Schlitz?" I said. "I don't think so. I know we brought a bottle of that IPA George likes back with us. I'm sure Matt must have programmed it in."

"Half a pizza and an IPA comin' right up," Asshole corrected.

"Your assembler has an interesting social module," Justus said. "And you gave it a name?"

I shrugged. "I programmed it to do a so-so imitation of a Brooklyn deli owner. And yeah, I like talking to things with names. Otherwise I feel like I'm just chatting with inanimate objects."

"You *are* chatting with an inanimate object. That's how voice control works."

"That doesn't mean it has to *feel* like I am."

"Order up!" Asshole announced. "Be careful, it's pipin' hot."

I opened the door and pulled out my half-pie and beer. I'd tried doing full-size ten inch pizzas before, but it totally threw off the crust to topping ratio and just wasn't the same. "Are you having anything?" I asked Justus.

"No, I ate already. Your assembler." He paused and smiled. "Asshole makes a really good loni sandwich."

"Loni? I don't know what that is, and I don't remember seeing a recipe for it."

"It's a bird," Justus explained. "About seven pounds, with blue feathers and a long neck. We farm them on Caprum."

"Oh, so they're like chicken?"

He shrugged. "I guess so?"

"What do they taste like?"

"Kind of bland, a little chewy. It's the seasonings that really give it flavor."

I nodded. "Yup. That's chicken." We both laughed. "You're not part of Kat's unit then?"

"No. We don't really go by ranks since we're such a small group, but if we did, he would be a sergeant and I would be closer to a colonel."

"So you outrank him?"

"In a sense. But we have different duties and roles we focus on. I don't tell him how to prepare his troops to fight, and he doesn't tell me how to fix things or strategize."

"Okay, but you do have a chain-of-command?"

"Yes. Definitely."

I put the pizza and beer on the table and sat, motioning to the opposite seat. "Can we talk?"

"Sure. You're the boss here, Captain." He accepted my offer to sit. "What do you want to talk about?"

"You have an interesting perspective on time travel," I said.

"Is it? That's the commonly accepted theory in the Spiral. Some pretty smart people have been working on proving it for a long time, without much luck so far, I might add."

"So maybe it's wrong."

"Could be. But I don't see how you eliminate all of the potential paradoxes otherwise. And since you're from Earth before the colony ship ever leaves Earth and it hasn't created some kind crazy apocalyptic vortex in spacetime, I think the circumstantial evidence holds up. Of course, we wouldn't know for sure unless Sedaya does blow up your planet, I suppose. Wouldn't that be something if we all just disappeared."

"It would definitely be *something*," I answered before taking a bite of the pizza.

He laughed. "I'm not implying I want that to happen. But that's the only thing I can think would happen if the accepted theory is wrong." He paused, eying me suspiciously. "You didn't just have me sit to theorize on time travel though."

"No. I wanted to talk to you about the neural link."

"What about it?"

"I have full access."

"Really? That was easier than I expected."

"Not because of me. Gia unlocked the neural link before she died. I've got the names of four companies that potentially helped build the ship that Prince Hiro was abducted in. If we can trace the ship to its last known location, we might be able to track down the prince from there."

"Great. But you seemed pretty sure Sedaya took the prince."

"I believe he funded the job, probably through the Dark Exchange. I don't think he's careless enough to let that trail lead directly back to him."

"Probably not, though he isn't known for being the most level-headed of nobles. Do you think whoever he hired is holding the prince captive, or might he already be dead?"

"They didn't need to take him if they just wanted to kill him. I'm working under the assumption he's alive, but might not be for much longer."

"Fair enough."

"I do think holding the prince is part of the job, but it's possible his abductors handed him off. Or they might be playing a shell game with the kid, keeping him on the move and ready to deliver to Sedaya at a moment's notice. Anyway, that's all conjecture right now. The first step is to figure out which of these companies might have a record of building the ship's chassis and learning who they might have sold it to. Since we're pressed for time, I thought maybe we could pass Gia's findings on to the duchess for her to pick up some of the investigative work."

"I don't know, Ben. It sounded to me like Her Grace had a lot of other tasks on her plate. Reaching out to sympathetic nobles to warn them about Sedaya without getting caught will be a pretty delicate process for her."

"Which is why I wanted to talk to you about the idea first. The fact is, if we recover Hiro and expose the Empress as a fake, we take the entire Royal Guard and any nobles still loyal to the Hegemony out of Sedaya's corner. At that point, he'll need to decide whether to try to take the seat by force, without the Royal Sentries, or run away with his tail between his legs. *Dominator* is powerful, but even one sigiltech ship can't stand up against the entire Royal Navy. I need you to convince Jaycee that's the higher priority play."

"Jaycee?" Justus replied.

"She told me I could call her that," I said. "I might be

able to convince her myself, but I think you have a better chance of it than I do."

"I don't know that she'll need too much convincing on this one," he replied. "Everything we might be able to pull together pales in comparison to the Sentry battlegroup orbiting Atlas, nevermind the entire fleet. If we can get Nattic back on the right side of things, we won't even need the call to arms."

"Ideally, she can do both. There's no such thing as too many allies or being too ready."

He smiled. "Are you sure you're just some kid from Earth who happened to buy a starship?"

"Yeah, why?"

"Because you remind me of my father. He was an Admiral in the Draconian Navy, back when His Grace, Matthias Dryka, was still alive. That's the kind of thing I can picture him saying."

"Is he still alive?"

"No. He died in the same battle that killed His Grace and made Her Grace the head of the Draconian duchy. He was a good man. A good father. Strong, confident, and loyal. He raised me to be the same."

"In that case, I appreciate the compliment. But I'm honestly nothing special. I've just read a lot of epic fantasy novels filled with this kind of game of thrones stuff. Plus, I'm pissed off."

His smile expanded. "That part reminds me of my father even more. He had a tremendous passion against injustice. If he was in your shoes, he'd be pissed off too." He stood up. "By your leave, I'll speak to Her Grace, Captain, and report back."

"Thank you, Justus. You're dismissed."

He bowed his head, leaving me sitting there staring at my pizza. Keep had told me I've matured since we first met, but being compared to an admiral? Thinking back on the conversation, I couldn't even completely believe the words that had come out of my mouth. Coming to the Spiral had definitely forced me to grow up a lot faster. It had also been so long since I was healthy enough to think so clearly. Maybe the brain tumor had robbed more from me than I'd even realized.

Either way, when it came to fighting back against Sedaya, I was just getting warmed up.

CHAPTER 14

The room on Deck Two that Alter and Matt had set up as a training area was empty when I entered it. The space wasn't huge. Twenty feet long and fifteen wide, it had been enough for learning hand-to-hand combat, sparring, and weapons handling, though obviously not live firing. Mats lined the floor and two of the bulkheads, while a small selection of weights, resistance bands, padded gloves, practice dummies, and other equipment waited neatly arranged in the corner. A couple of mirrors allowed users to observe their own form. I had only been here a few times, way back when Matt and I first purchased *Head Case*, starting just after we had escaped the warehouse on Caprum and defeated Sedaya's first round of goons in the hangar. Four months ago. On one hand, it felt like yesterday. On the other, it seemed like a lifetime. So much had happened. So much had changed. And it had all gone by so fast.

Not once had I ever been in this part of the ship feeling as healthy as I did right now. After meeting with Justus and having a bite to eat, I had gone to bed and slept a little too well, awaking nearly twelve hours later completely famished all over again. A quick breakfast of ham and eggs on an otherwise deserted Deck Three, and I was raring to go. My head was clear, my body strong. My blood glowed as brightly as it ever had, suggesting the mutated dark spots on my blood cells were nearly engorged with power.

I glanced at the weights in the corner, tempted to do a few curls, to see how well my body was recovering from the illness that had sapped so much of my energy and strength and had come so close to killing me. Looking in one of the mirrors, I could see that my musculature had filled back out, the wasting that had left me almost unable to stand no longer visible. It wasn't normal or natural. Restore had not only wiped away the cancer, it had pulled my body back into lean muscular perfection. Not that it had improved my looks. I wasn't ugly by any means, but I wasn't Matt. Not that I care about that. I was in a place I hadn't been in for quite some time. Scratch that. I was in a place, physically, that I had never been in before.

Even so, I hadn't come here to lift or practice my kung fu.

I had come to test my limits.

My sigiltech limits.

I started small, holding out a hand toward the weights, spreading my fingers.

Shirtless, I watched myself in one of the mirrors as the glow of my blood intensified from the *pull* sigil etched with the catalyst embedded in my skin. The glow traveled up and through my shoulder and around to the veins in the back of my hand. The weight lifted and snapped toward me like Mjolnir, but I stepped aside and reset the *pull*, grabbing it before it hit the wall and bringing it back. Stepping away again, I *pushed* it to the deck, where it came down on the mat with a passive thump.

"Not bad," I said, still feeling good. I wasn't operating at full strength, keeping the effort low. I didn't want to accidentally blast a weight through the hull and vent our atmosphere. What I didn't want to chance in a singular effort, I made up for by splitting my attention. I lifted the weight again with a *push* from the floor, while *pulling* a second weight toward me, negating its momentum before it could hit me in the chest. Dropping it straight down while *pulling* a different weight toward my chest, I absorbed its force. It hit me without effect, falling to the floor at my feet. I dispersed that energy into another weight, sending it shooting across the room. Meaning to *pull* it away, I was a little too slow, and it hit the other mirror, cracking the glass.

"Shit," I cursed, wincing as two other weights under my control dropped to the mat. And I was doing so well. A glance at my body in the mirror showed me that the glow of the chaos energy in my blood had diminished slightly, but I still felt good. Strong. "Again."

I breathed in deeply, holding it for a moment before *pulling* a weight up off the deck and *pushing* it at the wall. I *pulled* a second one to intercept it before it reached the bulkhead. Using *combine*, I watched as the two weights seemed to melt into one another. Keeping them held aloft with an equal measure of *push* and *pull* from the floor, the two weights merged. I used *separate* on them, an invisible blade slicing them in half before I hit one half with *excite*, which heated the molecules, the other with *dampen*, making it cold. The hot one melted the way the blade Matt threw at Admiral Lyke had, while I let the cold one shatter on the ground. When the liquified metal hit the mat, it ate right through, lighting the padding on fire.

"Shit," I said again, using *disperse* to remove the oxygen fueling the blaze before it could spread, leaving a messy puddle of iron goo on the deck. I had to be more careful. A lot more careful.

"Impressive," Kat said.

I spun around to face the entrance, not having noticed

the rebel and his unit had entered the room. I felt my face flush, embarrassed from nearly lighting the room on fire.

"Not so much," I replied.

"Don't worry, Captain," Ki said. "We saw the cool part before you almost killed us all."

I lowered my head. "I'm still getting used to this."

"Honestly, Cap," Kat said. "It's truly amazing what you're able to do with those marks on your chest. It seems more like magic than technology."

"It feels more like magic a lot of the time," I replied. "But you can see how dangerous it is, especially in the wrong hands. What if instead of freezing a weight, I froze you? Or split you in half? Or just touched you with calmed-to-death."

"Yeah, but you still need to see me to do it, right?" Kat asked. "If I came at you from behind, and you didn't know I was there—"

"You'd probably be able to kill me, sure," I replied. "Keep always told me that being an archon, even a Gilded, was like having the strength of a hundred soldiers. It doesn't make me a god."

"I wouldn't mind being able to melt people," Stearns said.

"But not if it means someone else can melt you back," O'Neill countered.

"We're sorry to disturb you, Captain," Kat said. "We just got finished at the gym. We planned to do a little sparring, and then run laps around the hangar. We can reverse the order."

"No, it's okay. I'm just trying to get a feel for how much energy I have stored up." I looked down at my chest. Only the restore sigil continued to glow, still pulsing like a heart. "More than when we ran into each other the first time."

"My back is still a little sore from being cracked into the bulkhead," Narayan said.

"Sorry," I replied.

He laughed. "All's fair in love and war, Captain. You didn't kill me, or even hurt me too bad. I'm grateful for that."

"Hey, maybe we could help you out," Kat said.

"In what way?" I replied.

"Well, let's say for instance that you find yourself in a dark alley."

"I don't think any alley I go in will stay dark," I interrupted.

They all laughed.

"True," Kat agreed. "But let's say a group of attackers comes out of the shadows to jump you. Five against one." He motioned to the others, who quickly formed a circle around me.

"I don't think this is a good idea," I said. "You saw what I did to the dumbbell."

"Yeah, exactly," Kat said. "Maybe you don't always want to kill a group of attackers. Maybe you just want to disable them. And let's say they're all armed with knives." He pulled a blade from a sheathe on his hip. The others followed his lead.

"I really don't think this is a good idea," I repeated, becoming uncomfortable with the scenario. "I don't want to hurt any of you, even by accident."

"We're Draconian rebels, Cap. We can take it. Just don't smush us to goo and we'll be good. Besides, you never know when the enemy might *attack!*" He shouted the last word, and all of them lunged at me with their knives.

I didn't move at all, simply *pushed* out in every direction, sending them all flying. They crashed into the bulkheads, remaining pinned against the walls as I held the *push*. Just like Kray had done. Just as Lyke had done. I realized there probably wasn't a manual after all. It was just a natural way to disable a group.

"Captain, do you think you can let us go now?" Ki asked.

I didn't respond, keeping them pinned, paying attention to how the effort affected me internally. It was subtle, but I could almost sense the drain of energy from my blood, my body slowly becoming weaker as I grew more mentally fatigued. I wanted to know my limits, but I wasn't ready to push myself to them just yet. I let go of the rebels, who all collapsed to their hands and knees on the floor.

"That was stupid," I growled, angry at what Kat had done. "I could have killed one of you. If that kind of recklessness is what I can expect going forward, thanks but no thanks. You can go back to *Radiance*."

I stormed out of the room, leaving the shaken fighters behind.

"Captain, wait!" Kat shouted before I could reach the elevator. I stopped and turned around, still angry as he ran to catch up to me. "I'm sorry, Captain. Maybe you're right. Maybe it was stupid. But I think we both know that the places we're going, you might not be the only, what is it you call yourself? Archon?"

"Yes."

"You might not be the only archon we need to deal with. Which means we need to come up with more effective strategies to fight them. Or in this case, you. I saw a chance to test you and to learn something about how to fight someone like you. Obviously, going in as a group doesn't work. You just knock us all on our asses. We need to know what does work."

Some of my anger drained in response to his explanation. "Honestly, I don't know. My crew had the same thing happen to them. Twice."

"Which kind of goes with my point."

"Your idea isn't wrong. Your approach was. At least right now, it needs to be more controlled."

"Yeah, I agree with you there. I'm sorry, Cap."

I couldn't stay mad. He was right. It wouldn't be enough to rely on archon versus archon to balance the scales. Especially since I had no idea if I could stand toe-to-toe with Lyke or any other Gilded. We had gone down that path already. Instead of using Keep to learn tactics against him, we had leaned on him to protect us from similar threats.

Big mistake.

"Bring your unit up to the conference room outside the flight deck," I said. "Let's talk about this in more detail."

He nodded. "Aye, Captain. Thank you."

Kat hurried away to round up the other rebels. I made it to the elevator, stopping on Deck Three to grab a shirt and down a couple of glasses of water. Realizing I was famished again, I had Asshole make a few pizzas and trays, plus a larger jug of soda to take up to the conference room.

"Captain," Justus said, finding me in the kitchen again. "You spend a lot of time here, don't you?"

"I'm always hungry," I replied. "I think the *restore* sigil is burning a lot of calories to keep me healthy."

"That seems logical," he said. "We can run some tests in sickbay to confirm. We should do daily check ups anyway, just to make sure you're remaining stable."

"That's a good idea. But we can do it after the meeting. I was about to message you. The rest of the crew is up in the conference room. We're going to discuss how to fight archons."

"I definitely want in on that," Justus said.

"Good. You can help me carry the pizza."

"Sure." He grabbed the boxes, while I hefted the jug and extra cups. "I spoke to Her Grace. She was hesitant at first, but that's not unusual for her. It didn't take too much back and forth to get her to agree to look into the information you provided. Obviously, we're limited while we're in hyperspace, but she'll be back near Caprum within a few days after dropping us at Windfall."

"But she understands the importance of tracking down Prince Hiro, right?"

"Of course."

"Awesome. Thank you for talking to her."

He beamed at the idea of talking to the duchess. "Any time."

"Unrequited love. Must be hard."

"Is it that obvious?" he asked, trying to straighten out his expression. "It was torture in the beginning. I've gotten used to it. And it's not like she doesn't care about me. But she sees me as a brother, not a lover."

"She's fortunate to have a brother like you."

He laughed. "Yeah, she is."

"Come on. Let's figure out how to kick archon ass."

"Sounds good to me."

CHAPTER 15

"*Head Case*, this is *Radiance*." Dryka said over the ship-to-ship comms. "Do you copy?"

"I copy," I replied, answering the hail.

"I know you already know, but we're dropping out of hyperspace in one minute."

I glanced at the countdown on the center console. "Yup. That's why I'm here."

"How are you doing with my fighters?"

"We're doing great. They've been incredibly helpful to me already. I appreciate you loaning them to me."

"Justus tells me you've been training them to combat archons."

"We've been training each other. Trying different tactics, seeing what works and doesn't work, both from my side and theirs. You're going to have the most skilled counter-archon unit in the Spiral."

"Great. I hope they won't need to use those skills very often. But I have a bad feeling they might."

"Not if I can help it. Anyway, one thing at a time, right?"

"That's right," she agreed, her voice softening. "How are you feeling, Ben?"

"I feel great," I replied. "Better than I have in probably over a year at least. Maybe ever. All of my markers are good, the mutation in my blood is stable, and I can pretty much eat anything I want. According to Justus, I'm burning close to twelve thousand calories a day just keeping myself alive."

"Lucky you."

"Maybe, maybe not. Justus is worried that the interaction between the chaos energy, my blood, the restore sigil, and my organs is going to put my overall health in a downward spiral."

"How so?"

I glanced over at him in the co-pilot seat, silently asking him to explain.

"Your Grace," he said. "Ben's current energy expenditure is much higher than typical. By needing to consume more calories, he's also putting more strain on his digestive system and all of his other internal support systems. They have to do more work, more quickly than they're really designed for. I could be completely wrong, but my concern is that this damage will accelerate over time, which will in turn require the restore sigil to use more energy to repair that damage, which means he'll have to eat more to provide the energy to repair that damage, which could cause more damage."

"And round and round we go," I added.

"It'll probably take some time," Justus said. "And the less he uses the other sigils, the less he needs to consume and the longer it'll take to really become a problem."

"But that isn't an option right now," Dryka said. "What about Avelus? You said it's the same sigil that's kept him alive all of these years."

"Not the exact same sigil, but similar," I replied. "The

difference is that he gained his sigil while he was still healthy. Also, he's using an optimal catalyst that his wife invented. A catalyst that can't be recreated. I was close to death, and to be honest the catalyst I used shouldn't work at all."

"We think it only does because of the restore sigil," Justus picked up. "And because of the mutation in Ben's blood. It's a pretty incredible interplay between the different variables, starting with the brain tumor and his ability to activate sigiltech in the first place. A perfect storm."

"Not completely perfect," I countered. "My cancer isn't really cured. It's just being held in check, which requires a lot more constant output to manage. Justus' theory is that the more I use the sigils, the more I shorten my expected lifespan."

"That's what I'm going with," Justus agreed. "But what we can't know right now is by how much. We could be talking going from infinite to a thousand years. Or we could be going from a hundred years to ten or less. Only time will tell."

"I understand," Dryka said.

"The way I see it, I should already be dead, so every extra minute is more than I ever thought I would have. And if I'm able to rescue my crew and deal with Sedaya, I can die at peace with the outcome. In that sense, nothing has really changed."

"Except that now you can bounce us around the training room like we're basketballs," Justus said, drawing a laugh from Dryka.

"Coming out of hyperspace now," she announced. Watching out of the forward transparency, the darkness was replaced with bright white which quickly spread out into stars in the distance and the silvery glint of starships surrounding a larger silver mass as we returned to slower-than-light speed. "Jump complete."

Even from a distance, Windfall Station looked large and chaotic. Pieced together from thousands of smaller modules that generally resembled shipping containers of various dimensions, it didn't appear to have a specific architectural design, but rather had grown organically as more pieces were added to support whatever the needs of the station happened to be. All sharp corners and rough edges, one section stretched off into the distance for nearly three miles, while another hung from the bottom like a severed spine.

Space docks the size of the one Archie had blown up were fused to the station in three different places, offering plenty of parking for incoming vessels. Smaller ships carried additional visitors to and from spoked airlocks separate from the larger space docks, keeping a constant flow of traffic moving around the station's exterior.

"Welcome to Windfall Station," Justus said, likely noticing my dropped jaw.

"Wow," I said, amazed by the activity as much as the overall scale of the entire endeavor. "I need to bring Matt back here."

I said it as if his rescue was already a done deal. After the work I had done with Kat and his unit over the last three days, part of me felt like it was. I had learned a lot about my own abilities and limits, as well as some tactics for different combat scenarios against non-archons. At the same time, the rebels had learned a lot about countering some of the sigils and landing hits on someone using sigiltech against them. That in turn had helped me formulate better ideas on how to fight archons myself. While I had watched Keep go head-to-head against Alonzo Dellacqua and attempt the same with Kray and Lyke, I knew now that his approach had been bad from the start. A straight up test of strength had clearly worked for him against the archons he spent centuries hunting. It didn't work against Gilded.

In fact, he had only beaten Alonzo because George and I had intervened, which was the starting point I had used with Kat and his unit to develop our tactics. Spreading out around an archon was a good thing. The element of surprise, essential. Staggered attacks could also be beneficial up to a point, but the real trick was coordination and knowing when to pour everything into a powerful strike. Even our training was mostly theoretical. We had done some limited live-fire exercises in the hangar with powered-down ion blasters, but until the group faced a real archon we wouldn't know for certain if we were on the right track.

I had a good feeling about it though.

"Ben, I'm deactivating the tether," Dryka said.

"Copy that," I replied. I felt the slight shudder through the pilot seat as the electromagnet released from the hull, the now limp wire being pulled back to *Radiance* by the same crew that had attached it. Floating free, I pulled back slightly on the stick, triggering vectoring thrusters to push us away from Dryka's ship.

"Request berthing at Windfall Dock Three," she continued. "Once you're on the station, ask for Charlie. He's the best starship mechanic on the station, though he won't come cheap."

"I don't need cheap, I need fast and reliable."

"Then Charlie's definitely your man. We're recalculating our next hyperspace route. You're on your own from here on out, but you know how to reach me. I'll keep you updated with anything I learn regarding the blueburn."

"Copy that," I said again. "Thank you, Duchess, for all of your help. Especially for getting me off that asteroid and lending me your fighters."

"Stopping Sedaya is the only thanks I need," she replied. "But you're welcome. *Radiance* out."

I watched Dryka's ship on the sensor grid as it slowly came about, turning away from Windfall Station and slowly accelerating along a nearly opposite path. I delayed adding much thrust to *Head Case* until the hyperspace field formed around the other ship and it vanished into the black.

On my own.

Justus, Kat, and the others were good people, and an able enough crew. They just weren't *my* crew. Thanks to Duchess Dryka, I was one step closer to getting my crew back.

"Windfall Station, this is *Nanofly*," I said, using the name and identifier Justus had given *Head Case*. While Dryka insisted I didn't need to worry about anyone here turning me or the ship over to the Royal Guard, I still didn't see any reason to broadcast our arrival. "Requesting berthing at Dock Three for repairs."

"Nanofly, this is Station Control. Copy that. Dock Three is currently at capacity. Estimated wait time is three days, six hours. Berthing is available at Docks One and Two."

"Shit," I cursed after muting the channel.

"Charlie must be busy right now," Justus said. "We can't afford to wait."

"No. Does it matter whether we shift to one or two?"

"I don't know any other mechanics here. I don't think it matters."

I unmuted the channel. "Station Control, this is Nanofly. Would it be possible for you to reach out to the ships at Dock Three and tell them I'm offering a million electro for a parking space?"

"What?" Justus said, raising his visor to look over at me with big eyes. "A million electro?"

"Like you just said, we can't afford to wait."

"Copy that, Nanofly," Station Control replied. "Standby."

"You could probably get the new reactor installed for a million," Justus said.

"Then what do you think I could get for ten million?" I asked.

"A new ship that's a lot nicer than this one."

"But it wouldn't be this one. Would it be enough to get Charlie to move us to the front of the repair line?"

"I'm going to venture a guess that it would. But it'll also leave you almost broke."

"I don't need electro. I need my crew back."

"Nanofly," Station Control said. "*Lakanti* accepts your offer. They'll clear the spot for you within the hour. Payment can be transferred to us plus a five percent handling fee. We'll hold the funds in escrow until *Lakanti* relinquishes the docking space."

"Five percent?" Justus complained. "That's a total rip-off."

"As well as a one hundred thousand electro docking fee," Control continued, ignoring Justus.

"Hyperspace robbery," he continued, throwing me the side eye. "You're being snowed."

"I don't care." I tapped on the center console as the payment request came through, transferring the electro without a second thought.

"Payment confirmed," Control replied. "Maintain position and standby."

"Copy that." I leaned back in my seat.

Waiting was always the hardest part.

CHAPTER 16

Careful not to plow into the bigger craft occupying the adjacent arms, I eased *Head Case* in toward the docking arm jutting out from the Dock Three spokes. Newer, cleaner, and much bigger, I figured the other ships had to belong to rich business owners, lesser nobles, or some very successful criminals.

"Huh, that's the *Ajira* on the starboard side," Justus said from the co-pilot seat.

"Who owns it? And don't say Sedaya."

"Not Sedaya, no," he replied, chuckling. "If Gia's the most famous singer in the Spiral, Katana, the owner of *Ajira*, is one of our most famous hop racers."

"Hop racer?" I asked.

"Starship races. Their ships are generally modeled after starfighters, and then modified to be smaller, lighter, and faster. But that's not all. Hop stands for hyperspace hops. Quick, uncalculated jumps into and out of hyperspace along a predefined route. Katana's the best there is."

I shrugged. "That doesn't sound all that impressive."

"Think about it, Ben. Drop a half second too early or too late, and you're nearly a hundred thousand miles from where you wanted to be. The better you time it, the better your time in the race."

"Good point," I replied. "I guess Hop Racing pays well. That's some ship."

"It pays well if you're one of the best. I bet he brought his racer here for Charlie to take a look at."

"I don't see it."

"It's tucked into the bottom of his flashy transporter. The hull is designed and molded to the shape of the racer."

"Cool."

I brought *Head Case* to a full stop a few feet away from the docking arm. It extended out toward the ship, latching on to the small hangar bay door. Looking down at the arm through my visor, it looked like a cigarette dangling from *Head Case's* mouth.

"Shall we?" Justus said, removing his restraints and dropping his helmet on the back of the seat.

"Absolutely," I replied, doing the same. We left the flight deck together, taking the elevator down to Deck Two before going to the hangar.

"You know, there's something weird about Deck Three," Justus said as we made our way to the armory. There hadn't been any discussion about whether we needed to go out onto Windfall Station armed, which made me think the need to carry a weapon was a forgone conclusion. Not as much for me, but I wasn't exactly keen to give away my status as an archon.

"What do you mean?" I asked.

"I mean, when I'm on Deck Three I feel like it's so much bigger than the other decks."

I glanced over at him, deciding to yank his chain a little. "Really? I never noticed."

"You didn't? Deck Three has an upstairs and a downstairs. I've been going over the layout of the ship in my head, and I can't quite figure out how that works."

"Levi, open the armory doors," I said as we approached. I feigned deep consideration of his statement. "You know, now that you mention it, that is strange. I never thought that much about how there are two floors on Deck Three."

He stared at me for a few seconds before laughing. "You're messing with me, aren't you?"

"A little," I admitted.

"Seriously, what's the deal? I know there's something funny going on there."

"The elevator has sigiltech in it. It shrinks you when you reach Deck Three, and grows you back to regular size once you leave."

"What? How is that even possible?"

"I have no idea. Keep did it. I think it has something to do with the action being constant, it doesn't need to be managed. He never really explained it that well."

"That's so weird. So what if the ship loses power while you're—"

"Everyone asks that. If you don't go out through the elevator shaft, you stay shrunk."

"So there's no emergency escape on Deck Three?"

"There is. But you stay shrunk," I repeated. "And no, that hasn't happened to anyone yet. That I know of, anyway."

He laughed even harder. "Is it just me, or do you feel like we should prank Kat?"

We each grabbed a simple blaster, slipping them into holsters on our hips. I had gone back to the Han Solo look, only now I wore a turtleneck and gloves to help cover my glow. It didn't cover the veins going up my neck, but they looked like they could be iridescent tattoos at a glance. I wasn't really trying to hide what I had become so much as I didn't want to attract extra attention.

"Stay focused," I replied. "We're still here on business."

"Right. Sorry, Cap."

We left the armory, returning to the elevator and taking it down to the hangar. Kat and his unit were there when we arrived, sitting on the deck near their sleeping bags and gear.

"Captain," Kat said, urging the others to their feet with him.

"Justus and I are going to look for Charlie," I said. "I'm going to arm *Head Case's* security protocols, but you're the second line of defense in case anyone tries to get through them."

"Aye, Captain," Kat agreed. "Not a likely scenario, but I'll keep a guard at the door at all times."

"Keep someone on the comms too," I said. "You can reach me on my phone in case of an emergency."

"Aye. Ki, head on up to the flight deck to listen in."

"On it. Good luck out there, Captain." She hurried up the steps and disappeared inside the elevator.

"Stearns, you and O'Neill have first watch."

"Sure thing," Stearns replied.

Justus and I left the ship through the smaller hangar bay door, passing over the threshold into the docking arm. We continued along it to the spoke, joining a few others in the corridor leading to the station proper. They were dressed similarly to us, standard space wayfarers hanging out in a place where asking too many questions about anybody was verboten.

I only had one question: where could I find Charlie?

The end of the spoke led to the outer ring of the space dock, which was connected to the primary station through the central pillar. Unlike the dock where *Dominator* was built, the top half of the ring was transparent, allowing a clear view of most of the station above it. The pillar was brightly lit by holographic advertisements for different services on the station—gambling, drinking, sports, entertainment. Vegas in space. I could just make out windows behind the holograms and the tiny silhouettes of people inside the rooms. A menagerie of interconnected modules loomed overhead.

"Your face right now," Justus said. "I can tell you're from Earth."

"I have an Earth face?" I asked.

"Jaw-dropping awe. Like you've never seen a space station before."

"I've seen a couple. This one's a bit bigger."

"Admittedly, it is pretty unique."

"Any idea where to find Charlie?"

"Yeah. He has space in the hub, on the lower decks. Prime real estate for starship repair. We'll keep going to the hub and take a lift down to him."

"It's a bit of a trek, isn't it?"

He laughed. "What, you expected to not have to walk in the future?"

"Well, yeah, I kind of thought there would be more options for getting places faster, sure. Even we have electric scooters back home. Not to mention escalators and moving sidewalks in airports."

"People have tried all kinds of gimmicky stuff over the years. In crowded places like Windfall, nothing beats good old-fashioned walking."

I looked around. There were other people in the corridor with us. There was even a Holthan—best described as a cross between Predator and a Wookie, only with a gentler disposition. But I would hardly call it a crowd.

"We haven't reached the main station yet," Justus said, reading my mind.

"I didn't plan to go to the main station," I replied.

"Charlie's good, but he can't install a reactor in a day. Not even for what you're willing to pay. We'll have some downtime."

"You're welcome to seek out whatever entertainment you want," I said. "I'm not interested."

"I wasn't talking about entertainment. I was talking about information."

"What do you mean?"

"Data brokers. Her Grace plans to look into the abduction as well, but she suggested that since we're here, we should bring your list to a broker and see what we can discover. Without revealing any details, of course."

"How do these brokers end up with more data than the duchess can glean on her own?"

"They have entire networks of contacts within all of the noble and occupational houses."

"You mean spies?"

"Informants and people down on their luck willing to spill their secrets for a price. Also gamblers looking to pay off debts other than with electro or addicts giving up intel for a score. The possibilities are endless, and they trade through them all."

"I guess it's worth a shot. I assume that intel won't come cheap."

"Not usually. But you have electro to burn, right?"

"I wouldn't put it that way."

"You're willing to spend for the right return."

"Let's go with that, yeah."

We made our way to the central hub, where the corridors did get considerably more crowded. I lost sight of the Holthan when he entered one of the many banks of clear elevators that moved up and down through the central pillar, ascending into the larger part of the station. Justus and I waited for a cab going down, joining a handful of others in the depths of the space dock's hub. Stepping out of the elevator, we felt like we had been transported to another location altogether. One that was darker, dirtier, and with the lingering smell of grease and metal. The bottom of the hub was clearly a mechanic's paradise.

A few other people stepped out with us. Two of them looked like mechanics themselves, a pair of women with petite frames, wearing fitted coveralls stained with grease and other fluids, their heads shaved to a peach fuzz. They hurried past us and around the bend.

We passed a handful of open hatches as we crossed the deck, the doorframes of each painted a different color. Repair shops, all of them, presumably under different ownership.

Peeking inside, I saw they were all similar in appearance. Large, open rooms filled with different parts and pieces of various starship related components, with workers in coveralls attending to repairs. Small airlocks ran along the outer bulkhead, some of which were occupied by drones like I had seen working on the sigiltech ships.

"This is Charlie's," Justus said, leading me over the yellow threshold and onto the floor of the shop. Almost immediately, one of the mechanics stopped what he was doing and approached us.

"Can I help you?" he asked. Young and stocky, the front of his coveralls stretched against a rounded stomach.

"I'm looking for Charlie," I said. "My ship needs repairs, and I hear he's the best."

"He was," the man agreed.

"Was?" Justus asked.

"He passed away three days ago. Heart attack. Went like that." He snapped his fingers.

I sighed audibly. It figured. "You don't seem very broken up about it."

He shrugged. "Nobody lives forever, right? Anyway, it gets worse for you. We were already booked for a month before Charlie's death, and the old man's passing ground us to a crawl for the last few days. We're way behind and not taking any new orders at the moment."

"Damn it," I cursed. "There's no way you can squeeze me in? I can pay over the standard rate. Like, way over."

He smiled. "I wish we could help you, but there's just no way, especially with Katana here. He has a race in two days and we're just getting started on his upgrades and repairs now."

"Maybe we can talk to whoever took over for Charlie?" I asked. "I assume you have a new owner? This is literally life or death."

He thought about it for a moment and then turned back to the floor and whistled. "Hey, Charlie!" A woman shut off her blowtorch and lifted the protective face shield to look over at us. "Customers!" He turned back to us. "Charlie's daughter."

"Yeah, I figured that out from her name," I said.

She put down the torch and took off the shield, hurrying over to us, obviously annoyed by the interruption. "Look, I'm sure you have electro and can pay for expedited service," she said, skipping over any pleasantries and either accurately jumping to conclusions or somehow having listened in to our conversation. "We just don't have the bandwidth. I'm sorry. It's not just about the money. It's about reputation, which is already going to be hard to keep up with my pops gone, and not getting Katana's work done on time and up to snuff could sink us. I've got a hundred employees counting on me." I opened my mouth, stymied by her diatribe. She didn't wait for my brain to catch up. "If you'll excuse me."

"Wait," I managed to say as she turned around. "My ship needs a reactor replacement. If you can't do it, who do you recommend?"

"How soon do you need it?" she asked.

"Yesterday."

She smiled. "Of course. You can check with Quaid, they're the purple door. If I had to rank the shops down here, I'd put them fourth."

"Who's second and third?" I asked.

"I wouldn't bother, I've sent them so much business in the last few days they're sure to be booked up, too."

"Is there something special going on?" Justus asked. "Why are so many starships coming in here for repairs?"

"It's the Hop Race," Charlie answered. "The starting line is hyper-ten out from here, so everybody's bringing their racers in for last minute checks, fixes, and mods."

"Hyper-ten?" I questioned.

"Ten minutes in hyperspace," Justus explained. "Seconds are hyper-oh. So hyper-oh-ten would be ten seconds."

"What about ten hours?"

"That's just hyperspace," Charlie said. "You've never seen a hop race before, I take it?"

"No."

"Were you born on Earth or something?"

I think she meant it as a figure of speech. "Actually—"

"We'll check in with Quaid," Justus said, cutting me off. "Thanks for the recommendation, and for coming over to shoot us down."

"No problem. Good luck with your search."

She returned to whatever she was working on, as did the other guy. Justus and I left the shop.

"We're screwed," I said.

"Nah, there are plenty of shops here. We might need to move to a different dock, though."

"After I paid a small fortune to get in here."

"That's the chance you take."

"I guess so."

"We should talk to Quaid first. The good news is, installing a reactor is relatively straightforward. I know you wanted the best, but even a mediocre mechanic should be able to get it done without mucking it up." He smiled. "Of course, they're going to wonder how it came to be that you're flying around in a giant robot head without a reactor. We can explain that away, and if—"

"Benjamin Murdock. Persephon Penal Station fugitive," a sharp female voice said behind us. "I suggest you turn around."

CHAPTER 17

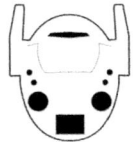

"Don't," I said to Justus when his hand drifted toward his blaster. I turned slowly around, not raising my hands since the woman behind us hadn't asked me to. "I thought I was supposed to be safe here," I added, loud enough for her to hear.

"You are," she replied, my gaze landing on the pair of pixies who had gotten off the elevator with us. They both had their hands in their pockets, looking pretty much harmless standing in the corridor. A longer look at them revealed two things. One, they looked enough alike that I was certain they had to be related. Two, only one of them was female. The other also had a small, childlike face and button-nose, and while neither had enough of a chest to create shape under their coveralls, his Adam's Apple gave him away.

"That was stupid," Justus growled, glaring at them. "I could have shot you."

"Sorry, I couldn't resist," she answered. "Although I had hoped for a more entertaining response. Maybe a little bit of fear behind those brown eyes of yours. Or at least a slight quiver in your voice when you spoke."

"Sorry to disappoint you," I said.

"No you aren't," the male said, his voice only slightly deeper than hers.

"Of course he isn't," the woman said. "Don't be daft, Leo." She sighed and shook her head. "Excuse my twin brother. He's a little slow."

"I knew he was being sarcastic," Leo said. "That's why I played it straight." He looked at me. "Excuse my twin sister. She's a little dense."

"You're both excused," I said. "Who are you?"

"Meg and Leo," Meg said. "We overheard you talking to Charlie and thought we should introduce ourselves. We're mechanics. Probably at least the third best repair crew on Windfall Station. Maybe the second after Charlie's group. From what I understand, you need a new reactor installed?"

"The second or third best repair crew?" Justus said. "How is it that I've never heard of you?"

"Have you heard of Plutus?" Leo asked.

"No."

"So you clearly haven't heard of everyone. Which is probably why you haven't heard of us."

"'I've heard of Quaid, and Charlie ranked him fourth. Which means I should at least find your names familiar. Which I don't."

Leo opened his mouth to retort. I interrupted him. "How do you know who I am?" I asked.

"Oh, we saw your ship come in. As far as I know, there's only one robot head gallivanting around the Spiral. So, basic deductive reasoning there. No sweat."

"Yeah, don't worry, Ben," Meg said. "You're right. Nobody will bother you here. At least, not about that. Individuals travel to Windfall because of its reputation as a safe harbor. Go into one of the pubs in the upper decks, you'll see sworn enemies tossing back quints together like they're the best of friends."

"Anyway," Leo said. "What my long-winded sister is trying to say is that we know you need some starship repairs, and we happen to be two very qualified mechanics who could use a job."

"According to Charlie, most of the shops on the station are booked because of the Hop Race," Justus said, sticking to his guns. "But you're available and good? I have a hard time believing that."

"We have some extenuating circumstances of our own that brought us to you," Meg said. "And we're only recently available."

"How recently?" I asked.

"The last hour or so," Leo replied.

"Do you have credentials?" Justus asked. "References?"

"Yes to the first," Meg said. "Not exactly to the second. Do you have a slab? I can send you our creds."

"I do." I pulled out my phone, setting it to receive.

Meg lifted a small transparent slab from her coverall pocket, tapping it a few times to send me the information. I opened it immediately, quickly looking over their certifications.

"It says here you're qualified in single occupant vessels," I said. "Not light freighters."

"We have hyperdrive certification," Leo said. "It's the equipment that matters, not the size of the ship."

"Then why do they break the licenses into classes?"

"I don't know," Meg said. "Probably because they charge a thousand electro for each listed qualification. We can work with bigger ships, we just didn't pay the fees to make it official."

"Ben, we're wasting our time here," Justus said. "We should go talk to Quaid."

"Quaid doesn't have any bandwidth," Leo claimed.

"How do you know?"

"You paid off *Lakanti* to give up her berth, right?" Meg asked.

"How did you know?"

"Because she got here a few hours before you did. The reason the captain was willing to leave was because he couldn't find a shop to do the repairs he wanted."

"Shit," I hissed angrily. "Wait. If you knew *Lakanti* couldn't find a mechanic, why didn't you offer to fix that ship?"

"Because her captain is a total asscrab," Leo said. "Unlike yourself."

"How do you know I'm not an asscrab?" I asked.

"We can tell by looking at you," Meg replied. "Besides, no self-respecting asscrab would be caught dead flying around in a robot head."

I laughed despite myself. I kind of liked Leo and Meg, even though I was fairly certain they couldn't be trusted. "Let's say I hired you. I need a reactor install, not a repair. You obviously don't have your own shop here. Where are you going to get the reactor?"

"An excellent question," Meg said. "We're on Windfall Station, Ben. Anyone can get anything with enough electro and determination."

"Ben, we can go up to Dock One. Ask around there," Justus said.

"Yeah," I agreed. "Sorry. No sale." I turned to leave. Leo danced past me to block my path.

"Ben, come on. You're a fugitive from Persephon Penal Station. That's why we came to you. Because you understand what it means to be misunderstood. To be honest, we need more than a job. We need to get off Windfall Station as soon as possible, with someone who knows what it's like to be on the run."

"We're good mechanics," Meg said, slipping in front of

me to stand beside her brother. "Our size means we can get into places other people can't, which saves costs on bots and drones and all that shit."

"You're in trouble here?" I asked.

"Not here, specifically. We'd rather not go into detail. But when we saw your ship coming, it was like our luck had finally changed for the better."

"Please, Ben," Leo begged. "Just give us a chance. Have us fix something small and we'll prove we know what we're doing."

"Ben," Justus said. "Forget about these two. Let's just go."

"Please?" Meg added. "You don't have to pay us for the install. Just the cost of the reactor and a ride out of here on your ship. That's all we need."

"Well, maybe a little payment so we can get back on our feet when we get somewhere more permanent," Leo said.

"We're wasting time, Ben," Justus said.

"The last person who just wanted a ride somewhere else wound up dead before I could drop him off," I said, doing my best to cut through the noise of the competing voices. "And where I'm headed next, the odds are good that it could happen again."

Leo and Meg froze, each looking at the other at the same time, silently questioning each other on how they felt about my statement. As one, they looked back at me.

"It's a risk we're willing to take," they both said. "Please?"

"Ben, no," Justus resolutely ground out.

That did it. I whirled on Justus. "What did you just say?" I growled, getting in his face. "I appreciate your advice, but *Head Case* is my ship. The electro is my money. You don't get a vote. Understood?"

Justus kept his composure, accepting the outburst. "Aye, Captain. I'm only trying to guide you in the right direction.

No offense, but you already lost a million electro on your last big idea."

I almost yelled at him again for that comment, but I couldn't argue that he was right. I thought I was so smart with that move and it had backfired on me. Even so, I couldn't afford to start questioning my decisions. That wouldn't lead anywhere good, especially in a fight. I had to trust my instincts.

I turned back to the twins. "If you two can procure a reactor that's suitably sized for my ship within the next two hours, I'll purchase it and bring you on for the install. I'll need you to fix the ion cannons, too, but that can wait until we're in hyperspace."

"Oh, thank you," they both said. "Thank you so—"

"But I'm also going to have Justus here watching you the entire time you're working. He's not a certified mechanic, but he is an engineer and he'll know if you sabotage anything."

"Sabotage?" Meg said. "We wouldn't dream of it."

"Not a chance," Leo added.

"Then you won't mind him keeping an eye on you."

"Not at all," Meg said. "We'll get you a reactor and everything else we need to set it up. No problem."

"Here's my identifier," I said, passing it to Meg's slab. "Two hours. Clock's ticking."

"We'll be in touch," Meg said as she and Leo disappeared around the bend ahead, dashing for the elevator.

"You know you can't trust them. That's why you put me on babysitting duty."

"Yup. And?"

"How can we go to the data brokers if I'm stuck watching the dunder twins operate?"

"*You* can't. I don't need an escort."

"For protection, no. To ensure you don't get ripped off? Yes."

"I can take care of myself. Besides, it's my electro to throw away."

He shrugged. "Suit yourself. I was just trying to help."

"I know. I do appreciate that. I'm heading to the upper levels of the station. I'll meet you back at *Head Case* when I'm done."

"Okay." He smiled. "Make sure you do some exploring while you're up there. Grab yourself a stiff drink and maybe a girl at the Pink Parlor. At least get yourself a lap dance. You have time, and frankly, you could stand to vent some tension before you implode."

I scowled at him. "I thought we established I'm not here to have fun." And the last thing I wanted or needed was to lose my virginity to a prostitute.

He didn't respond. He just shrugged and looked away.

I hesitated before asking my next question. "So, do you think Meg and Leo will come through with the reactor?"

"Gut feeling?" He glanced back at me.

I nodded.

"Yeah. I do. But whether or not it will break at an unbelievably inconvenient moment for us is another story."

"So you think this is a con?"

"It sure looks like one. But hey, you never know. Maybe they do just need a ride somewhere far away from here." I couldn't tell if he was being facetious or not. He didn't give me a chance to ask. "See you back at the ship, Captain."

He clapped me on the shoulder and hurried away, making it onto the next elevator. I had to wait for the next one, giving me time to think. On my own and not in immediate mortal danger.

That was a first. Maybe Justus was right. Maybe I should at least give myself a minute or two to enjoy it. Grab that stiff drink somewhere, maybe try my hand at a game of chance.

No. I couldn't enjoy the experience. Not when Matt and

the others might be out there shoveling rocks and burning in the heat of Melchior's suns. Business first. We could always come back here and check out the entertainment later.

All of us. Together.

CHAPTER 18

I wasn't sure where I was going inside Windfall Station. Maybe I had dismissed Justus a little prematurely, but getting *Head Case* hyperspace-ready was my top priority. Hitting up a data broker and possibly tracking down the blueburn was a nice-to-have, but I was also willing to rely on Duchess Dryka to figure that part out, at least until Matt and the others were safe. In any case, it didn't take long for me to get my bearings. I figured Windfall must receive a lot of first timers, because an assistance kiosk waited just off the elevators incoming from the various docks, brightly lit and easily noticed as soon as I stepped off the elevator.

A woman and a robot occupied the kiosk, which currently didn't have any other newcomers asking questions. The woman wore a red jacket that resembled patent leather over a green shirt, her hair molded into soft waves, her face heavy with brightly colored makeup. The robot was humanoid in shape, an image of a human face displayed on the screen that occupied the flat front of its head.

As I approached them, I wondered why the kiosk

needed both a human and a robot. By appearance, the robot seemed like it could handle the duties alone.

"Hello," it said to me when I reached the edge of the round desk. Its voice was male, smooth and rich like a radio announcer. A spotlight activated overhead, shining down on me and making me feel like I had stepped into an interrogation room. "Benjamin," it added after a brief pause. "Welcome to Windfall Station."

"Uh, thanks," I replied.

"How can we help you today?"

"I just need some directions," I said. "Or maybe a map? This is my first time here."

"Where is it you'd like to go?"

I glanced at the woman. She hadn't said a word and seemed more interested in filing her nails than helping me, further bolstering my confusion regarding why she was even there. "I'm looking for information." I paused trying to come up with a delicate way to phrase the request. "Special information."

"I'm sorry, can you be more specific?" the robot asked.

"Information that may not be available in the public domain," I said, looking back at the robot. "Potentially sensitive information that other people might not want just anybody knowing."

"I'm sorry, can you be more specific?" it asked again. I shifted my attention back to the woman, trying to convey with my expression that I needed some *human* help. What else was she there for if not to smooth out the disconnects between man and machine?

"What?" she said, finally speaking up.

"Do you work here?" I asked.

"Yeah," she answered.

"Maybe *you* can help me."

"If you have a question, Winston's got you." She kicked

the back of the robot. It stumbled forward half a step before catching itself, unbothered by the action.

I wanted to ask her why she was there since she clearly didn't want to be helpful. I didn't. "I'm trying to ask it about how to locate someone selling information."

"You mean a data broker trafficking illicit intel?" she asked, raising her voice. She laughed when I looked around, nervous about her drawing so much attention our way. "Relax, Benjamin. Nobody cares about your illegal interests here. Most of the folks come to Windfall to do something the Hegemony or their duke doesn't want them to do. And it gets a lot spicier than data, if you know what I mean. In other words, be direct."

I had a feeling that what I thought she meant was only the tip of the iceberg in terms of the things that happened here. I nodded and turned to Winston. "I need directions to a data broker."

"I'm sorry," Winston said. "I can't locate any data brokers among the registered business units."

The woman laughed. "It's obvious you're a newbie. Were you born on Earth or something? Just because nobody cares if you break Hegemony laws here doesn't mean the illegal businesses set up storefronts with billboard advertisements. You can't just ask for directions."

I made a face, regretting coming up here without Justus. Every time I thought maybe I had a handle on how things worked in the Manticore Spiral, something threw me off. "So how do I find a broker?"

"It's all about networking. I can give you a hint to get you started." She pulled out her slab suggestively.

"Right," I said, smirking as I took out mine, receiving a request for a thousand electro a few seconds later. I accepted it, sending her the funds.

"All of the sections of the station are color-coded. That doesn't mean the things you can find in those sections are only available there, but it helps give people directions and of course different colors have different reputations which you would learn if you stuck around long enough, but I have a feeling you won't be here too long. You want to go up to Purple. It's about halfway up the station in the central elevators, and then you'll take a tram out toward the edge. Here." She sent me a file. I accepted and opened it. A basic three-dimensional, color-coded map of the station rendered on my screen. "This should help you get around."

"I had to pay you a thousand electro for a map?" I asked.

"No, the map was free. The destination cost you a thousand."

I looked at the map. Purple still had over a hundred businesses in it, along with additional modules for housing. "How much to dial in the specificity of your advice?"

She smiled. "You're a fast learner." She sent me another request. Ten thousand electro. Part of me was tempted to just pay it, but I realized she was testing me. Seeing how much she could milk from me based on my resistance. I had paid her the thousand too easily.

"Purple," I said. "Got it. Thanks for the map." I started turning away. The original request vanished, replaced with one for half as much. "No deal. I can find my way from here."

"It's not that easy," she said.

"No? I'm guessing if I hit up enough of the pubs up there a bartender will give me a name for a lot less than five thousand."

"Suit yourself," she said, dropping the request.

I didn't hesitate to leave, even though internally I wondered if I had pushed too hard. I wanted the easy way forward for the sake of time. But Matt had taught me a long time ago that once you showed someone you were an easy mark, they would use that to your disadvantage.

I returned to the elevators and waited for the next one going up. According to the map, I had to climb to the Red Zone to catch the tram to Purple. No problem.

The cab arrived, newcomers spilling out before I climbed in with a handful of others. The elevator was crowded, keeping me shoulder-to-shoulder with the other riders as we ascended.

"Benjamin," the woman from the kiosk said, tapping me on the back. I hadn't even seen her get in.

"What is it?" I asked, glancing over my shoulder at her.

Something smaller pressed into my lower back. "I know you have funds. I have a family to take care of."

A new request popped up on my phone. Ten thousand electro.

"Do you even work at the kiosk?" I asked.

She smiled. "Not officially." She shoved the blaster into my back again. "I'd like to finish this transaction before we arrive."

There was no way the others in the elevator didn't know what was happening, but none of them reacted. Clearly, this wasn't an isolated incident. "You don't want to threaten me," I said.

"It's only a threat if you don't intend to make good on it," she replied.

I imagined my jacket becoming a surface for the *reflect* sigil, sending the point-blank energy blast back into the gun, silently activating it to blow up the weapon, taking the woman's hand with it, if she took the shot. I locked eyes with her. "Then pull the trigger. But I guarantee you won't like the result."

The statement confused her. She hesitated. I didn't break eye contact with her.

"Come on, man," she pleaded. "Do you think I want to do this?" She shoved the gun into my back again. The reflect reversed the force, pushing her hand back. She flinched in confusion. "What the hell?"

The elevator stopped. The doors opened. Enough people got off that I was able to turn and face her. "You can't hurt me," I said.

Her eyes drifted to the vein in my neck, examining it more closely. "I thought that was a tattoo. What are you, some kind of experimental super-soldier or something?"

"Not even close," I answered. "I'm better than that. And if you don't want to lose your hand, you won't fire that weapon."

She considered for a moment as the cab filled again. Then she lowered the blaster, putting it back out of sight. "Marsh is going to kill me."

"Who's Marsh?" I asked.

She leaned forward, coming in close so she could put her lips up near my ear, speaking softly enough nobody else in the cab could hear over the other murmured conversations. "He runs the Junket. It's sort of a pawn shop slash black market slash indentured servant brokerage. He'd beat me just for telling you about it. Shit, I don't even know why I'm telling you about it. I may have run up a decent sized gambling debt. I may be working it off by shaking down newcomers."

"Gambling debt?" I responded. "Am I supposed to feel sorry for you?"

"I did it for my daughter," she replied. "She needed medical treatment I couldn't afford. I thought if I could win a few rounds of Jackal, I'd be able to take care of her. I knew it was a risk, but I didn't have any other choice. I gambled. And I lost." She backed up, tears in her eyes. "She died two months ago, and I'm stuck doing this to pay Marsh back. If you're some kind of superhero, maybe you can superhero me out of this."

She managed to tug at my heartstrings. At the same

time, I couldn't be sure the sob story wasn't all an act. "I'm not a superhero," I said. "I don't know what you want me to do, and I have no way to know if any of what you just said is true."

"It is," she insisted. "Every word. Ask around about the Junket. Make it known you're looking to buy. You'll see." She sent another electro request. Two thousand instead of ten. "Please?"

I locked eyes with her again. Either she was sincere or she was a really good faker. Mom had always taught me to assume the best about people, and I really didn't want the Spiral to make me so cynical. I approved the request, sending her the money.

Her face afterward suggested I made the right choice. Her lip quivered, ready to cry. Her body shook. "Thank you," she mouthed. The elevator stopped again and she hurried past me, getting off and disappearing into the station.

I spent another minute on the elevator before it opened at my stop, thinking about what the woman had said and realizing I didn't even know her name. The Junket. It had left me curious, but I didn't have time for that right now.

My phone rang. I answered, putting it to my ear.

"Hey, Captain Ben," Meg said. "We've got a reactor for you."

"Already?" I replied, surprised. "That was fast."

"We're pretty resourceful with the right motivation."

"How much?" I asked.

"Two million."

"What?" I replied. It seemed expensive for one part of a starship rather than an entire starship.

"You thought you could get it fast *and* cheap?"

"No, but maybe not that expensive."

"We can ask around a little more. Your call, Captain."

"No. Send the request. How long will it take you to

install it?" I had been ready to pay Charlie ten million if it came to that. I would give up every electro I had if that was my only option.

"If we work nonstop, maybe a day or so."

Dryka had estimated two or three days. That was a huge difference. "Awesome. Let's get it done."

"Aye aye."

A payment request came in right after I hung up. Two million electro. I accepted without hesitation. A smile crossed my face as the elevator stopped in the Red Zone and I stepped out, one step closer to helping my friends.

CHAPTER 19

It took a bit of time wandering the Red Zone for me to locate the tram that moved across the station to Purple. I didn't stop at the assistance kiosk because I thought I knew where I was going, only to wind up passing through the open hatch of a large module into a smaller, more crowded section. It was lined with tiny storefronts selling all kinds of electronic gadgets and gizmos. Not the tactical gear Miklos had traded in. Rather, gimmicks and toys.

Among them, I saw pins that activated holograms to turn the wearer into a monster, lightsaber-like play swords, and a wide assortment of slabs in every shape and size. The shop owners standing behind their wares were dressed in colorful pants and shirts, with wide, toothy grins that made them look friendly but predatory. Whenever I passed one of them talking to a customer, I could hear them engaged in intense negotiation over the prices. Checking the map, I realized I was in some place called Beeping Bazaar. At least the name made sense.

The tram was four modules over. I reached it without incident, passing other businesses along the way. Pubs and restaurants, clothing stores, and gambling halls were the most plentiful, reinforcing my impression of Windfall as Vegas in space. The corridors between the storefronts were relatively crowded, making it necessary to weave around backed up traffic and constantly dodge individuals who plowed through the horde without ever giving way. After a while I wondered if I should do the same, until I saw two such immovable objects collide and get into a pretty violent fight. That's when I quickly learned the station had cop-like enforcers that didn't tolerate disturbances. The use of high-tech cattle prods stopped the fight in an instant, leaving both combatants motionless on the deck and me unsure if they were unconscious or dead.

Reaching the tram station, I found myself waiting at the back of a massive crowd lined up on both sides of a heavy cable that crossed the length of the module. It passed through a pair of sealed airlock doors similarly to how the space elevator from Kasper to Persephon Penal Station worked. Confused, I checked the map again, only then realizing that the Purple Zone wasn't directly connected to Red, but rather was an almost separate station linked by concentric coaxials to the main part of Windfall.

My phone rang, and I pulled it out of my pocket, the screen indicating the call was coming from *Head Case*. "Hello."

"Captain," Justus said. "Leo and Meg are here. They don't have the reactor with them, but they asked for access to the engine room."

"So?" I asked. "Is there a problem?"

"Well, you do have that part of the ship locked out to us," he replied. "I'm not able to give them access."

"Oh, shit. Sorry." I lowered the phone and tapped on the screen until I disabled security for the rear compartment on Deck Six, also the internal location for the main thruster. "I unlocked the section. Make sure they stay away from the workbench at the front of the deck."

"Aye, Captain. How's your hunt for a data broker going so far?"

"You knew it wouldn't be straightforward to find one," I said accusingly.

"I tried to warn you," he replied.

"You did. It's going okay. I'm waiting to board the tram to Purple Zone. I got directions from some hard-luck woman who said she's paying off a debt to some guy named Marsh. It only cost me three thousand electro."

"Junket Marsh?" Justus asked.

"Yeah. You know him?"

"I know of him. I would have steered you away from getting involved with any of that, but what can you do?"

"Should I be worried?"

"You?" He laughed. "Not unless you try to steal from him. From what I've heard, he's more of a businessman than a criminal, even if he trades in mostly illegal items."

"Like people." I said.

"Yeah, mostly indentured servants. Usually addicts of one kind or another, desperate for the next fix. But there are some decent people who make bad decisions and get caught up in his bullshit."

"Not that different from Earth," I said.

"Leo and Meg are on their way up to Deck Six. I'm going to meet them. Talk to you later, Cap."

"Thank you for the update."

As I disconnected, the airlock to my right opened to allow the tram to enter. The vehicle wasn't far off from what I expected. Sealed against space, long and narrow, it apparently had standing room only. From the clomp of maglocked boots as the departing passengers fought through the boarding passengers to get out into the Red Zone, I realized the machine didn't have artificial gravity. Pushed and shoved by people heading the opposite way, I didn't make the first tram, ending up squeezed into the middle of the crowd waiting for the next one. I kept a firm grip on my blaster and my phone to make sure nobody stole either, figuring the masses made for a target rich environment. Especially if Marsh's indentured servants came down here with sticky fingers to help pay off their debts. Fortunately, the next tram arrived within a couple of minutes, the same boarding procedure repeating. I just managed to grab one of the last open spaces on the transport, pushing my way aboard as the doors butted into my sides a couple of times, trying to close. I made it through and they slammed shut against my back.

Nobody spoke, averting their eyes from one another as the airlock ahead of the tram opened. The transport paused again between the doors to let the outer hatch open and then zipped away, shooting through space toward a collection of modules and another space dock a few kilometers away. We reached it within a few minutes, passing a returning tram, not packed quite as full as mine, on a second line. Like the Vegas Strip, it seemed Purple Zone was where most of the action could be found.

We pulled to a stop at the Purple station, the trim color making it easily identifiable. There weren't as many boarding passengers here so I didn't have to shove my way out. I walked briskly but steadily to stay away from the masses who got off behind me, one benefit to being shoved against the door. Impeccably timed, a message popped up on my phone just as I left the tram station.

TALK TO MACEY AT THE SCHNOCKERED UNICORN. <3

The message wasn't signed unless the heart was the signature. I figured it had to be from Marsh's servant, giving me a little more guidance in return for the electro I had passed her. I didn't know if she was watching me somehow, if she knew I had just reached Purple, or if it was a coincidence. Whatever the reason, I was glad for the extra hint. I wrote back a simple thank you and set about finding the facetiously named pub.

It wasn't hard to find.

I'd barely stepped inside the first module when one of Gia's lollipop hits assaulted my ears. The increasing volume led me down the concourse, past a busy restaurant, a game arcade and other businesses to the hologram of a unicorn drunk-dancing on the rainbow floor in front of the establishment. A huge doorman stood to one side of the wide entryway behind the hologram, his sullen eyes daring someone in the long line of people standing outside to get unruly as they waited to get in. I didn't count heads, but there had to be a hundred people in line. Obviously, it would take me a long time to work my way to the front.

I had maybe a day before Leo and Meg got the reactor installed, but I didn't want to wait. It might take more than one data broker to score any useful information, if I could learn anything at all that I didn't already know. And standing in line for hours felt like a total waste.

I walked right through the unicorn hologram to get to the bouncer. He noticed me coming and turned to face me, puffing himself up to make himself look even bigger. Nearly seven feet tall and bulging with muscle, it wasn't necessary at all.

"Line's over there, kid," he said, motioning with his hand, unconcerned by my approach.

I caught the gripes of the others in line telling me to wait my turn in the background. "How much to skip the line?"

"Sorry, no bribes."

"Seriously? You do know what station you're on, right?"

He smiled. "Yeah. I wish I could. Honestly. But my boss forbids it, and I need this job."

It surprised me to be shut down so completely. I gave it one more try. "How much do you make here?"

"Not enough. But that's not the point. You could give

me a hundred million electro, and two hours later, you'd find me floating away from the station with a blaster hole between my eyes. Because I know what station I'm on." His grin expanded. "Line's that way." He pointed to the end of it.

Stymied, I nodded and turned away. I didn't go to the end of the line though. Instead, I walked across the street to a clothing store, wondering why the place even existed when assemblers could make anything an individual needed. Maybe it was cheaper for some to buy already assembled stuff than to purchase a whole bunch of different materials to make whatever you wanted. Or maybe assemblers weren't quite as ubiquitous as I thought.

I browsed through the clothes while I thought about how I might get inside. A long coat with a high collar caught my eye. Black and glossy, I picked it off the rack and slipped it on.

"You have good taste," the shop's apparent proprietor said, appearing from seemingly out of nowhere. "That's made from the finest recreated Hijun hide on the market."

"Is it waterproof?" I asked.

"Are you worried about rain on Windfall Station?" he asked jokingly.

"You never know," I replied.

"It's waterproof. Also puncture and burn resistant."

"How would it hold up if I accidentally shot myself in the chest?"

His eyes drifted to my blaster. "From point-blank? Probably not that well. If your arm was a bit longer, I think it could absorb a few...accidents."

We smiled at one another. "How much?"

"Eight hundred."

"I'll give you two."

"Two hundred? The protective coating module for the assembler cost more than that. Seven-fifty."

I didn't really want to haggle. "Fine," I said, pulling out my phone.

He looked confused. "Really?"

"Yeah, I don't have time to bargain."

"Very well." He pulled out his slab and sent me the payment request, looking a little disappointed by the loss of the hunt.

I accepted the request, paid for the coat, and left it on as I stepped back out of the shop. Glancing at the unicorn, I grabbed the collar and stood it up so it covered my entire neck and rose over my head. I had an idea. Probably a bad one, but worth a shot. Worst case, the Rock look-alike would smell what I was cooking and knock me on my ass.

Becoming invisible wasn't easy. I closed my eyes, imagining the long coat and my pants *pulling* and *reflecting* the incoming light to bend it around me. Being a geek, I had looked into the feasibility of invisibility before. I knew a time delay would create a distortion as the light moved around me, but I hoped it wouldn't be enough for anyone to really notice. It wasn't as if anyone was actually watching me.

I knew when the relevant sigils activated from the tingle on my chest. Requiring multiple sigils and a longer duration, it left the intensity of the glow from my neck obviously reduced, the reflection off the collar of the coat diminishing by almost half. I nearly laughed out loud at the idea of how I was using the artery as a charge indicator as if I were a laptop or an electric car.

Hoping for the best, I started across the passageway, watching the reactions of oncoming pedestrians. A couple of them seemed to notice something strange as I passed them, and they tilted their heads or narrowed their eyes, trying to figure out what was off. Neither one of them cared enough to actually stop and assuage their curiosity. Others didn't seem to notice at all, nearly colliding with me as if I wasn't there.

Pleased with the initial reactions, I made my way around the unicorn hologram to the front of the pub, slipping in behind the bouncer and through the open door. I heard someone in the line say "did you see that?" as I dropped the sigiltech action.

I took a quick look around, determining nobody had noticed me appearing out of thin air.

I was in.

CHAPTER 20

I followed the rainbow path into the Schnockered Unicorn, taking the branch that led directly to the large, circular bar at the center of the floor. The place was as packed as the bouncer would allow, which was busy but not exceptionally crowded. Plenty of open tables ringed the bar, while booths covered the outer suitably darker and more private perimeter.

The setup reminded me of Cestus, except it was a lot less shady. Several groups of patrons circled the pool tables on my right, while others danced in and around another holographic unicorn on my left. Both men and women wearing glittering bodysuits and wigs with long, colorful manes and horns drifted through the crowd serving drinks.

I moved off the rainbow path onto an etched metal floor and dropped onto one of the stools. It was only a few seconds before the bartender made her way over to me.

"Nice coat," she said with a smile, though I questioned her sincerity. "You got that at Yimbo's, just across the mod, didn't you?"

"I did," I admitted.

"My friend had his eye on that coat. He couldn't afford it, though."

"Yeah, it didn't come cheap."

"What are you drinking tonight?"

"I'm not sure. I'm looking for something exotic. Something maybe I can only get here."

"First timer, huh? I know exactly what you need." She reached under the bar to grab a glass.

"I'm also looking for Macey," I added.

She paused to glance at me. "*You're* looking for Macey?"

"Why is that a surprise?"

"You're so young."

"I'm old enough to be looking for Macey."

She laughed as she removed the cup from the bartop. "You don't want this if you want to talk to Macey." Her hands lingered out of sight, and my phone vibrated as a payment request came through. I pulled it out of my pocket to look.

"Three hundred?" I said.

"That's a nice coat," she repeated.

I accepted the request. She pointed to one of the booths along the wall. "Who gave you the name, by the way?"

"I don't know her name. But she didn't *give* it to me. I'm going broke just trying to get where I want to be."

Her amusement intensified. "Welcome to Windfall. Nice doing business with you."

I smiled back at her and made my way to a table along the wall where an elderly woman sat, nursing a green-colored drink with an umbrella in it. "You're Macey?" I asked when I reached her, finally noticing there was something alive swimming around in her drink.

The woman had to be in her sixties. Her short hair was peach fuzzed on one side. She had a dozen rings in each ear, and she looked as if her lithe curves had been poured into her Hijun hide leather jumpsuit. Stiletto-heeled knee-high boots rounded out the senior citizen cool look.

"Who's asking?"

"My name's Ben," I said. "I'm looking for information. I hear you're good at finding it."

"Sit down, Ben." She motioned to the opposite side of her booth. "So, what kind of information are you looking for?"

"I'm looking for a specific starship," I said, sliding into the booth and folding my hands on the table. "I've narrowed the builder down to four potential sources. I'm trying to cut the list to one."

"I see." Her eyes danced over me, stopping to stare at my neck. "I thought that was a tattoo, but it's your blood that's glowing like that, isn't it?"

"Good observation," I replied.

"Comes with the territory. How'd you do that?"

"Long story."

"I love long stories."

"I don't have time for long stories. Do you think you can help me or not?"

"Maybe. What's in it for me?"

"I can pay you well for anything that gets me closer to a single source."

"What if I don't want electro?"

"Who doesn't want electro?"

"What if I want to hear all about your glowing blood instead?"

"Do you think that data's worth more?" I asked.

"Possibly. Information is a commodity. Some investments pay off, others fizzle out. My intuition tells me you're a gold mine."

"Don't you mean ivory?" I asked. Keep had said gold wasn't worth as much here as it was on Earth because there were moons and asteroids and the like practically made from it. Ivory on the other hand...

"Ivory," she said. "Aha!" She shouted it loud enough it made me flinch, especially when she thrust her finger at me. "You're Murdock. The Persephon fugitive. The Earthian."

I glanced around to see if anyone had noticed her outburst. If they had, nobody showed it. "Is it that obvious?"

"It's my job to know things," she answered. "And not many people who aren't already inordinately wealthy, such that they would have a data broker on staff, know ivory is even a thing that exists. Unless they're from Earth or know someone from that backwater world."

I shrugged. "I guess you caught me. I can't tell you about my blood though."

"Can't or won't?"

"Okay, won't. It's too risky for me. I can pay you well in electro however."

"I have enough electro to last me three lifetimes. Information is the only currency I need nowadays."

"Well, thanks anyway," I said, sliding out of the booth. "I'll find another broker."

"Sure, Ben. You can find lots of other brokers. But I'll tell you right now that Gilson Heavyworks isn't the company you're looking for."

I froze in place. She had named one of the companies on my short list.

"Didn't see that one coming, did you?" she asked, laughing. "I know why you're here. I know what you're looking for. Not a ship, that's for sure."

I frowned as I fell back into the seat. "If I tell you about my glowing blood, you'll tell me everything you know?"

"That's the deal."

I leaned back in the seat but didn't immediately start talking. Keep had spent years trying to wipe sigiltech from the Spiral, and if I told Macey the truth about my blood, I would ensure that Pandora's Box could never be closed. Then again, hadn't we already reached that point of no return?

"I'm ready whenever you are," Macey said.

I exhaled sharply and started talking. She listened attentively as I went through everything from the moment we arrived on Omega Station almost until now, leaving out a lot of details that didn't answer her original query. She didn't need to know about Gia or Alter, or even Keep for that matter. I only told her about sigiltech, a little bit about David, and a lot more about how I had hacked the system to become my own personal light show. After I finished, she didn't say anything for nearly five minutes. The pause left me growing more nervous and uncomfortable, and wondering if she was going to take the intel and run.

"That's some story," she finally said. Why had that comment taken so long? "I see the glowing blood, but what about the rest? Prove it."

I glanced around the bar. "Do you see that table?" I motioned to a smaller freestanding table where a pair of men were having a couple of drinks.

"What about it?"

It didn't take much effort for me to pull it onto its side, spilling the drinks and leaving the men scrambling back in confusion.

Macey laughed, maybe a little too loudly. "That is amazing."

"You think that's funny?" one of the men said, glaring at her.

"I said *amazing*," she replied. "Not amusing."

"You ancient bitch," he snapped, storming toward us. I lifted my hand to *push* him back, but Macey unholstered her blaster and shot him in the leg before I could unleash *push*. He stumbled to a knee, crying out in pain and glaring at her. "What the hell'd you do that for?"

"Respect your elders," she snapped back. "And stop whining. It's only a flesh wound."

The man's friend picked him up and helped him limp away. Nobody else in the place batted an eye. No guards came to arrest her. I got the feeling the lack of response was more because of who Macey was then because fighting like that was acceptable here. I felt guilty for causing the altercation in the first place.

She turned her attention back to me. "Amazing. And true, which is even more mind blowing. Completely worth the price of admission. Remind me not to frig with you."

"So what else can you tell me about the object of my desire?" I asked.

"I already gave you a pretty juicy tidbit."

"Is that all you have? For the price, I expected more."

"I have more. Though I can't help you whittle your list by more than one. What I can tell you is that you aren't the only one asking similar questions for a similar reason."

"Someone else came to you about this?"

"Not to me directly. To the network."

"Another broker?"

She nodded emphatically. "Yes."

"Who?"

"I can't spill the identities of my clients. What kind of broker would that make me?"

"Then why tell me someone else is doing the same search? That's not really a surprise considering the bounty involved."

"What I can tell you is that the individual asking the questions was a Niflin."

The small detail stopped me in my tracks, the implications massive. "You're not bullshitting me?"

"Brokers don't lie. It would be awful for business."

I stared at her while my mind tried to make sense of the new information. If Sedaya had sent one of his Daft Punks to find out more about the ship that had stolen Prince Hiro, then he wasn't responsible for taking him.

But if not him, then who? Sucaath? That didn't make any sense. He and Sedaya were in cahoots. There would be no reason for the duke to be hunting for the boy if his partner in crime had him. Did that mean there was another player in this game I didn't yet know about?

Either way, the news blew my entire theory about Hiro's abduction out of the water.

"I love when I do that to people," Macey said. "Just that stone-faced, glassy-eyed look of shock and surprise. Gets me every time."

"I still expected a little more," I said. "What I told you is stuff that's been buried for a thousand years."

"In a pretty shallow grave, it seems," she replied. "You have the list of suspects? Give me the names."

"You already know Gilson Heavyworks," I said. "I'll cross them off. Then there's Bracken Shipbuilders, Orinu Heavyworks, and Mushari Technical."

Macey stared at me for a few seconds, giving me the impression she was accessing a neural link. "Okay, Ben. I'm only giving you this because what you shared with me was so juicy. Even if I can't sell it, just knowing about it makes it worthwhile. That, and I think you're adorable." I felt the heat rise through my cheeks. "Mushari hasn't announced yet, but they're on the verge of declaring bankruptcy and going under."

"What happens to their records when they go out of business?"

"By law, the most confidential data will be destroyed. The rest will be sold off to the highest bidder."

"You?"

She smiled. "Possibly."

"That seems suspicious though, doesn't it?"

Macey shrugged. "That's not for me to say. I deal in data, not conjecture. Anyway, that's all I have for you."

"What about my story? You aren't going to gossip with the other brokers, are you?"

She laughed. "That's not how it works. We barter with one another the same as we do with outsiders. We don't even offer each other discounts. This one won't come cheap, I'll tell you that. There's a good chance I'll never find a worthwhile trade for it. I am getting older."

I stood up. "Thank you. I appreciate your time."

"Be safe out there, Benjamin Murdock. You're one of the good ones, and there are far too few of those these days."

My face heated up a second time. "I'll do my best. Thank you again."

I left the Schnockered Unicorn, catching the attention of the bouncer on my way out.

"Hey," he snapped. "How…what?"

"See you around," I replied with a grin and a wave. There was nothing he could do but stare.

CHAPTER 21

My meeting with Macey went better than I expected, leaving me with more time to kill before Meg and Leo finished the reactor install. My decision to give three thousand electro to Marsh's woman in the red coat had turned out to be the right one. As I made my way toward the Purple Zone tram, I wondered if I should seek out a second opinion, talk to another broker in case they could give me a bit more intel. From the way Macey knew what I was looking for before I even brought it up, I had a feeling none of the others in her field would be able to provide anything more.

With nearly an entire day of waiting ahead of me, I considered spending more time exploring Windfall Station. Vegas in space. There had to be plenty of things to see and do on board, especially given the scale of the place. There was a certain appeal to taking a little shore leave, especially after the events of the last week, but I couldn't get my heart behind it. Every time my mind wandered toward the bright sign of another bar or a holographic poster for a live show, I couldn't help thinking about my crew, my friends, and what I imagined they were going through. It felt wrong to enjoy anything right now.

It didn't take long for me to make my way back to Red Zone, and from there, down to Space Dock Three. I got a little turned around in the hub, heading down the wrong spoke, which became less busy the further I moved from the center. I didn't realize I was in the wrong place until I reached the spot where I thought *Head Case* should be, momentarily panicked by the absence until I saw *Ajira* was missing as well. Turning around, I froze in place, my eyes landing on a contingent of Niflin making their way down the corridor toward me.

All of the Niflin I had ever seen, male or female, looked the same to me, their body shapes relatively androgynous. This group wore breathing tubes in front of their noses rather than going full Daft Punk. They all had bluish skin, long silver-blonde hair, and delicate features. The leader walked a couple of steps ahead of the others.

"Shit," I cursed under my breath, quickly raising the high collar of my new coat and turning away. Macey had given me the impression the Niflin she had spoken to had been by to see her days ago. Was this the same group? Had they lingered to enjoy more of Windfall's offerings, or was their visit with the broker more recent than I realized?

I moved to the side of the passageway, looking out at the closest starship. With its slender nose, a small cockpit like that of an X-wing fighter, and a massive ass where six huge thruster ports jutted out from the main fuselage, it appeared to be a hop racer. The compartment to the reactor, thruster assembly, and hyperspace engine were visible through an open port on the side where a spider-like drone worked on some kind of upgrades or repairs. The whole starship had been painted bright yellow, *Kraken* written in script beneath the transparency of the cockpit. It was a cool looking ship. Cool enough I almost forgot about the Niflin as they neared my position.

"Are you sure you can trust him?" one of the Niflin said.

"As far as you can trust anyone in a place like this. Marsh has a lot to gain by going along with the Master's plan. He's already benefited greatly from our arrangement."

"And a lot to lose if he doesn't," one of the other Niflin said.

A chill tickled my spine as I recognized the first voice. Daft Punk Remix. The last time I had seen him was in the bazaar on Furion, where he had threatened me before launching an all-out assault on the planet that had ended with my capture. I sensed the *restore* sigil pulsing on my chest, subconsciously activating the outer edge of the construct in preparation to use the sigils. I couldn't lash out at Sedaya right now. His Niflin lackey might be the next best thing.

I turned to face their backs as they passed, my hands curling into fists, chaos energy pooling near the construct. I could call them out and take them down before they knew what hit them. I could squeeze DPR's throat until his eyes bulged out of their sockets and he begged for mercy. I could but…

I forced my hands open and exhaled, watching them continue toward what had to be their ship at the end of the passageway. Killing a handful of Niflin wouldn't get me any closer to helping Matt and the others or taking down Sedaya. It would only draw more attention to me and possibly get the guards involved. The last thing I needed was to wind up locked up on the station or sent back to Persephon.

Turning away from them, I couldn't help wondering what they had enlisted Marsh to do. Keep an eye out for me maybe? But they had no reason to think I was still alive unless they had seen *Head Case*, unlikely since they were berthed on the complete opposite side of the dock. Were they here to neutralize Windfall and make sure it didn't become a safe haven for people trying to fight back against Sedaya? Test people he bought into slavery for sigiltech aptitude? Search for additional sigiltech ship debris? There were too many possibilities to assume any of them were correct. All I knew for sure was that if it was good for Sedaya, it was most likely bad for the Hegemony at large, and probably me too.

I hurried back the way I had come, crossing the dock's hub to the other side and making my way back to *Head Case*.

"Captain on deck!" O'Neill announced as I stepped through the hatch into the hangar. Stearns flanked the entry and he turned to face me, coming to attention.

"Okay, you don't have to do that," I said. "How about a *Hey, Ben* or *Hey, Captain* instead?"

Both rebels smiled. "Hey Captain," Stearns said. "How'd it go out there?"

"That's better," I replied. "I have some intel to pass on to the duchess. And I made it back here in one piece, so it went as good as I could hope for."

They both smiled. "The two mechanics you hired are in the engine room," O'Neill said. "The reactor arrived thirty minutes ago. I had Kat and Ki take it up to them."

"Thank you for the update," I said. "I'm going to head up to Six to check on them. Everything else good here?"

"Sure is, Captain."

I headed for the stairs, wondering what a reactor actually looked like that it had been dropped off like Meg and Leo bought it on Amazon. The elevator opened ahead of me, Kat standing in the cab.

"Captain," he said, coming to attention.

"You don't have to snap to attention," I repeated. "I'm not comfortable with military protocol."

He relaxed his posture. "As you wish, Captain. I left Ki up on the flight deck. I was just coming down to wait for you."

"Wait for me? What's up?"

"I wanted to show you something. You aren't going to believe it."

"Is this a bad something or a good something?"

"I'm not sure."

I stepped into the elevator with him. He punched the control button for Deck Three.

"Lead the way," I said as we stepped out of the cab. I followed Kat toward the lounge.

"I was just scanning the news streams when it came up as one of the headlines," he explained. "I'm not really sure how it's even possible."

"How what's possible?"

We reached the lounge. Kat picked up the remote control for the television and switched it on, revealing a news feed. The process hadn't changed all that much in the future, except the anchors narrating the headlines were all computer generated, the text written by AI. They looked and spoke naturally enough that I had only known they were fake because Alter told me so. A few quick taps on the remote and Kat navigated to one story in particular. My eyes shot to the header.

GIA RETURNS HOME. ANNOUNCES ALL NEW SHOW! PFCL EVENT DATES AND MATCHUPS ALSO REVEALED.

What the hell?

CHAPTER 22

"It has to be Blorb, but why is it impersonating Gia?" I asked, as the news report shifted from the fake anchor—rendered as a handsome male in his mid-forties wearing a traditional business suit—to images of Gia in concert at her castle, performing to a sold-out show. It could make itself look like anyone. Even Gia. Yet, that didn't make any sense.

"Maybe it's always dreamed of being a pop star?" Kat suggested.

"Not likely. Are you sure this isn't an old feed?"

"I double-checked the timestamp and byline. It's definitely from today."

"I don't get it. Blorb would have had to absorb her persona, which I never saw it do. Besides, it already has a lot on its plate, pretending to be the Empress. Even if it wanted to do lollipop, it wouldn't be able to be on Atlas and Gia's world at the same time."

"Then maybe the woman who was on the ship with you wasn't really Gia," he suggested. "A body double or something. You didn't ask her to sing, did you?"

"I was with her in her suite at the castle. And I have her

neural link. The Gia who died on Omega Station was the real Gia. I'm sure of it."

"Evil twin, then?"

I laughed. That would be so soap opera, and yet somehow fitting. "She never mentioned a twin sister."

"Clone," he said confidently.

"You have cloning here?"

"Officially, no. It's outlawed. But so is sigiltech, and well…" He motioned to my chest.

I considered it before shaking my head. "I can see Sedaya cloning himself. Gia doing that, not so much. She cared too much about authenticity. I can't completely rule it out, but it seems unlikely."

"Well, whatever the reason, as far as the public's concerned she's back. I thought you'd want to know."

"Thanks. Maybe we'll have time to look into it more later. I'm going up to engineering to check on the new mechanics' progress."

"Aye, Captain."

I glanced at the television one last time before leaving the lounge, still confused by what I had just seen. Gia had made arrangements for her untimely demise. Was this one of them? If so, had she found some way to deliver new live performances from the grave or was this some kind of mind game she was playing with Sedaya?

Ultimately, it didn't matter right now. My priorities hadn't changed.

I took the elevator to Six, the loud commotion of an argument between Meg and Leo assaulting my ears as the doors slid open. Their backs were to me, facing the large central cylinder that had once held the Star of Caprum, now empty.

"I'm telling you Megamoron, we need to run a splice from the conduit there…" He motioned to the wires leading away from the Star's casing. "…to the new generator."

"You can't splice a conduit like that, Leodiot," Meg shot back. "We need to cut the line completely and rewire it."

"Not if we replace the power boxes behind the converters!" he shouted, pointing at one of the large machines that sat near the curve of the bulkhead. "Judging by the rest of the ship, they're probably a hundred years old at least. Updated models will ensure stability against source variations." Stepping back, he swung his arm toward the battery, and once again, his voice rose. "And the muckheads who wired that relic in are lucky they didn't short the whole damn thing out!"

"I'm not arguing with that," she bit out. "What I'm arguing about is that it'll take another half day to make those kinds of changes, and Ben was very clear we need to do this fast."

"We should do it right," Leo countered. "Half a day isn't a lot."

"It is when you're imprisoned on Melchior," Justus said. I couldn't see him from inside the cab, but it sounded like he was sitting on Miklos' workbench. "Every hour feels like another year."

The statement tied my chest in a knot. "That's not very comforting," I said, stepping out of the elevator.

Justus' head snapped in my direction. "Oh, Captain. I didn't see you there." He started to rise.

"Don't stand up," I said, putting my hand up to stop him. "I'm not military. I don't need or deserve the formality."

"If that's how you want it," he replied, remaining on the stool. "As for Melchior, it's not as bad as I said. A little bit of exaggeration to make a point."

"Good try," I said. "I know you're lying."

"For your benefit though," he admitted.

"Captain," Meg said. "We have the reactor." She pointed to my left. I turned my head, surprised to see a black box no larger than an oversized armoire. "It's a little overpowered for your ship, but bigger is better, right?"

"That's a nuclear reactor?" I asked, gawking at what I thought was too small to be a nuke.

"It's a cold fusion reactor," Leo explained. "FreezeFire Twelve by Gilson Heavyworks. Only a year old. An excellent vintage. And a lucky find."

"Cold fusion is a myth," I said. "It's bullshit."

"Does that look like bullshit to you?"

"It's not cold fusion the way you're thinking," Justus said. "It's based on chemical reactions and energy transfer that occurs at absolute zero. That black box is essentially a fancy fridge."

"What we can't figure out is what you had in here," Meg said, tapping on the Star of Caprum's case. "It's all wrong to be any kind of reactor I'm familiar with."

"It was called the Star of Caprum. A miniature star," I said.

"Where did you get a miniature star?" Leo asked. "Is that even a thing that's possible?"

"Apparently it is possible, because it does exist," I replied. "I don't know how or where it came from. I just know that it used to power the ship."

He shrugged. "What happened to it?"

"Duke Sedaya stole it from me to supply power to his new warship. I still intend to get it back."

"In which case, we'll need to splice the lines," Leo said, directing his comment at Meg.

She looked at me. "We actually have two options for the repair. One involves cutting the cables to this container and connecting them directly to the reactor. The other is to splice new lines in from the reactor. The second will take longer, but it will allow you to use the Star again right away if you get it back. Otherwise, you'd have to reverse the install to use the Star again."

"And the splice will take a bit more time," I said. "I caught that part."

"Yeah, almost fifty percent more time," Meg said. "And if every hour feels like another year where your friends are, that's a long time."

"It is," I agreed, considering the dilemma. Short term, faster was undoubtedly better. The sooner we left, the sooner we could help Matt and the others. Long term, supporting both the Star and the reactor could have its benefits.

But getting the Star back would mean retrieving it from *Dominator*. What were the odds that would happen anytime soon?

"Forget the splice," I decided. "Get the reactor online asap. Okay?"

"Your wish is our command, Captain," Leo said, suddenly not bothered at all by my choice of Meg's suggestion. "We still need to do some work to the control board on the reactor to make it compatible with your system, and I believe we'll need to make some changes to the ion thruster controllers to ensure they can handle the additional power output."

"Handle the power output?" I said. "The electrical system was being powered by a *star*. I don't think you can have higher power output than that."

"Yeah, that's probably true," he agreed. "I'm sorry. I was comparing it to the battery, not its prior primary power supply. We can probably shave a few hours off our original estimate if you're confident the ship's wiring is capable of handling the load."

"I'm confident."

"We'll continue our work then, Captain," Meg said. "Believe me, we're as eager to get out of here as you are."

"Thank you." I shifted my attention to Justus. "Can we speak in private for a moment?" I pointed at the elevator.

He hurried over and ducked into the cab ahead of me. I used the control panel to keep us on Deck Six. "What do you think of these two?"

"The blunder twins? So far, they've had a fight about every single detail involved with hooking up the reactor. When they talk about it, they sound like they know what they're doing, but the fact that they can't agree on an approach is a little worrisome. Not to mention a waste of time."

"Maybe it's a good thing. Matt and I always argued a lot on which songs to cover, lyrics for songs we were trying to write, chords in the riffs, all of that. I think it made our music better overall. Hopefully it's the same thing for them."

Justus grimaced. "I hope so. Technology doesn't usually have as many ways to do things as creativity. How'd it go with the broker?"

"Pretty well, I think. Next time we can contact the duchess, she can strike Gilson Heavyworks from the list. The broker didn't go into detail but she was certain they're a dead end. She did tell me Musashi is about to go bankrupt, which will lead to destroying a lot of their confidential info."

"Sounds convenient."

"That's what I said. I think they're the priority out of the three remaining builders."

"I agree."

"One other thing. Sedaya is looking for Prince Hiro, too."

"What? I thought Sedaya took him."

"So did I. I was sure of it. I went the wrong way when I reached the hub and happened to come across one of Sedaya's main goons. He didn't see me, but just the fact that he's here and he spoke to the broker confirmed Sedaya doesn't have Hiro."

"So who does?"

"Possibly Sedaya's partner in crime in all of this. Someone named Sucaath."

"That's not the name of a duke, or any other noble I've heard of. But if they're working together and Sucaath has Hiro, shouldn't Sedaya know about it?"

"Yeah, that's my sticking point, too. I'm worried there's someone else involved in all of this."

"Worried? Why? Maybe they're on our side and they took him to protect him."

"I hope so, but that's not how the Spiral seems to work."

"There are some good people here. We're not all just out for ourselves."

"I know. Maybe Keep will have more insight once we get him back. Knowing him, there's probably some powerful long-lost sigiltech-wielding civilization he forgot to mention that may have taken the prince."

Justus laughed. "Let's hope not."

"I'm going to head down to the kitchen, and then try to get a little rest. Let me know immediately if Meg and Leo either need help or do something shady."

"Will do, Captain. You're hungry again?"

"I used the sigils to make myself invisible so I could slip past the bouncer at the Schnockered Unicorn. Whenever I drain the chaos energy in my blood even a little, I seem to get famished."

"I can't believe the sentence that just came out of your mouth. Worse, I can't believe I understood every word of it."

We shared a short laugh before he got off the elevator to rejoin Meg and Leo. I rode the elevator down to Deck Three, suddenly lamenting the fact that I had nothing to do except eat, sleep, and wait.

CHAPTER 23

Three hours later, after already having downed a burger, fries, and milkshake, I was in the lounge watching *That Darn Cat* and eating pizza in memory of Alter. I paused the movie when I heard someone running down the corridor from the elevator, heading my way.

"Captain!" Meg shouted. "Captain!"

I looked over my shoulder as she reached the top of the steps leading into the sunken room. "What's going on?"

"It's Leo," she said. "I sent him out to pick up a couple of parts we needed an hour ago and he still hasn't come back."

"Are you sure he's in trouble?" I asked. "Maybe it's just taking longer than you expected."

She pulled out her slab. "I tried contacting him. He isn't responding."

And to think I actually had three hours without a problem. "Has he ever disappeared on you before?"

"A few times," she admitted.

"What usually happens when he does?"

"He turns up again a few hours later. Maybe I shouldn't worry, but he knows how important it is for us to finish installing the reactor. For you and for us. He wouldn't vanish like this. Not now."

I couldn't argue with that. I shut off the television and pushed the pizza box away so I could stand up. "We'll have to go look for him. Is Justus still on Six?"

"Yes. I'm surprised he didn't follow me down here. He's been breathing down my neck since we boarded."

"He's watching you under my orders," I said. "I'm not convinced I can trust you two." I paused after saying it. "I'm actually not sure I can trust you right now. How do I know you aren't setting me up for an ambush?"

"Why would I do that?"

"I don't know, but it wouldn't be the first time that's happened to me."

"Please, Captain," Meg said, her eyes meeting mine. "I'm not lying. Leo is in trouble. I know it. We need your help."

She seemed sincere, enough so that she was either ready to collect an Oscar or she was telling the truth. I only had one way to know for sure. "Okay, go up to Six and get Justus. I'll meet both of you in the hangar."

"Thank you, Captain." She rushed back to the elevator. I followed behind her at a slower pace, sliding on my new coat by the time I reached the elevator. Taking it to the hangar, I found Ki and Narayan guarding the door.

"Ki, do you have comms with Kat?"

"Aye, Captain. What do you need?"

"Can you tell him I need him in the hangar? Armed."

"Is there a problem?" Narayan asked.

"Almost always," I replied. "Were you here when Leo left, about an hour ago?"

"Leo?"

"The mechanic installing the new reactor. He's wearing coveralls, probably has grease on his face."

"Oh. Aye, Captain. He said he needed to pick up some doohickeys I've never heard of before."

"I think he said thingamabobs," Ki said with a smile as she hurried over to the rebels' small camp to pick up her helmet. "Kat, do you copy?" she said into its comms.

"I copy," Kat replied.

"The Captain requests your presence in the hangar, formally attired."

"Copy that. On my way."

"Formally attired?" I asked. "Does that mean what I think it means?"

"That depends on what you think it means," Ki replied with a smile.

"Does the black tie have a trigger?"

"Yes."

"Then it means what I think it means." My hand drifted to my blaster, still strapped to my thigh and hidden from view by the length of the coat. Whatever had happened to Leo, I really hoped I wouldn't need to use it.

Justus and Meg arrived first, descending the stairs to the main hangar deck. Meg's initial worry had subsided a little, probably from knowing we were trying to do something about her brother's disappearance. Justus didn't seem concerned at all. In fact, when his eyes met mine they seemed to be shouting "I told you so."

"Meg," I said. "Do you have any idea where Leo might have gone? You've said multiple times you want to get off the station. Is there someone who may be looking for you? Or who may have wanted to hurt you or your brother?"

"I don't know," she replied, shaking her head.

"Then why are you so eager to get away from Windfall?" Justus asked.

Meg froze. "We just...we...we were born here. Our parents died when we were eight. We've never known anywhere else, but we've outgrown this place. We're twenty-five now. We've wanted to get out for years, but couldn't."

"Why not?" I asked, glancing up at the elevator as the doors opened and Kat stepped out. In full combat armor, he had a blaster on each hip and a plasma rifle in hand. Formal attire.

"It's not so easy to get off Windfall when you come from Windfall. There are…complications."

"Why do I get the feeling there's something you aren't telling us?" Justus said.

"Or maybe a lot you aren't telling," Ki added.

"I'm telling you what I know," Meg replied.

"Who took your brother?" Justus pressed.

"I don't know." Justus grabbed her by the arm and squeezed, hard enough she cried out. "You're hurting me."

"Justus!" I snapped. "Let her go."

"Who took your brother?" he shouted in her face before letting go of her arm.

Kat skipped the last half of the steps, vaulting over the side and landing cleanly before rushing over.

Meg's eyes teared up, lip quivering as she clutched her arm.

"Justus, what the hell?" I said. "That's the second time you've gone out of—"

"Marsh," Meg said softly.

"What?" I said, the anger at Justus draining as quickly as it had come into play.

"If anyone grabbed Leo, it was Marsh," she repeated, lifting her head.

It hit me all at once, coming out in a sharp sigh. "You're indentured to him, aren't you?"

She nodded.

"Son of a bitch," I said. "And that's why nobody wanted to hire you?"

"Yes," she admitted. "Our parents died when we were

eight. Children on Windfall don't make it alone. Ever. We had two choices. Either become prostitutes for one of the pleasure parlors or go to Marsh. If there's one good thing about him, it's that he doesn't use kids as whores. He paid for us to go to engineering school and then arranged our apprenticeship. We were good enough to earn positions on Katana's primary prep crew, making sure everything was one hundred percent before each race. The job itself was a dream. Everything outside of it was a nightmare."

"How so?" I asked.

"When you're on Katana's team, you don't get time off. There's always something to be done. And he's not his father. He's violent, angry, demeaning, and abusive."

"He always seemed pretty nice in his interviews," Kat said.

"It's bullshit," Meg said. "An act. He's not like that with his crews. Anyway, we owed Marsh some money, plus interest. Except the rate is so high we can never pay him back. We can never get out. And he won't take us off Katana's team because he's done so well with us and the rest of his crew. He's superstitious and thinks any change will make him lose."

"Wait. What does Katana have to do with Marsh?" I asked.

"Katana is Marsh's son," Meg answered. "His real name is Mason; he just likes katanas. It's a sword."

"I'm familiar."

"He has one he carries around with him sometimes." She pulled back the sleeve of her coveralls, showing a row of neat scars. "He likes to test the sharpness on us when he gets mad. I've got more cuts all over. So does Leo."

"He gets mad that much?" Justus asked.

"Every time he races. Even when he wins, there's always something we should have done better. Or if he misses a hop by a fraction of a second, that's our fault even though he's the damn pilot."

"Have you told Marsh?" I said.

"Of course. He doesn't give a shit. That's his kid; he can do no wrong." She shook her head. "I wish I could take that katana of his and shove it up his ass."

I cringed at the visualization. "So Marsh knows you're trying to get away and he grabbed Leo?"

She bit her lower lip. "Not exactly."

"I don't understand."

"Since we're on Windfall, Mason's spending more time off *Ajira*, probably hitting up the pleasure parlors and drinking himself into a stupor before the race in a few days. Which gave us an opportunity to get off *Ajira* too. When I saw your ship docking, I saw our chance. I knew who you were and that you likely needed repairs, and that the other shops were all busy. And I knew Mason wouldn't notice we took a job for someone else right away. I figured we'd be long gone before anyone caught on. But I didn't expect you to need a reactor of all things, and we both wanted off the station as soon as possible."

"So you stole one," Justus said.

"Technically," Meg replied.

"There's not much gray area in taking something that doesn't belong to you. That's called stealing."

"She didn't steal it, I paid for it," I said. "Didn't I?"

"Technically," she said again. "Leo and I have spent the last six years on Mason's team. His junior mechanics make over two hundred thousand electro per year. With the interest and everything Marsh decided we owe, we make zero. The way I see it, he owes us two million electro, easy. Or one reactor. Which we promptly sold to you, Captain."

"So the electro I sent you is in your account?"

"Yes. We can't leave Windfall and go somewhere else with nothing. We'll end up right back in the same place."

"But as far as Marsh is concerned, you stole it, right? And so when his people spotted Leo, they grabbed him."

"I guess so. Maybe. I don't know how they knew we took the reactor already. Why do I always have such horrible luck?"

"Believe me, I've asked myself that question plenty of times lately," I said. "So what if we go to Marsh and pay him for the reactor? Do you think we can get Leo back?"

"He might let him finish the job, but he won't let us leave. You'll get your ship fixed, but we'll still be stuck here."

"I'm okay with that," Justus said. "You lied to us and got us mixed up in all of this garbage."

"Can we pay to have you released from his service?" I asked. "How much do you owe him?"

"Ben, you aren't really thinking—"

"I'm entertaining the idea, yeah," I said, cutting Justus off. "I can't believe I need to say this in a society founded by future Earthians, but slavery is wrong."

"They're not slaves. All they have to do is pay off their debt."

"It's slavery with a bow on it," I said. "And we already went through that on Earth too. How much do you owe Marsh?"

"I don't know," Meg replied.

"How can you pay off a debt when you don't know how much the debt is?"

"Exactly. I swear he just makes up numbers."

"Do you know where to find him?"

She nodded. "I can lead you to the Junket."

"Kat, Justus, you're with me," I said. "Ki, if we aren't back in three hours, come find us. Formally attired."

CHAPTER 24

The Junket was Marsh's domain. Located in the hull of a former salvage freighter converted to a station module—which was how it got its name—it wasn't all that close to Space Dock Three. It was officially part of Yellow Zone, a short tram ride from Green, which sat above Red in regard to its gravitational orientation.

The largest zone on Windfall Station, the sealed off cargo compartment of the freighter made up only a small portion of Green. The rest of it was dedicated to services that had apparently sprung up around the business that occurred inside the Junket. Bonds, loans, pawn shops, and of course casinos ringed the compartment, along with pleasure parlors and betting saloons that streamed live competitions from around the Spiral to wager on. I recognized the multitude of places as additional opportunities for someone to lose all of their money and borrow more so that they could lose it too. At which point, they would need to go to Marsh if they wanted to escape the bookies and loan sharks with their lives.

The whole setup was a total racket, an obvious yet elegant trap for anyone down on their luck or desperate.

Like Meg and Leo, or the woman in the red jacket. If anyone deserved such penance, maybe it was the individuals who had gambled their lives away. But a pair of orphans or a mother trying to save her son's life definitely didn't.

I knew Justus didn't agree. All he saw was the fact that Meg and her brother had lied and gotten us involved in their mess. Maybe it was my Earthian background, maybe it was just my personality, but I wanted to think I saw past that to an untenable situation with very few options to escape it. Maybe because I had been in a similar place a few times myself, including less than a week ago, I couldn't wash my hands of the whole thing. And anyway, I still believed it would be more efficient to pay off their debt and get them back to work on the reactor than it would be to find another pair of mechanics. Especially if they were as adept at their profession as they appeared to be.

The full expanse of the Junket became visible as a pair of blast doors slowly groaned along their tracks, opening in front of us. A central avenue in the center ran nearly the entire length of the module. A series of tiered landings occupied both sides while a large pagoda waited at the far end. A completely different category of shops were set up on the tiers.

Markets that would be illegal in most other places.

Meg had said Marsh had enough scruples not to sell children to pleasure parlors. That didn't mean he wasn't involved with selling children. A group of them stood in front of one of the ground-level shops. Tight shock collars like the one the police had put me in on Kasper clung to their necks. Their posture was perfect, straight up with their arms at their sides, but whenever one moved even a little, an adult woman would hit them with a small rod, bringing them back to perfect attention.

I spotted adult servants on display on the other side of

the center lane, two decks up, and additional slave markets further ahead. Sprinkled among them were gun dealers and drug dealers. There was even a shop advertising cyborg surgery at cut prices. All in all, the place wasn't as busy as I feared, or as empty as I hoped. Hundreds of visitors moved from floor to floor and shop to shop, browsing the so-called merchandise.

It all left me sick to my stomach, my hands clenching tighter and tighter as we crossed the threshold into the Junket and made a beeline for the pagoda. Marsh's estate. It was where Meg was certain we would find him holding court with all kinds of riffraff, from shop owners to station guards trading criminals for electro.

I had the power to stop them from selling kids. All I had to do was flick my thumb and forefinger and I could bury the adults involved in the bulkheads. But I couldn't stop everyone, especially with Marsh's guards patrolling the center line and standing watch along the tiered sides. For all of the power sigiltech had granted me, it hadn't made me a superhero like the woman in the red jacket claimed. I was at best the super soldier Keep had claimed I could become, possibly worth a hundred of the guards. I didn't even feel close to being that capable, even after eating my fill of junk food and recovering a good portion of the spent chaos energy.

Beyond my silent, nauseated rage and white knuckles, I couldn't do anything for the collared children. And it sucked.

I could tell by Justus' expression the sight bothered him too, but not to the same extent that it tore at me. How had future generations from Earth ended up in a new part of the universe and turned it into this, with feudal system dynamics, slavery, and who knew what else? What kind of people had been on the colony ship and why did they make decisions that had led to this shit? They had all of Earth's history to work with. A chance to start fresh and do everything better. And this was where they ended up.

"We were lucky," Meg said, noticing my anger. "Leo and I. We were smart enough to get into a trade. Those kids you see, even Marsh thinks they're nearly worthless. He'll get a few hundred electro for them, at best."

"What'll happen to them?" I asked.

"Marsh makes buyers sign a contract that stipulates they won't be abused. But most of the sales go off-station, and Marsh doesn't check in on them after the fact. There are rumors that word got back to him of kids being mistreated a few times and he dealt with it violently, which maybe keeps some of the buyers in line, but not all, I'm sure."

"Meg." The whispered hail drew our attention to the woman in the red coat as she materialized from between two of the shops. She came to a stop in front of us, offering me a quick look of acknowledgement before returning her attention to the mechanic. "Marsh has your brother. He sent me to find you."

"Well, you didn't have to look very hard, did you Latreese?" Meg replied harshly. "I'm on my way to speak to him right now. But I'm sure you'll report that you brought me in so you can write down your debt." She smirked. "How much do you still owe him?"

"Enough," Latreese replied.

"How much exactly?" I asked her.

"I don't know," she admitted. "A few hundred thousand still, probably."

"Only until next week when the interest goes up," Meg scoffed. "But you're welcome to claim you rounded me up."

Latreese smiled. "Thank you, Meg. I'm just trying to get out from under this. We all are. You know that."

"Leo and I, we're trying a different way."

Latreese looked at me again. "Did my advice work out for you, Ben?"

"It did, actually. Really well."

"I'm glad. One good turn deserves another. That's what my mother always used to say."

"I can get behind that," I agreed.

"How do you know Meg?" She paused. "Oh, let me guess. She and her brother are fixing your ship."

I nodded. "I didn't expect this drama to come along with the decision."

"Do you remember what I said to you before?"

I was sure she meant about being a superhero. "Yeah. Maybe that's part of the reason I'm here."

"Maybe you can put in a good word for me."

"Do you have to snake your way into everything?" Meg spat at her. "You'll get your credit, leave it at that."

She shrugged. "I'll do whatever it takes. Just like you. Anyway, you should pick up the pace. You know how much Marsh hates waiting."

I hoped that was the only thing the Junket's owner and I had in common.

We crossed the bazaar quickly, Latreese leading the way, Justus and Kat following behind, the other patrons steering around us as if they knew we had business in the pagoda. I did my best not to look at any of the shops and stalls along the way, but it was close to impossible to ignore the places with people, and in one case, a rare, intelligent spider-like alien I think was called a xixitil. It hunkered back in its cage, multiple eyes seeming to plead with me when it noticed my head shift slightly to look at it. There was also a stall where a handful of elderly men and women sat, grim determination on their faces as they waited to have their debt transferred.

"It's hard to say this without sounding like an asshole," I said. "But why would someone take on their debt?"

"It's called Voluntary Inheritance," Latreese replied. "Which makes it sound better than it is. Those people took out loans from Marsh and passed the proceeds to their children, intentionally becoming indentured servants. Marsh sells them to different manufacturers who use them for testing. New drugs, new implants, new armor, whatever requires the real deal for trials. They'll spend the last year of their lives in hell to care for the ones they're leaving behind." She shook her head. "The shame of it is they have no idea what they're really in for."

I swallowed the lump that had grown in my throat. At least their presence in the Junket was voluntary.

"What about the xixitil?" I asked. "It owes Marsh money too?"

"She was a stowaway on one of Marsh's freighters. Probably owed him a few hundred electro for the ride. It's either this or prison."

"I bet the loan's up to a few thousand by now," Meg said.

"I think prison would be preferable," I said.

"Not for a xixitil. Most people hate them. She wouldn't last a day."

"What if someone bought her just to kill her? Or abuse her?"

Latreese shrugged. "That's the chance you take, I guess."

We reached the base of the pagoda, where a couple dozen small steps led up to the entrance. A half-dozen well-equipped guards in intimidating dark red combat armor flanked the steps and the pair of golden doors at the top, currently open. The guards didn't react to us as we began the ascent to the golden doors but closed ranks when we neared them, quickly surrounding us.

"Come on, Vasli," Latreese said pointedly to one of the guards. "I'm bringing them to see Marsh."

"No guns inside," Vasli replied, orienting himself toward Kat. "You all need to hand over your weapons or wait out here."

Kat turned his head toward me, a silent question in his eyes.

"Why don't you wait out here?" I suggested, pulling my blaster from its holster and handing it to him.

He nodded. "Aye, Captain."

Justus turned his gun over to Kat as well. He nodded to the guards before returning to the base of the pagoda. The guards didn't give us any more trouble, returning to their posts as we finished the climb, passing through the golden doors and into the building.

A long, ornately decorated corridor continued along the center line of the Junket, all the way forward to an even more ornately carved wood door I assumed opened into a throne room. Stairs on either side led to higher floors of the building.

Latreese led us past open doorways that led to a library and a conference room. We had nearly reached the doors to the throne room when a thin, short-haired woman in dark pants and a suit jacket walked through a third door and approached us.

"Latreese," she said. "Oh good, you found her. Hello, Meg."

"Hi, Sarah," Meg said coldly.

Sarah's eyes shifted to me. "And you are?"

"Ben," I replied. "And my friend, Justus."

"Just Ben?" Sarah asked, apparently amused.

"Just Ben," I answered.

"No need to be coy, Just Ben. We know who you are. Your electro is welcome here."

I smiled at her. "That's good to hear."

"Marsh is finishing up with a meeting. He'll..." She paused, her eyes losing focus as she obviously listened to an internal comm, probably much like mine. "Oh, he's actually ready for you now." She turned over her left hand, revealing a series of raised bumps beneath the skin of her wrist. She tapped one, and the throne room doors started opening. Her hand swept forward as she backed away, a smile on her face that gave me the impression she knew something I didn't. "In you go."

CHAPTER 25

Marsh's throne room wasn't as large as the doors leading into it suggested. A shimmering red and gold rug ran fifty feet from the doorway to a large rectangular table, its legs carved in the shape of oriental dragons. A man who had to be Marsh sat in a large, red velvet chair behind it, a ten or eleven-year-old girl on his left, another man on his right. A pair of guards stood at attention on each end of the table, two more behind the throne, and another two on the inside of the doors.

Leo was there, too, seated in front of the guard on the left end of the table, hands folded in his lap. He stood up when he saw us enter, glancing at Marsh before resisting the urge to rush to his sister. Marsh and the others at the table stood as well.

Older, with thick white hair, a wild beard, and sharp eyes, the owner of the Junket wore simple brown pants and an ivory shirt that left him looking more like a hobo than one of the most powerful people on Windfall Station. An expensive-looking gold watch dangled from his boney wrist, conflicting with his otherwise ragged appearance. The young girl had long golden hair and a small, cherubic face, although her eyes hinted at a level of maturity or experience well past her age. The man on his other side was the total opposite of Marsh. In his twenties, he wore rich blacks and reds and plenty of bling.

"Oh shit, that's Katana," Justus whispered, recognizing Mason.

"And Marsh's daughter Eliza," Meg added.

"Benjamin Murdock!" Marsh shouted, his voice echoing around the room. "What a treat. What a pleasure. What good fortune. Please, come in, come in. Don't be shy." He waved his arm emphatically as if he was pulling us in.

We approached at a normal pace while Marsh and his children returned to their seats. At the same time, a line of young servants in formalwear began pouring into the room through side doors, carrying trays of food and drink.

"Not specifically intended for you, Ben. Can I call you Ben?" Marsh asked.

"Sure," I replied.

"However, your timing is impeccable. I'll have the help bring two more plates."

"That's not necessary," I said. "We've already eaten."

"Are you sure? There's plenty here. More than we can eat."

"I'm sure. If we'd known you would have food, we would have come hungry."

Marsh laughed, leaning back in his seat as one of the servants began scooping something like mashed potatoes onto a plate in front of him. Another on his other side put a hunk of meat on the plate. He picked up his knife and fork, ready to dig in.

"Daddy, I don't like roast poyn," Eliza said, complaining about the meat.

"Then don't eat it," Marsh replied before looking at us again. "Well, if you two aren't going to eat, then we should get down to business, yes?"

"That sounds like a good idea," I answered.

"I see you brought Meg back to me. Did you hear I was looking for her and her brother?" He motioned to Leo, who had sat down again.

"Actually, I—" Latreese started to say.

"Did anyone talk to you, Lottie?" Marsh snapped. "Be quiet."

Latreese lowered her head subserviently.

"Actually, Lottie came to my ship and retrieved Meg," I said. "I wanted to come along to meet you and talk about purchasing the twins' debt. Her debt as well."

"What?" Latreese said, surprised.

"Meg and Leo aren't for sale," Mason said with his mouth full.

"What have I told you, Mason?" Marsh said. "Everything has a price. We never refuse to negotiate."

"What have I told you, *Marsh*?" Mason answered back. "Call me Katana. And I am refusing to negotiate. The biggest race of the year is coming up and I need them in my stable." His eyes met mine. He reminded me of the jerk from *VR Awesome!*, Bloodstain, or rather, Jeff. "Maybe you can come back after the race and we'll discuss it. Until then, piss off."

Marsh slammed his hand on the table, rattling the silverware. "Katana! That's not how you treat potential business partners. Benjamin here is one of the only people to ever escape from Persephon Penal Station. He's earned our respect."

"Whatever," Mason said, taking another bite off his meal.

"How much do Meg and Leo owe you?" I asked.

"Latreese owes me six hundred eighty-four thousand, three hundred and seventy-three electro," Marsh said. "With the ten percent transfer fee, that comes out to—"

"What about Meg and Leo?" I asked again. He had spit

the number out so quickly he either had a neural link like Gia's or he had just pulled the number off the top of his head. Probably the latter, though I was sure he did have a link.

Marsh glanced at his son. "Sixty-three million," he replied.

"There's no way we owe sixty-three million," Leo shouted, jumping up. The guard grabbed him and shoved him back into his seat.

"That's impossible," Meg agreed.

"It's not just your debt," Marsh said. "Katana says he needs you for the race. You have a value beyond what you owe." He looked at me. "That's the price, Benjamin."

"I don't have that much electro," I replied.

"Care to take a loan?" Marsh questioned wryly.

"With you? Not a chance."

"I'm sorry you can't afford them. Would you like to continue negotiations for Latreese?"

I nodded. "But I'd like to continue negotiations for Meg and Leo first. Besides becoming indentured to you, what will it take to get them on my ship, fixing my reactor."

"*Your* reactor?" Marsh said, his entire demeanor changing suddenly. "*Your* reactor? I'm afraid not, Ben. That reactor was stolen from my warehouse. My inventory. You didn't pay me for it, so it belongs to me." He relaxed slightly. "But I will sell it to you for twenty million electro."

I felt my hands clench anew as I realized Marsh was trying to push me into the same desperate trap he had pushed all of his servants into. I smiled at the ridiculousness of it. "I'll return the reactor to you."

"I do appreciate that. We may still have a problem. The reactor was brand new. If even a single thing has been altered on it, that makes it used and vastly diminishes its value."

Of course. "Meg?"

She looked at me, her terrified expression answering the question before her words. "We already started the install."

"There you have it," Marsh said. "It's lost at least fifteen million in value."

"That's ridiculous," Justus said, finally speaking up. "A reactor like that one sells for three million tops on the open market."

"Under normal circumstances, perhaps. But you've been to the docks. You've seen how busy the station is. Right now, all it would take is one reactor failure on the right ship and I could easily get that much for it."

"I would pay that much if *Ajira* needed a new reactor," Mason said.

"See?" Marsh added. "My point is made."

"I don't have fifteen million electro," I growled, running out of patience.

"Oh, that's too bad. Well, I'll be happy to loan you the funds so you can pay me. Sarah!" He shouted and clapped his hands. When I looked over my shoulder, she was coming up behind us.

"Yes, sir?" she said.

"We need a standard loan contract drawn up for Benjamin Murdock, in the value of..." He trailed off, waiting for me to fill in the amount I needed.

"Forget it, Marsh," I said. "I'm not playing your game. You can't just inflate the value of something because it suits you."

He stared at me for a second before taking another bite of his food, not answering until he had chewed and swallowed. "Actually, Ben, I can. It's all perfectly legal here. If you don't like it, take it up with Adam Winthorpe."

"Winthorpe?" I said.

"He owns Windfall Station," Justus explained. "And he's not wrong."

"You should have warned me about bullshit like that before we even came here," I said.

"I didn't think it would become an issue."

"Sarah, draw up our standard loan contract for Benjamin Murdock in the value of—"

"I'd rather go to prison," I said, cutting him off.

Marsh smiled back. "If you won't cover your debt, perhaps there's someone else who will. Sarah?"

I looked over my shoulder at her.

"Yes, sir," she replied. "Legrond, please come in."

I kept my eyes toward the rear as Daft Punk Remix and his backup assholes moved into the doorway. I should have known.

It was a trap.

CHAPTER 26

"Benjamin Murdock." Daft Punk Remix, or rather, Legrond said. "We meet again."

"Better never than late," I replied. "But I guess there's nothing I can do about that now."

He smiled. "There's an insect on your planet, if I'm not wrong, known for being able to survive every attempt to exterminate it, no matter how violent that effort may be. Are you familiar with what I'm talking about?"

"Yeah. You mean a cockroach. I'll take that as a compliment."

"You should be dead."

"Surprise."

"Well, however you survived, I'll be sure not to make the same mistake that Blorb apparently did by leaving you alive."

"Blorb?" I heard Mason say behind me, followed by his laughter.

"You know Blorb?" I asked Legrond.

"For a long time," he replied. "A valuable tool, though he outdid himself this time. I'll forever be grateful to him for disposing of that wild bouncing murder doll of yours."

I did my best to contain my desire to *push* him into the ground so hard he popped like a cyst. "What are you even doing here?" I asked.

"As you know, change is coming to the Hegemony. Duke Sedaya sent me to Windfall to discuss the future with both Windthorpe and Marsh. Imagine my surprise when Marsh informed me he had caught one of his mechanics coming from a starship called *Nanofly* that coincidentally is a robot head. But of course, the mechanic said the ship was named *Head Case*."

I gave Leo a side glance, who looked sincerely apologetic about the slip. Marsh had set me up, but at least he and Meg weren't involved. I doubted Legrond needed confirmation that the giant robot head was my ship.

Only my eyes moved as I returned my attention to Legrond. "So you came here to what? Take me prisoner? Again? That didn't work out well for you before."

Legrond smiled, pulling a blaster from his hip. "I think I'll try the straightforward approach this time." He leveled the gun at my chest.

"Wait a second," Marsh said. "He owes me. I expect to be paid."

"You'll get everything you have coming to you, Marsh," Legrond said. "I guarantee it." He returned his attention to me. "That's an interesting tattoo on your neck, by the way. I'm curious to know where you got it, before I kill you."

I activated the construct, feeling the energy gathering around the sigils, invisible to everyone in the room.

"Oh, I almost forgot.." Legrond's attention turned to rivet on the doorway behind me. "Jessica?"

My attention went to a woman who now stood there, her hand raised in my direction. Immediately, I felt pressure surrounding me, a *push* and *pull*, or maybe a different sigil I didn't know. Either way, I could tell she wasn't strong enough to be Gilded. She could hold me in place, but I knew she wasn't strong enough to contain me.

"You're an archon now, aren't you, Ben?" Legrond continued. I don't see any catalyst on you, but there are ways to hide it. So, the tattoo. Where did you say you got it? Maybe I'll get one myself."

"It's not a tattoo," I growled, at the same time I *pushed* back. The force holding me shattered as Jessica was thrown to the floor. "Get down!" I shouted as Mason pulled his gun, followed by Marsh and all of his guards. None of the people I wanted to help were armed.

Or so I thought.

Mason might have gotten a shot off at me if Latreese hadn't dug into a hidden pocket in her pants and come out with a knife she threw at Mason so fast it was almost a blur. The blade did nothing but bounce off his chest, it distracted him long enough for my people to hit the deck.

And it gave me the extra half-second I needed.

I *pushed* a second time, initiating a circle of force around me from the waist up and violently throwing the guards around me into the bulkheads. It shoved the table into Marsh and Mason, blowing them backward like rag dolls and pinning them against the wall. Only Eliza escaped unharmed, smart enough to duck when I said to get down. She scrambled away from the scene on her hands and knees, vanishing through the side door as I dropped the action.

"Let's go," I barked at the others, who jumped back to their feet and hurried ahead of me toward the door.

"Murdock!" Marsh screamed at me. "You're a dead man!"

His guards were still stunned, and a dazed Legrond struggled to get up. Jessica had made it back to her feet. She stepped forward, raising her hand.

I activated *reflect* ahead of her action, a tingling sensation confirming it had done its job. She cried out as her energy bounced back at her, wrapping her up in its energy. Since it was her action, she canceled it almost immediately, but it still gave Justus time enough to scoop up one of the Niflin's discarded blasters and shoot her in the chest. Crying out, she fell to the floor, pulling herself into a fetal position to suffer through the pain.

"Benjamin," Legrond said, making it to his knees. I whipped my hand toward him, ready to make good on my desire to smash him like a grape. Only his hands were up, the fight knocked out of him. "We surrender."

I didn't have time to take him prisoner, and he knew it. He was counting on me to be the better person now that I had the upper hand, and as much as I wanted to take him out, I couldn't bring myself to kill in cold blood. I moved ahead of the others, throwing up a wall of *absorb* as the guards in the long hallway started shooting from the cover of the columns.

Energy blasts hit the invisible shield and seemed to stick there, rapidly creating a pincushion of energy that started obscuring my view. I held the action for as long as I could, watching through the hanging flares as the guards from the steps rushed into the pagoda.

I didn't drop *absorb*, but I did tack on *disperse*, releasing the stored blasts toward the incoming guards. A barrage of firepower slammed into their line, taking out half of them before the rest could dive behind cover. Realizing their error, the guards stopped shooting as we ran for the exit. I already knew they would pick it up again once we had passed, possibly thinking I could only work my magic in front of my face. I considered pulling the columns from the pagoda, but rejected the idea because I didn't know how much energy I had stored up or how much I would need. It didn't make sense to waste it. I could already feel myself growing weaker.

Kat appeared in the pagoda's entrance a moment later, plasma rifle in hand. He opened fire on the guards nearest him, catching them by surprise. It seemed they had completely forgotten about him in the chaos. Further back, the guards in the throne room must have recovered because more blasts began zipping past us from behind.

"This is crazy," Leo shouted as I activated *disperse* all around us. The energy from the bolts dissipated as it hit the field, creating lines like lightning but leaving us unharmed.

"Keep going," I urged them once everybody got ahead of me and the gunfire. Coming to a stop and spinning around, I dropped the action. A few random blasts made it through to me, my new coat absorbing one of them. I turned my hands over and *pulled*. The floor tiles lifted from the floor, sending the shooters tumbling. It bought me enough time to catch up to the others outside the pagoda.

"Sorry, Captain." I saw that Kat had already distributed all the weapons he had collected. "You didn't look like you needed a gun."

"Look out!" Latreese warned as the guards on the tiers around us started shooting, the sellers in the shops scattering. I barely managed to activate *disperse* in time to cover them as they escaped the chaos. Kat tried to fire back at the guards through my *disperse*, only to find his rounds fading out of existence. The other guards were no doubt regrouping behind us.

"I can't hold this long enough to get us to the other end," I grunted. "We need to split up and use the available cover so I can focus the effort."

"Copy that," Kat said. "We can't fight back like this anyway."

"Everyone go with Kat. They want me. I'll pull their fire away from you."

"What if you don't make it?" Latreese asked.

"That's not an option," I replied. "I'm dropping the defenses on three. Ready?"

"Ready as we'll ever be," Meg answered.

"Ready," Kat said, sending everyone dashing to different spots on the port side of the Junket.

With everyone already finding cover , I just hollered, "three!" and ended the *disperse* as I broke starboard.

Kat immediately shot a pair of the guards, Justus a third, using the element of surprise to their advantage. Energy blasts sizzled against the deck, zipping so close by my hip I could feel the heat. Another grazed the tail of my coat as I angled toward the stalls and dove behind one right before a blast would have taken my head off. I found myself in the midst of a group of cowering elderly people who had signed up for Voluntary Inheritance.

"Who are you?" one of them asked.

"Name's Ben," I replied. "Nice to meet you. If you're having second thoughts about signing your lives away, now's your time to get the hell out of here. If your families care about you, I think they'd rather have you here with them than a one-time payday based on your suffering."

"What do you know?" a grizzled old woman hissed. "No wonder the guards are shooting at you."

I shook my head at the violence of her retort and wrote them off, dashing away from the stall as a barrage of plasma and blaster fire poured into it. Glancing back, I knew none of the old folks had survived, but I didn't have time to lament their pointless loss. I spotted nearly two dozen guards moving out of the pagoda, most of them facing my direction. At least that part of the plan was working.

I stood to face them, gritting my teeth as I *pulled* their guns out of their hands. It was a big mistake on my part. Pulling from that distance used excessive energy, more than I could spare. My arms tingled from the sudden drain, warning me I was going to run out of fuel completely if I wasn't more careful. The guards' weapons fell to the deck halfway between them and me.

I made it to the next stall, hitting the deck before a shooter in front of me came close to blasting my head off. Finding myself behind a rusted cage, I nearly screamed when the xixitl spun around, six black orbs and long, menacing chelicerae right in front of my face.

"Helpsss," she rasped, pushing out a lot of air to form the word.

I didn't hesitate, *pulling* the cage apart from both sides. She spun around again, powerful legs pushing her out through the weakened container. She landed on the guard who had shot at me, stabbing him with thick, barbed claws at the end of the tarsus bone of one of her limbs. She picked up his rifle and tossed it to me before jerking her head to indicate I was clear.

I ran forward to join her, expecting more gunfire from our backs. I looked over my shoulder, surprised to see some of the servants had hurriedly captured the guns I had pulled away from the guards, picking them up and putting them to good use. A quick glance across the center of the deck showed me that my people were pinned down. I turned my rifle on the shooters across the way, hitting them from the flank and taking the heat off Kat and the others.

"I have a ship," I said to the xixitl, doing my best to ignore the fear factor of her appearance. "You're welcome to come with us."

"Yessss," she replied, just before bouncing toward a stairwell a short distance away. Landing at the base, she spun and raised her abdomen, launching spider silk from it. Spinning again, she pulled a guard down the steps to her and speared him with a tarsus before scrambling up to the second level.

With the firefight behind me losing steam, the servants

likely on the losing end, a guard popped out from cover ahead of me, ready to shoot. I *pulled* his rifle away and shot back, the plasma piercing his armor and burning a hole in his chest.

I jumped over his body, closing in on the blast doors that marked the Junket's exit. I barely avoided a pair of shooters further up, throwing myself down behind a metal counter. Waiting a couple of seconds, I popped up again and *pushed* the crate into the pair hiding behind it, laying them out flat on the deck. They were still trying to get back up when the xixitl dropped from the side of the tier on a strand of webbing, swinging into them and stabbing them both. She released the web and landed cleanly on the deck in front of me.

I flashed her a smile that summed up my appreciation of her timely save. She made a hissing chuckling sound before scurrying off to locate another target.

As I neared the end of the module, gunfire zipped across the Junket toward us from the rear. I dove behind the last of the stalls, while Kat and the others remained crouched on the opposite side of the center aisle. They opened fire on the guards coming forward from the pagoda, forcing them to find their own cover.

I didn't expect the blast doors to open on their own accord, so I turned to face them and *pulled.* The motor holding it in place was strong, forcing me to up the ante to budge the doors. They finally started sliding open, creating a breach just large enough for us to slip through. Kat broke for it first, leading the others as they continued shooting down the length of the Junket.

Seeing that we were about to escape, the guards redoubled their efforts, launching a barrage that surrounded the others and pounded the doors. Hit, Latreese cried out and fell to the deck, clutching her arm. Another round hit her before she could recover. She fell flat on her stomach, and I lamented her loss when she didn't move again. The others made it through the door, but flashes from the other side suggested they'd run into opposition there as well.

"Time to go," I said to the xixitl.

Before I knew what was happening, she scooped me up in her two frontmost legs, tucking me under her cephalothorax and bounding into the air toward the opening. She grabbed onto the side of the blast door, protecting me with her body as she scurried along it to the edge and around to the other side. I let go of the *pull,* and the door slammed shut with enough force to shake the whole module.

We were out!

CHAPTER 27

Unfortunately, escaping the Junket didn't make us safe.

I knew that starting a fight with Marsh would have repercussions, but Marsh had already been working with Sedaya, so there was a limit to how bad it could get.

I just didn't know what that limit was yet.

When the xixitl and I entered the Yellow Zone, Kat and Justus had already downed the guards at the blast door. Flashing red lights and a monotone voice warned everyone there to find shelter. It meant the whole station, or at least this section of it, was gunning for us. The xixitl lowered me to the deck, placing me gently on my feet and letting go before scurrying off again, a dark mass vanishing quickly into the shadows. An energy blast zipped past me, the spidery alien taking out the shooter a moment later.

"We need to get to the tram," Kat said, sidling up beside me. "I see you made a new friend."

"Someone should have told me xixitl are such badasses. I would have set her free *before* we went into the pagoda." The blast door behind us started opening again. "Shit, let's go."

The crowded, enclosed environment of the station was

perfectly tailored to the xixitl's strengths. As she ranged ahead, the rest of us shot our way through several more unsuspecting guards, taking them out before they knew we were even there. With the civilians all fleeing or taking cover inside the shops, it allowed her to quickly overpower any opposition that got in our way. We took only limited fire from the guards coming out of the Junket as we ran through the entrance to the next module.

We found the entire place nearly deserted, the shops closed up, the stalls abandoned. The station guards had set up a portable barricade in the center, with narrow slits they could see and shoot through. Their rifle muzzles punched through the small openings, helmets lined up beside them.

"Hold!" one of the guards shouted from behind the barrier. We came to a quick stop. "Drop your weapons!"

Kat and Justus glanced at me. I shook my head almost imperceptibly. "Don't do it." I was getting tired, but I still had some gas left in the tank. I breathed in, gathering the chaos energy into the construct.

The *push* rattled the module with its force, tearing away the barricade and sending the guards sprawling. The xixitl scurried into their midst, quickly stabbing one after another as we raced through the module toward the tram entrance.

Would they shut down service to Yellow Zone in light of the emergency? Did the system even have that capability?

We made it more than halfway across the section before Marsh's remaining guards made it into the module, their fresh blaster fire exploding around us. I *pulled* the shattered pieces of the barricade back together, landing it between us and our attackers, rounds sizzling against its thick metal instead of tearing into us.

The xixitl reached the entrance to the tram first. She stuck her two front tarsus into the crack between the doors and pulled them apart, holding them open while the rest of us dashed in beneath her. Bringing up the rear, I patted her on the side as I went under, feeling short coarse hairs on a leathery carapace.

"I don't even know your name," I said on the way past.

"Ixitat," she breathed out.

"Ixitat, nice to meet you. I'm Ben."

She twisted through the open doorway without losing her grip on it, releasing it to close again once she was clear. All of us safe inside. I watched as the airlock on the left side closed just behind the end tram. The module was otherwise empty, everyone either having boarded a transport or otherwise evacuated from the area.

"Not a bad place for a last stand," Kat said, backing away from our entry door with his rifle aimed at it.

"Last stand, my ass. Ixitat, can you web the module doors closed?" I asked. I figured if Spiderman could do it, she should be able to as well.

She clicked out something that sounded like affirmation and turned her abdomen to the door, spraying silk across it in a disgustingly impressive display.

Behind me, without a word, Justus collapsed, the sound of his body hitting the floor drawing my attention. A large plasma burn covered half his abdomen, leaving him in rough shape.

Restore was a passive symbol. I couldn't help him that way. But I wasn't powerless. I hurried over to him, putting my hand on his forehead. "*Pax*," I said softly, activating *calm*. Warm energy flowed through my hand into him and he relaxed. A temporary pain blocker, but hopefully it was enough for us to get him back to *Head Case*.

"How do we get out of here?" I asked, shifting my attention between the blast doors and the empty tram line.

"Hold on," Leo said. He ran to the bulkhead beside the airlock and opened a hidden access panel, revealing a touchscreen. Tapping frantically on the interface, he growled and shook his head. "Meg, I need you!"

She rushed to his side as the blast doors tried to open, held in place by Ixitat's web. I didn't know how long the thick threads would last. I hoped long enough.

"What are you doing?" I asked, watching the twins navigate through screens on the panel.

"We missed the last tram before the emergency shutdown," Meg replied. "I'm trying to override the system so the trams will resume running."

"You can do that?"

"We've worked on them before," Leo said. "As long as they haven't changed the passcodes."

"They haven't," Meg said, a big, mischievous grin filling her face. "Trams are back online."

"For how long?" I asked.

Her smile turned mischievous. "Well, I just changed the passcode, so until they figure out what I changed it to. Which will take them a few hours to a few weeks."

"Nice work," I said, patting her shoulder before turning back to the door. "How long until the next transport arrives?" I asked, the web stretching enough to allow the doors to part a few more inches each time they tried to open.

"About twenty seconds," Leo said. The guards, finally able to shove their muzzles through the opening between the doors, got off a couple of wild shots before Ixitat pushed one of her legs through to stab at them, forcing them to retreat.

"Captain," Kat said. "Ki reports station guards are in the docking spoke, moving toward *Head Case*."

"Of course they are," I replied drolly. "I can remote the ship out of there to a closer dock." I grabbed my phone from my pocket.

"No you can't," Meg said, rejoining us. "We were in the middle of repairs. The engines aren't hooked up yet."

"What? Our plan was to get back to the ship and get the hell out of here. And now you're saying we can't do that?"

"Well, we can once we restore the connection."

"How long will that take?"

"I don't know. An hour?"

"Pretty much every guard on this station is coming for us. I don't think we have an hour."

"There's only so much I can do, Captain."

The airlock on my right opened and the tram slid into the station. "All aboard!" Leo shouted.

With the emergency shutdown in place, the tram was completely empty, giving us the entire thing to ourselves. We piled in, Ixitat the last to retreat. With her legs no longer stabbing through the gap, Marsh's guards immediately blasted the webbing, allowing the doors to open the rest of the way.

It was their turn to make a big mistake.

As the inner airlock door unsealed, I pulled the outer airlock open, exposing the module to the vacuum of space. Right away, the air began evacuating through the opening. The guards froze within seconds as they realized what was happening, turning tail and scrambling back through the door and closing it behind them. The airtight tram moved into the airlock, its automated controls pausing it there while the inner airlock closed and the outer one opened, at which point I released my *pull*. Our transport slid out of the station, riding the line back toward Green Zone. We would need to remain on the line while it dropped to Red.

"How likely are the guards to blast the tram out of space?" Justus asked, head swiveling back and forth in search of incoming ships.

"And shut the whole line down for weeks?" Meg replied. "It won't happen. We aren't worth that much to Winthorpe or Marsh."

"Besides, they can just wait for us at the ship," Kat said.

"Ki says they've taken up static positions in the spoke. They aren't trying to actually board *Head Case*."

"They might not realize your unit is on board," I said. "As far as Legrond knows, my crew is all captured. He probably thinks I got here on my own."

"Without a reactor?" Justus asked.

"He's not bright enough to figure out if I needed an entire reactor or just repairs. Also, nobody else has left the ship. Kat, put your team in position to ambush them once we get to the dock."

"Aye, Captain."

"How are you holding up?" Justus questioned. "With the sigiltech, I mean. Your neck is getting dim."

"I'm tired," I replied. "And starving. What about you?"

He looked down at his burned belly. "It hurts, but whatever you did made the pain manageable."

"It will. I don't know how long the *calm* will last though. Keep always used enough to put me to sleep for hours."

Ixitat approached us, bowing her head to me. "Thankssss," she rasped.

"Thank *you*," I replied. "We wouldn't have made it without you."

She bowed her head again, acknowledging my gratitude.

"Captain, we're approaching Green Zone," Leo said, watching our progress.

"I'll pull the outer airlock open once we get inside. That'll keep the guards away from the tram. We'll be fine until we get to Red."

"And then what?" Meg asked.

"Then we have to fight our way down to the dock," Justus said. "But even if we do, we'll still be stuck there for over an hour. I don't know if we can hold out that long."

"We have to," Kat said. "There's no other option."

I glanced at Meg and Leo, a crazy idea worming its way into my head.

"What?" Leo asked defensively.

"You worked for Katana on *Ajira*, right?"

"Yeah. Me and Meg, both. Why?"

I matched Meg's earlier mischievous grin with one of my own.

CHAPTER 28

"Where is everybody?" Kat asked as we stepped off the tram back at the Red Zone. We had expected to have to fight our way from the tram module to the elevators. Instead, the area was deserted.

"I guess they're afraid of us," Justus replied, his arm over Kat's shoulder for support.

"Not us," Kat countered, thrusting a thumb at me. "Him."

"Yeah," Meg agreed. "Making blaster rounds vanish into thin air has that effect on people."

"They aren't vanishing," I said. "They're dispersing. The energy scatters."

"Same difference," Leo said. "You're putting on a show I don't think Marsh or Winthorpe will be too quick to forget."

"That might not be a good thing if they decide they want to know how it all works. Besides, I already told you I can't keep this up forever."

"You don't need to," Meg replied. "The coast is clear."

"Not down at the dock, it isn't," Kat said. "According to Ki, reinforcements are moving in. They're going to do their damndest to prevent us from reaching and boarding *Head Case*."

"They must figure there's strength in numbers," Justus said.

"They aren't wrong," I pointed out. "But we still have some element of surprise."

We remained cautious despite the solitude, crossing the tram platform to the exit and pausing behind the bulkhead while the blast doors slid open. Peering through the opening, I marveled at how the next module, teeming with activity an hour earlier, was now completely abandoned. Shops boarded up. Stalls covered over with tarps. Lights dimmed.

"Are we sure this isn't a trap?" Leo asked in response to the eerie look of both this habitat and the one after it, equally dark and foreboding.

"Pretty sure it may be," Justus replied.

Ixitat tapped me on the shoulder to get my attention, motioning with another leg to herself and then to the darkened module.

"You want to scout ahead?" I asked. She nodded in affirmation. "Be my guest."

She scuttled through the door and to the left, her dark coloring allowing her to quickly vanish into the darkness. She appeared a few seconds later on top of one of the shops before leaping to the ceiling and crawling upside down to the other side of the aisle. Making a zig zag as she traveled the length of the module, she dropped at the far end and rose up on her hind limbs, using her forelimbs to wave us forward.

I almost laughed at the absurdity of it. I never thought I would be taking directions from what amounted to a giant spider. Correction. An intelligent giant spider. An alien. It should have been creepy as hell, but it was actually pretty awesome.

As Ixitat scouted the next module, we walked straight down the middle of this one without incident. Our spider friend was already waiting at the far end of the next module by the time we reached it. We continued the process all the way to the elevators a few habitats away.

Justus tapped on the controls, only to have the screen flash a red OFFLINE back at us.

"What a surprise," Meg said.

"I can get us down," I said. "You just have to trust me to *push* you up from the ground after you jump into the shaft."

Kat looked at me like I had just suggested he throw himself out of an airlock. "That's a lot of trust, especially with you getting tired. Have you ever done anything like that before?"

"Once. Sort of. And it left me temporarily paralyzed."

"No thank you," Justus said.

"Things were different then."

"There must be stairs here somewhere," Kat added.

"On a space station?"

"Don't worry about it, Captain," Leo said, digging a screwdriver from his pants pocket. "We've got this." He quickly removed a hidden panel next to the control screen, revealing the guts of the system's electronics. He reached into the guts to flip a switch. The UI on the screen changed, asking for the maintenance passcode.

Meg punched it in and navigated to a list of shafts with sliders. Of course, the whole thing was currently set to OFFLINE. She flipped the master slider at the top back to ONLINE. "If the guards are waiting at the bottom, they'll know we've regained access," she said.

"I don't get it," I said. "Why bother locking out the elevators on an empty deck when all of your defenses are in between us and where we want to go? It doesn't make sense."

"Unless they were trying to slow us down," Kat replied. "Stalling for time."

"Time to do what?" I asked.

He shrugged. "You got me. But it did take us nearly twenty minutes to get across the module. And if the lockout had actually worked…"

The first elevator cab arrived, cutting him off as he spun toward it and brought up his rifle. The rest of us trained our weapons on it too, ready to disintegrate any guards who might be inside.

Empty.

A second elevator cab reached the deck. We trained our weapons on it.

Also empty.

The third and fourth cabs arrived on the top level of Red Zone at almost the same time, splitting our attention.

Both of those were empty too.

"More stalling," Justus decided. "Do we go down in one cab or split up?"

"You do what you want," Kat said. "I'm sticking with the human battering ram."

"Me, too," Meg and Leo agreed. I thought Ixitat would as well, but she indicated she would go another way, through one of the shafts a cab hadn't ascended.

"Level Six, Spoke Nine," I told her. If there were guards waiting for us at the bottom, she would be a nasty surprise for them.

"Yesss," she replied. Prying the doors open with her forelimbs, she crawled through and vanished as the rest of us boarded our elevator.

"Do you make strange new friends everywhere you go?" Justus asked me as we started the descent.

"Are we friends?" I asked skeptically.

"I'd like to think so."

I smiled. "Then yes, pretty much."

"What's your secret?" Meg asked. "Because friends have been hard to find on Windfall. Leo and I have always only had each other."

"I don't know," I replied. "I'm just being me. But you don't only have each other anymore."

Both she and her brother smiled. "I knew you were the right person to come to," she said. "I knew things would change for the better."

"Yeah," Leo said. "I believe her exact words were, 'let's hope he doesn't screw us over.'"

"I never said that." She looked at me. "Captain, I never said that."

"Yes you did," Leo insisted.

"Whether you did or didn't doesn't matter," I said. "You're on Team Hondo now."

"Hondo?" Kat asked. "That's almost as bad as Blorb."

"Not quite," Justus added.

The elevator slowed as we approached Deck Six of the space dock, our tension-relieving chatter fading with it. All eyes and muzzles turned to the doors. My chest tingled in response to the chaos energy building in the construct, ready for release.

"Kat, tell Ki to get ready," I said. "But wait for my signal."

"Copy that," he replied, passing the message on through the comms.

The elevator came to a stop, and the doors began to open.

CHAPTER 29

Knowing we needed to return to *Head Case* to leave the station, Ki had warned us the guards were setting up outside the ship. With only the ship's external cameras to work from, she had no way to see how many additional forces had taken root near the elevators, waiting for us to arrive.

We expected resistance. I had steeled myself to burn a lot of my remaining energy against it. But I hadn't planned for the enemy to learn so quickly from what I had already accomplished in the Junket. Maybe I should have, considering Legrond was up there with Marsh, able to provide as much information as he could about sigiltech and its limitations. I should have killed the Niflin when I had the chance. Even after everything I had already been through, I was still too forgiving. Too damn nice. For better or worse, I wasn't sure if I could change that personality trait.

I had *reflect* ready to go, figuring we were packed too tightly for *disperse* to drain the enemy's firepower before it could hurt us. But *reflect* wasn't rubber. It didn't mean everything bounced off it. The action countered velocity, and Legrond must have told Marsh so, who passed the message along.

As the doors slid open, instead of being immediately fired upon, a mass of guards pushed forward, rushing into the elevator. I dropped *reflect* only a moment after I activated it as a dozen hands grabbed me and pulled me out of the cab. Wary of hitting me, the others held their fire, and once I was pulled clear, it left them unprotected from a deadly offensive barrage.

I only saw it in quick glimpses between the armored shoulders of the station guards, who funneled me away from the elevator banks as quickly as they could. Kat and Justus started shooting as soon as I was clear, but so did a line of guards waiting for their line of sight to open up. The exchange only lasted a couple of seconds, a mass of blaster rounds pouring in on my companions before Meg had the wherewithal to again close the elevator up and send them all back up a level. At the same time, fists found my chest, pummeling me and disrupting the construct, making it hard for me to activate my sigils. Opaque helmets looked down at me with expressionless contempt. One of them turned their rifle toward me, putting the muzzle only inches from my face, finger moving to the trigger.

"Twenty million to the individual who kills you," he growled. "Enough to make us all—" He looked away from me in response to sudden shouting back at the elevators. I didn't need to see Ixitat to know she had arrived, emerging unnoticed from her shaft and launching a sneak attack on the guards.

I *pushed* myself to my feet before lightly *pushing* outward, just enough to off-balance the guards. I didn't want to throw them into Ixitat. I just wanted to throw off their aim.

Ixitat skittered across the ceiling and dropped onto a guard. At the same time, she shot webbing at the guards behind him, entangling them in the sticky stuff to send a wave of palpable fear through their defenses. Reaching forward, I put my hand between the helmet and armor of the guard closest to me, only my fingertip touching skin. It was enough. I activated *calmed-to-death* for the first time, sending it through the light touch.

The guard froze and collapsed, instantly placed into a coma that would lead to death within seconds. At least, that's what David's computer model had suggested the sigil would do. I stood in shock with my hand still outstretched for a moment, until another guard wrapped their arms around me from behind. He lifted me off the ground and spun me toward a second guard, already waiting with his rifle leveled. I just barely activated *reflect* in time. At such a close range, the plasma bolt seemed to misfire, reversing into the gun. It exploded in the guard's hands. He screamed and fell to the deck, writhing in pain as he stared with horror at his bloody stumps.

I grabbed the guard behind me by his forearms and activated *enhance*. It made my hands strong enough to break his grip on me, and with a *push*, I sent him sprawling into the guards behind him.

Fresh gunfire filled the corridor, launched from a fortified guard position further down Spoke Nine. One of the bolts caught me in the back, the sizzle of the plasma's heat filling my ears as it tried to burn through my coat. I ducked low and spun around again, ready to raise a wall of *reflect* to send it back at them. I didn't have a chance before someone tackled me from behind, flattening me on the deck. Pinned, I *pushed* myself up, taking my attacker with me as we rose the height of the passageway and I slammed him into the ceiling, bones cracking from the force.

I *pushed* myself forward to get out from under him, twisting and landing on my feet in time to see another guard coming at me. An *enhanced* punch drove him into the bulkhead, knocking him out. A third guard pointed his blaster at me. I *pulled* it from his hands, catching it awkwardly as he froze in place. Before I could turn the weapon in my hand to use it, a plasma bolt hit him in the side of his helmet, killing him.

Looking back toward the elevators was a live version of one of those cheesy cavalry-to-the-rescue shots in the movies. Ixitat was in the center of the line, flanked by Kat and Justus on one side, Leo and Meg on the other—all of them stepping over the downed guards between us—as they walked toward me.

I raised a hand to activate *absorb* before immediately switching to *disperse as* the approaching guards shot plasma bolts at me. I realized my mistake almost too late. I couldn't dole out *disperse* like a time-released medication. It was all or nothing. If I *absorbed* too much energy, I would have nowhere to put it without destroying the space dock and killing us all.

The bolt blasts created a light show between us and the second wave of defenses as Ixitat and the others reached me. While I was able to hold the attack at bay, I knew every second I held the sigiltech action left me that much close to running out of chaos energy.

"Sorry to have left you in the lurch like that, Captain," Meg said, referring to escaping the onslaught of plasma bolts pouring into the elevator cab. "I didn't know what else to do to get out of the line of fire."

"You did the right thing," I replied. "And you came back. That's what's important." My eyes swept across them. "I can't hold out much longer. We have to go straight through."

"Considering how hard they're trying to slow us down, I think that's a good idea," Justus said.

"Then we make a run for it. I'll try to keep them off us, but if they get too close…"

"We've got it," Kat said. "We'll make it."

"Can I say it?" Leo asked. "I've always wanted to say it."

"Don't," Meg said.

"I'm saying it," he decided.

"Saying what?" I asked. "Leeroy Jenkins? For Frodo?"

"Don't ask," Meg said.

"You'll see," Leo replied. She shook her head, annoyed with her twin.

I didn't know what he planned, and I didn't care. As long as we made it out of here. "Let's go," I said, not waiting to break into an all-out sprint.

"Freeeeddddooommmm!" Leo cried out behind me.

We barreled headlong toward the defenses, though I had no intention of actually doing battle. Energy blasts and plasma bolts filled the passageway, crossing through my dispersion field and sliding around us like liquid light, unable to land a solid hit.

We raced toward the enemy at full speed. "Don't slow down," I shouted as we neared the bolted-down barricades, similar to the one the guards had erected in the Purple Zone. The guards continued shooting through the barrier while we closed the gap. The intensity of firepower was both a plus and a minus, draining my strength while it reduced the amount of heat and energy that reached us. "Get ready!"

I held out for as long as I could, the heat of the energy blasts biting and burning at my face as the barrage closed in on us, too powerful to fully dissolve. Without hesitation, without slowing, I canceled *disperse* and *pushed*.

Like before, the force was enough to dislodge the barricade. But this time, the grated decking gave way, curling up before tearing into large pieces of shrapnel that hurtled into the barrier and the guards behind it. Guttural screams filled the air as some of them scattered. Those who didn't move fast enough either went down where they stood, crushed under the weight of their defenses, or were thrown against the passageway bulkhead.

I entered the resulting chaos, forced to slow as I jumped over the missing section of deck, landing on the other side. A guard still left alive picked himself up and lunged at me, his arms wrapping around my waist. I spun with him, using my free hand to shove him back a step. He lost his grip on me and stumbled back, teetering on the edge of the deep hole. Kat slammed him with the butt of his rifle, the man's arms windmilling as he fell from view.

Ixitat skittered overhead, gaining the lead as the bulk of the guards had just enough time to get up before she dropped onto them. They cried out in raw terror, wailing in pain as she stabbed them with her forelimbs or shredded them with her razor-sharp chelicerae. I *pushed* others away, pinning them against the bulkheads as we raced past.

Breaking through the second line of defense, I could already see the third further ahead, set up just in front of *Head Case*. Looking out through the corridor transparency, I could see the ship's damaged ear as well as *Ajira* still parked behind it. We were almost there.

"Kat!" I snapped, looking back as the guards behind us regrouped, their first few poorly aimed rounds zipping past us. "Now!"

He passed the signal to Ki as I fell to the rear of the group, raising a fresh barrier between us and the guards at our backs. Ixitat scurried well ahead of us, bum rushing the last wave of defenders. They had to be more careful than the second wave to avoid hitting friendlies, which we were able to use to our advantage.

Even though I couldn't see them, I knew the moment Ki and the other rebels emerged from *Head Case*. Shouts rose from the third placement of defenders, reflections of light and energy revealing a quick and intense firefight. A few potshots still came toward us from behind, but the ambush took the pressure off me of trying to cover both sides of the passageway. It allowed me to keep the rear protected while we closed on the enemy ahead of us.

All of the forward gunfire stopped when Ixitat leaped over the barricade and dropped on the guards. Stabbing, biting, and stinging, she had them screaming and trying to run as she decimated their numbers. We were almost to the barricade when they broke completely, squeezing around the barrier and running toward us with their hands in the air. None of them slowed as we crossed paths. I went around the barricade to the right, smiling when I saw Ki and the other rebels spreading across the passageway, claiming victory over the routed station guards.

I let go of *disperse*. The sudden release washed over me like a tidal wave, a crushing fatigue hitting me like a sledgehammer. I stumbled and fell to my knees, the entire passage spinning around me.

"Ben!" Kat was at my side right away, hand under my arm to help me back up. I lifted my head to look up at him, attention stolen by the view of space through the clear top of the corridor. Or rather, the lack of space. My body immediately started trembling. Fear, anger, and desperation coalesced within me as an unmistakable, unnatural black scar blotted out the stars.

"What is that?" Leo asked, spotting it.

"The reason they were trying to slow us down," I replied, gritting my teeth and letting my anger motivate me back to my feet. "We need to get out of here, now. Meg, you're with me. Leo, you need to get *Head Case* away from the station." The mains were offline, but vectoring thrusters would be enough to separate the ship and the dock. "Everyone else, get on board and cross your fingers." I glanced at Ixitat. "Or your forelimbs."

She clicked out what sounded like sharp laughter, but the moment was short-lived as my fear became realized.

The ship that created the passage through a tear in the fabric of space and time began to emerge, sigils along the hull glowing brightly, powered by the Star of Caprum.

Dominator had arrived.

CHAPTER 30

My fury kept me planted as I watched *Dominator* complete its transit, no doubt summoned to Windfall Station by Legrond. Meg jogged me out of my rage-paralysis, grabbing my hand and tugging me toward *Ajira*. "Ben, come on!"

I looked at her, my mind so warped by the sight of the sigiltech ship that I didn't respond to her right away. Then I nodded and stopped resisting, joining her in a fresh sprint toward Mason's ship. The others hurried to board *Head Case*, vanishing up the ramp without so much as a *good luck*.

I had suspected *Dominator* would have the sigils to transit, but knowing how much power it required I was also certain only the Star had made it possible to use on something so large. Even as I followed Meg to the airlock leading into *Ajira*, part of me wanted to stand my ground and wait for Admiral Lyke. The saner side knew it would be suicide. I wasn't sure I could beat her at full strength. There was no way in hell I could defeat her in my current state. If she reached the dock before we made it away, the same thing would happen to Justus, Kat, and the others as had happened to Matt, Shaq, and my crew.

Instead of rescuing them from Melchior, we would join them there. And Lyke wouldn't make the mistake Blorb had of leaving me alive to suffer. That was assuming she even intended to dock the sigiltech ship or her smaller transport and deal with me in person. Maybe she would wait to see if we managed to get away first, and then sic her warship on my robot head. Under the best of circumstances it would hardly be a fair fight, and we weren't even close to the best of circumstances.

If we were, I wouldn't have been running to the ship next to *Head Case*.

My phone vibrated in my pocket as we reached *Ajira's* airlock, sealed tight. But not for long. Meg used a control panel on the station side to access the ship's hatch controls while I pulled out my phone and glanced at the screen. A notification had popped up, informing me of an incoming hail from an unknown identifier.

Maybe unknown to *Head Case's* datastore. I knew exactly who it was since she knew I was still alive, thanks to Legrond. The only question was whether or not I should answer the call.

"Ben," Meg said, getting my attention as the door slid open. A pair of large men in coveralls stood immediately behind it, large wrenches raised overhead, mid-swing. They pulled up as they recognized Meg.

"Meg," one of them said. "Geez. What are you doing here?"

"Klath, this is Ben," she replied, laying the back of her hand against my lower chest. "He's a new friend of mine. We're trying to get away from the fighting. We barely made it here in time."

"That's why we locked the door," Klath said. "I thought maybe someone was trying to get to *Starbright*, to sabotage the race."

"*Starbright*?" I said.

"Mason's hop racer," Meg answered.

"Meg, you know he doesn't like when you call him Mason," the other man said.

"Come on, Jonah. I know for a fact Mason isn't here."

My phone vibrated in my hand a second time. I couldn't see *Dominator* from inside the airlock, but it was a stark reminder that we needed to hurry up. "Meg," I prodded.

"Right," she replied. "Permission to come aboard?"

Klath lowered his wrench but rubbed at his chin with his other hand. "I don't know."

I pushed both mechanics against the bulkhead, holding them there. "We're coming aboard," I said, trailing Meg past them.

"This way," she said, guiding me into a carpeted passageway. Holographic images lined both sides between the hatches, every one of them an image of Mason holding up a trophy or standing at the top of a podium.

"At least he's not proud of himself," I said.

"Meg!" Klath shouted from further back. "Meg!"

She stopped and turned around. "Klath, I'm just going to show *Starbright* to Ben. It's fine. Mason gave me permission."

"He did?"

"Yeah. I just came from dinner with him."

Klath made a face. "I'm going to call him."

"You go ahead and do that." Both mechanics went in an alternate direction. "It'll take them at least three minutes to get to the bridge to contact Mason, assuming you didn't disable him when you smashed him with the table. Which was one of the best moments of my life, by the way."

"I don't really like hurting people, but he was definitely an asscrab."

My phone vibrated a third time. I tapped on the notification, the phone scanning my face before allowing me to remote access *Head Case's* comms. I tapped a few more times to open the hail.

"Can't this wait?" I asked before Lyke could say anything. "I'm a little busy at the moment."

"How did you get off Omega Station?" Lyke asked. "You've earned my respect for that much."

"*Lego Elrond* said it's because I'm a cockroach," I replied. "I tend to agree. Or maybe a cat. Nine lives, you know."

She actually laughed. "Regardless of the circumstances, it must have been a lot of effort for only a few more days of breathing."

"No pain, no gain, right?"

"I hope your friend Matt feels the same way. If so, he stands to gain quite a lot. So do Quasar, Druck, and your little pet."

Renewed fury burned through my veins, but I refused to let her push my buttons. "What about Keep?"

"He refused to give me what I wanted, so I tossed him out of an airlock."

A cold shiver ran throughout my body, free hand clenching. "You..." I trailed off. Alter, Gia, and now Keep too? I couldn't believe it. "You'll pay for that." It was corny and cliche, but it was all I could come up with. At least I'd lowered my voice, adding a good deal of menace to my words.

"Yes, Ben, I can see from where I'm standing that I'm in deep trouble. Are you going to come after me in your little toy robot head?" She laughed. "Since I have the Star of Caprum, your ship doesn't even have a power source, which is why I hailed you. I wanted to give you a chance to surrender."

We reached an elevator which opened at Meg's approach. The cab was carpeted too, the walls lined with thick red velvet and accented with gold. Ugly and ostentatious as sin.

"I might be willing to surrender if you let Matt and the others go," I said as the doors closed and the elevator descended.

"Sorry, Ben. I can't do it. Sedaya's orders."

"But he'll allow you to let me surrender?"

"To be delivered to the same place as your friends. Or Avelus. That'll be your choice once you're on board."

The last two words, *on board*, nearly got me to tell Meg we were calling our plan off. Once I was on board, I could challenge Lyke and try to recover the Star. Or better yet, gain control of *Dominator*.

Except I was tired and hungry, and I knew Lyke would kick my ass right now. It would be better to live to fight another day. Windthorpe and Marsh had tried to stall me for her. Now it was my turn to stall back.

"Honestly, it's kind of tempting," I said. "You didn't mention David. Where is he?"

"I passed him to Sedaya before returning Blorb to Atlas. He has a Hegemony to run, after all. I must say, Ben. When the duke first told me about the Star of Caprum, I believed he was speaking in hyperbole. But after completing a month's worth of travel in a few days I think he may have been underselling the potential."

"I'm so glad you're impressed. I guess that means I can't convince you to give it back. You know I'm having a bitch of a time trying to get into hyperspace without it."

The elevator doors opened, revealing a short corridor with an airlock at the end. We hurried to it, and I looked through the small window at the top half of Katana's hop racer, which seemed to be fused with the hull of the larger vessel. Coated in glittering chameleon paint, the racer shimmered and sparkled like a Swarovski storefront during Pride Month. *Starbright* was written in thousands of small crystals, in a font smaller than the flat black of *Katana* above it. I hit the mute button on the phone and glanced at Meg.

"You want *me* to fly *that*?"

"Unless you'd rather surrender to the Ice Bitch," she replied, getting the nickname solely from Lyke's voice. "Or die."

I motioned for her to let us in, unmuting the phone before Lyke finished laughing at me.

"Enough with the games. I want an answer now, Ben," she growled, probably realizing I was stalling for time.

"What if I choose not to surrender?" I asked.

"Then I'll do to you what you very nearly did to me with that bomb of yours."

The airlock hatch slid open. Meg and I entered the strange hangar, where she approached *Starbright* and opened a panel on the ship's side, tapping on a control screen. The sleek canopy opened and she motioned for me to get in.

"You know what I don't get, Admiral? May I call you Admiral?" She didn't respond, so I kept talking as I dropped into the pilot's seat, nearly verbalizing how comfortable the padding was as it sank into it and it wrapped around me like a hug. "What I don't get, Admiral, is, well, two things. One, what exactly are you an Admiral of? You only have one ship. Two, why can't you and Sedaya make up your minds? Capture me, kill me, capture me, kill me. If I'm being frank, the indecision is exhausting."

I hoped maybe to get her goat and have her explode in anger at my defiance. Instead, she started laughing again.

"Is this your response, Ben?" she asked. "Are you going to try to just float away?"

I smiled at the statement. Leo was using the vectoring thrusters to maneuver *Head Case* from the space dock, getting the ship into position. "Is it working?" I replied as Meg lowered herself into my lap and pulled the restraints over both of us. Thankfully, she was a lot smaller and lighter than Keep. While the fit inside *Starbright* was snug, I was able to see over her head and reach all of the controls, though she would handle most of the non-flying part. She tapped on the touchscreen at the front of the cockpit, initializing the reactor.

"Here's my answer," Lyke said. "Goodbye for good this time, Benjamin Murdock." The comms disconnected.

It was just as well. I didn't have a chance to respond before a sudden, violent force yanked my phone from my hand and threw Meg and me against our shared restraints, first in one direction and then another. I reached out, trying to grab my phone as it smacked against the inside of the canopy. Meg did her best to work the touch controls against constantly changing g-forces. Judging by the way it felt, my guess was that we were spinning. But what had Lyke done to make it happen?

"Bad design decision," I growled, *pulling* my phone back into my hand.

"Hop racers weren't meant for this," she groaned back, using her left hand to stabilize the right. "Whatever this is. Bombs away."

She hit the button to release *Starbright* from its cradle, vectoring thrusters automatically firing to push us away from the ship. The asynchronous movement nearly got us killed as the larger vessel's rotating hull swung toward us. Acting purely on instinct, I put up my hand and pushed against it, just barely getting us out of the way.

"That was close," I said as we gained a little more distance from *Ajira*. A large square of metal zipped past the canopy, missing it by less than a meter. That was closer. I stabilized our rotation and craned my neck to find its cause.

My heart jumped into my throat, my entire body shaking once more.

Space Dock Three was gone.

CHAPTER 31

Looking down at where the space dock had been, I really couldn't tell what had happened to it. All I knew for sure was that before, there had been multiple levels of spokes and hubs with dozens of ships connected via docking arms and airlocks. Now there was debris everywhere, as if every bolt, screw, and anchor in the dock had been ripped out all at once and the resulting pieces had been hurled through space in every direction, except toward Windfall Station itself. Those chunks of debris had slammed into the parked starships, in every case tearing them away from their moorings and scattering them with the rest of the junk, in many cases puncturing them with accelerated particles and exposing them to vacuum. That in turn caused more material to be pulled out of the ships, including people.

"Take this," I urged Meg, handing her my phone as cold shock continued chilling my entire body. I finished leveling *Starbright* out, freeing my hand to put it on the ship's throttle. A combination of pure luck and the small size of the racer prevented us from being struck with additional debris, though a lot of it continued zipping past all around us, making navigation tricky.

Looking up through the canopy, I saw *Ajira* continuing to drift away, hit suddenly by another ship that had been thrown on a different course. The collision tore open both ships, and I nearly cried out when I saw Klath emerge from *Ajira* to certain death in the cold of space.

"That bitch," Meg hissed softly, tears streaming down her cheeks. "Those people…"

"Meg, I need nav. We have to find *Head Case*." I hit the throttle, tapping it lightly to give us some forward acceleration, my eyes darting everywhere, trying to keep track of all the debris.

"What if they're gone? Destroyed? What if we're alone out here?"

I pushed the throttle a little harder, surprised not to feel any of the inertia as the ship jolted ahead of an incoming segment of space dock. Of course a ship like this would have the most current and advanced form of counter-inertial technology. "They weren't destroyed, and we aren't alone out here."

"How do you know?"

"This ship has to have sensors," I pressed. "Focus on our lives and get us the grid."

She nodded curtly. "Display sensor grid," she said.

The grid projected onto the canopy in front of me provided a translucent heads-up display of our surroundings. There were so many objects around us I thought the ship's computer would struggle to render it all, but it handled the task without lag. Of course, a ship like this would also need the most powerful onboard computers in order to calculate jumps as rapidly as possible. And since this was Mason's ship, it probably had the best-of-the-best.

"Why didn't you tell me it was all voice activated?" I said.

"It isn't until everything is initialized," she replied.

"Now it is, except for the hop trigger on your stick. Racers usually calculate the route between hops and keep it ready until they've reached the hop point on the course nav. Anyway, you need to be careful what you say. There's no activation word. Usually only one person is in the racer at a time, so they're either talking to the computer or themselves."

"Got it," I replied, scanning the grid. *Dominator* was easy to spot, hanging above the destruction a few hundred kilometers away. Like in the asteroid field, anything that should have collided with the warship bounced off an invisible field laid against the hull. I knew Lyke would stick around, waiting to see if *Head Case* made it through her overkill effort to destroy me. She had no way to know I wasn't on board.

I'll do to you what you very nearly did to me, she had said. I understood now. She was at the space dock when Archie detonated his candy bomb. She had made it back to *Dominator*, although she had to have barely escaped the fireball. She wanted me to know what it felt like to be put under that kind of pressure, to either die or come close to dying, while leaving Windfall Station in one piece. How many people had she just killed to create those conditions? What kind of psycho had Sedaya enlisted to command his most powerful asset?

She was probably his sister or something.

"Do you see *Head Case*?" Meg asked nervously. "I don't see it."

"Keep looking," I replied. "More of my attention is on all of the junk coming at us. Does this thing have shields?"

"Bare minimum for random dust particles and stuff. They're automatic. It'll tell you if any of the nodes are down."

I turned the stick and hit the thrusters, avoiding another

piece of metal. "What about the phone? If you can still remote access the ship, then it's still out there."

Meg looked down at the screen. "We're still connected. That doesn't mean the ship has air."

"You're so negative," I said. "They're out there and in one piece. We just need to find them." I looked up at *Dominator* again as the large warship's main thrusters began emitting ions again, pushing the ship into motion. "Or wait for someone else to find them for us." I turned *Starbright* in the same direction *Dominator* was moving. "Focus on the grid in front of us."

I directed the command at Meg, but the ship's computer took it as an instruction, *Starbright* zooming ahead. Luckily, my less than careful wording had worked out for us.

This time.

"There," she said, pointing at the unmistakable outline of *Head Case* drifting away from the rest of the debris. The level flight path toward clear space suggested someone was behind the stick. *Dominator* continued accelerating toward *Head Case*. Moving in to capture or kill? Either way, I needed to get there before Lyke did.

At least I was in the right kind of ship for a race.

"Hold on," I said. "This is going to get tense. Can you set us up for a jump?"

"Yes, just don't say anything else," Meg replied. She opened a small compartment in the sidewall of the cockpit and threw my phone into it, slamming it shut again to keep it from floating around loose in the cockpit. As soon as she grabbed onto the restraints, I pushed the throttle forward.

The sudden acceleration overcame the counter-inertial systems, pressing Meg into me and me deeper into the seat. The thrusters burned bright enough right behind the cockpit for me to see everything around us. We shot through the debris field like a bullet, the distance between us and *Head Case* shrinking in milliseconds.

Of course, increasing speed made it harder to avoid everything in our path. I had to focus closely on ducking, diving, and dodging around everything larger than a baseball and letting the shields handle the rest. I was able to keep to a predominantly straight line toward the ship, swaying only a little to slip around the obstacles. I nearly lost my focus when a frozen body passed just ahead of us, Charlie's shocked eyes staring accusingly back at me. In a sense, it was my fault she was dead. It was my fault all of them were dead. If I hadn't come to Windfall Station...

I stopped myself there, rejecting the blame. Lyke had a million ways to grab me without destroying the entire space dock. She had chosen mass destruction. For me, it was a preview of what the Spiral would be like under Sedaya's control.

I cut the throttle just after passing the dead engineer, maintaining velocity and angling toward *Head Case*. *Dominator* was closing in, but we had managed to gain on the warship. We were coming in fast. Too fast? Like hop racing, the timing would need to be perfect.

"Set a jump path for course checkpoint alpha," Meg said, instructing the computer to prepare for hyperspace.

"Calculation complete," the computer replied a few seconds later. "Recalibration active."

I wanted to ask Meg what recalibration was. I didn't want to say anything that might mess anything up. But there was something she had omitted.

"Computer, recalculate with hyperspace field extended one hundred meters around," I said, prefacing the instruction for my own sake.

"Good call," Meg said. "Sorry."

"Recalculation complete. Warning. An enlarged field will drain the power supply beyond requirements to complete the race."

"I'll take that under advisement," I said, shifting my

finger to the hop trigger. Nearly to the edge of the debris field, I updated our vector, aiming *Starbright* directly at *Head Case*. From the path *Dominator* was taking, it seemed they either hadn't noticed the racer or didn't think we were a threat. Not that anything was really a threat against the enormous warship.

That didn't mean we couldn't ruin Lyke's day.

Like an arrow, I aimed the racer toward *Head Case*, the racer on a perfect course to move into position just below it. At a steady velocity, I could count down the seconds until our paths intersected.

Ten. Nine. Eight…

Head Case suddenly climbed higher than should have been possible, course and velocity changed as it seemed to turn on a dime. Understanding what was happening replaced my instant of confusion. I adjusted vectors, throwing the racer into a hard turn. The force of it shoved both Meg and me against the side of the seat. Looking up and to the left, I spotted *Dominator* a little further back, sigils glowing as the warship *pulled Head Case* in with what amounted to a tractor beam.

"No you don't," I growled, finishing the tight course correction and sweeping around toward *Head Case*.

Seven. Six…

I rolled *Starbright* over, bringing the racer hull-to-hull with *Head Case* and easing the vector down just a hair.

Five. Four. Three.

My finger touched the hop trigger while I activated the construct on my chest, quickly visualizing what I wanted to happen.

Two. One.

With the smallest tap of retrorockets, I depressed the hop trigger and simultaneously activated *combine*. Unlike *Head Case* or *Radiance*, *Starbright's* field formed in a fraction of a second, quickly surrounding the two ships as they merged together into a single form. The difference in velocity at the time of the joining caused *Head Case* to be yanked backward, which in turn pulled us forward, throwing us into a wild backspin inside the field. It was a result *Starbright's* computer definitely didn't like.

"Warning. Warning. Hyperspace navigation error. Abort. Abort."

"We aren't aborting!" I shouted through gritted teeth, fighting the stick to get both ships under control. Even though we were in hyperspace and even though *Dominator* had vanished from the grid as we darted away faster than light, we definitely weren't out of the woods.

"Ben, we need to abort!" Meg cried. "We're way off course. We could crash into anything."

"Not yet," I snarled back, adjusting thrust to slow our spin. It actually felt like I was trying to fly a snail or a hermit crab, lugging around a huge appendage that only made everything harder.

"Warning. Warning," the computer started again.

"Shut up!" I barked at it. Surprisingly, it complied. "Come on, damn it!" I screamed next, adjusting the mains and adding vectorying thrusters, finally slowing the runaway train. Within a few more seconds, I had us resting comfortably inside the field, smooth and steady. "Now you can abort."

The ship's computer pulled us out of hyperspace, nearly a minute away and over eleven million miles from where we had started. The sudden stillness allowed me to finally exhale, which brought its own problem.

My stomach churned, bile rising to my throat. "Meg," I said softly. "I'm going to be sick."

"Don't you dare," she said. "There're no sick bags in here, nowhere to—" She stopped talking as I vomited down my chest and into the back of her coveralls. "Oh, gross."

I imagine she could feel it soaking through her coveralls

to her skin. "Sorry," I breathed out, panting for air and still feeling uneasy.

"Well, at least we're alive," she replied. "I can deal with puke oozing down my back for that. Nice work, Captain."

"You too, Meg. I couldn't have done it without you."

Finally, we were safe.

CHAPTER 32

Transferring from *Starbright* to *Head Case* wouldn't be easy. In order to get from the hop racer, fused to what was essentially *Head Case's* chin, and then up and into the hangar, I had to do something I had never tried before. Maybe in a way no archon had ever tried before. Even though I had formulated the usage idea while we were riding the tram from Purple Zone to Red, I had also questioned whether or not it was even possible.

The only reason I believed it might be conceivable was kind of dumb. Keep had gone through a lot of effort to save my life. He said I was important and special because I could do things with sigiltech that nobody else could do. I figured maybe this was one of those cases, and that my creativity with the technology could be what separated me from the likes of either him or Lyke, even if I might not have the same overall level of power output as a Gilded.

Of course, believing you could do something and actually doing it were two different beasts. And I had drained nearly all of my stored chaos energy getting us away from Windfall Station. It left me exhausted, beyond hungry, and at the same time perpetually nauseous. The only good news was that I hadn't fallen unconscious. Although, with the amount of discomfort I was in at the moment, maybe that wasn't good news.

What saved Meg and me, in the end, was Mason's love of chocolate.

When Meg opened the compartment to retrieve my phone so she could check up on Leo and the others, she found an entire stack of chocolate bars. Half a dozen in all, the eight ounce bars claimed to be made from a classic recipe that came all the way from Earth via the original settlers.It turned out the marketing was on point. Branded as Killgor's Finest, they tasted just like Hershey's.

My upset stomach made it hard for me to take the first few bites, but I knew if I didn't, I wouldn't be able to get us out of the tight confines of the racer's cockpit. Eating them didn't end the nausea, but between the calories and time, it did help replenish some of my energy. Within an hour, I was ready for my next Houdini act of activating a construct. I closed my eyes and visualized what I wanted to happen before carrying out the combination of necessary actions.

First, I used *pull* to hold in the air around us, keeping us surrounded by oxygen. Next, figuring we would lose warmth in a hurry once we opened the canopy, I activated *absorb*, holding onto the heat inside the cockpit. To that end, and this was the trickiest part, I also added *reflect*. Except I didn't add it to a solid surface like my clothes, but rather to the air surrounding us so it would keep the light, heat, and oxygen contained.

Then there was the fact that even though I would feel the activation of the sigils and the pull of energy from my body, I didn't know for sure if any of it would work until we actually allowed space to enter the cockpit.There were no verbal commands that would affect anything having to do with life support. Meg had to open the canopy manually, overriding the controls so is the cockpit would depressurize in space.

"Are you ready?" I asked.

"I'm ready," Meg replied, quickly tapping the screen to initiate *Starbright's* shutdown sequence. There was no sense leaving the racer running. "I hope we don't die."

"Me too. Do it."

My heart raced as she tapped the touchscreen and the seal of the transparency signaled its release. I had to force myself not to hold my breath while I waited to feel the cold of the vacuum or have the air sucked out of my lungs as the canopy swung open.

"So far so good," she said, still able to speak in our magic little hamster ball. "Ready to go."

"Set us loose," I said.

She released our shared restraints and I *pushed* off from the outside of our air bubble, sending us floating upward like a helium-filled balloon. My body shivered as we cleared *Starbright*, my ability to hold the complex action already wavering. It took too much focus to maintain all of it. I let go of *reflect*, immediately sensing the change in temperature as the warmth began siphoning out.

"Ben?" Meg said, feeling it too.

I ignored her, pushing our bubble out and up. We weren't that far from the hangar door. Kat and Ki would be in spacesuits, waiting for us.

We rose upward under *Head Case*, the light of the hangar interior a beacon as were the two rebels silhouetted in the threshold. I pushed us toward them as my limbs began shaking more violently, my muscles cramping, my strength nearly spent.

I lost my grip on *absorb*, and right away, a biting cold hit me like a hammer, threatening to steal *pull* from me too. If that happened, we'd be exposed to the vacuum of space. I let loose a primal scream, fighting with everything in me to hang onto the action while knowing its failure was imminent. Once we lost air, the vacuum would suck the oxygen from our lungs, all of the moisture on us would evaporate, and we would have ten to twenty seconds max to get out of it before we died.

My vision blurred, but I held on as we drifted ever closer to the hangar and the two rebels. Ultimately, all the desire in the universe didn't matter. The last molecule of chaos energy spent, the action faded, the harshness of space about to hit us like a brick.

At least, I thought it would be space. But something slapped down over my face and I found I could still breathe. Within seconds, I was on the hangar deck, the door closing behind me and atmosphere rushing back into the compartment. I didn't move, choking at first on the thin air but quickly pulling in enough to get coughing gulps of air, my lungs heaving and spasming, my muscles moving but my mind unable to control them.

"Captain," Kat said, standing over me. "Captain!"

I tried to turn my head to look at him, but couldn't. I had read about deep sea diving and the bends before, and I imagined this had to be what it was like. Painful and terrifying. And at the same time, I had survived worse.

"We need to get him to sickbay," Ki said.

Kat ripped off his helmet. "Ben, you're going to be okay. Just hang in there." He scooped me into a fireman's carry and ran. I saw Ki and Meg trailing a little behind him, and despite the pain of the spasming, I was grateful she had made it without suffering the same agony.

I was still awake when we reached sickbay, convinced that falling unconscious was a much better way to handle the aftermath of sigiltech overexertion. Like a car that refused to turn over, it was as though the hemolytic catalyst I had used in place of the golden catalyst was being rejected, and the restore sigil was trying to keep me going.

Only the fuel lines were clogged.

"Justus!" Kat shouted as we entered the sickbay. "I need you!"

He came out of Room One, shirtless with a bandage over his burned stomach. His eyes widened when he saw me. "Damn, you're pale, Ben," he said. "Hang in there. Take him to Room Two," he told Kat, crossing sickbay to the storage compartment to gather two bags of IV nutrients. When he came through the room's door, Kat was holding me down in the chair to keep the convulsions from throwing me out of it onto the floor. "Get his arms cuffed," Justus ordered.

It took both Kat and Meg, who ran into the room right behind Justus, to keep me steady enough to lock me into the chair. Justus loaded the nutrient bags into the autodoc and quickly set the controls. The machine lowered over me, the IV needle hovering over my arm, but I was still thrashing around too much for it to pinpoint the vein.

"Hold him still!" Justus roared.

All three of them had to lean on my arm, keeping it immoveable enough for the autodoc to stab me. Fluids immediately began flowing in a cold stream that started at my vein, spreading quickly throughout my body. The moment it hit the construct, an unbelievable pain overwhelmed me, exploding outward from my chest as every muscle in my body tried to expand and my vision went totally white.

A sudden peace found me there, and in that blinding millisecond or two of light, I saw a shadow of something that stole the peace. Just the hint of it was enough to frighten me more than anything had ever frightened me before. Enough that as the pain subsided, as my muscles calmed, as my body settled, I sensed the warm moisture of my urine running down my leg, and I was pretty sure I had shit myself, too.

"Ben," Justus said. "Can you hear me?"

I still couldn't turn my head, but at least I had stopped spasming. "I hear you. I can't move." Even though I could talk well enough to be understood, I couldn't move my mouth. A wave of panic swept over me. What if this was it? I had gambled against sigil sickness. What if I had just lost? What if I were paralyzed for good?

"Okay," he replied. "Don't freak out. The same thing happened to you on Omega when Her Grace brought you to sickbay there. I'm going to put you to sleep, give your body a chance to recover, okay?"

"Yeah. You should have done that five minutes ago. Before I made a mess of myself."

"We'll get you cleaned up," Kat said. "Don't worry about it, Captain."

I closed my eyes. "Yeah, okay." Embarrassed, I didn't want to be conscious for the indignity of them having to clean me up. I barely knew them. Used to Nurse Alter cleaning me up, it was times like this that I most wanted her back.

I wanted all of my crew back. My friends. I refused to believe that I wouldn't recover after everything that had transpired. My strength would probably return while Meg and Leo installed the reactor. After that?

Payback time.

CHAPTER 33

"Hey Captain, how are you feeling?" Justus asked as he entered my room in sickbay, carrying one of the medical slabs.

"Making progress," I replied, bending my legs at the knees. "Kind of sick of fluids, though." I tapped on the IV line. "I'm ready for pizza. Burgers. Beer. What about you?"

Justus laughed. "Me? Most of the stuff on this ship is at least sixty years old. The autodoc thankfully isn't one of them. The burn still hurts, but it's manageable, and it'll heal. Just like you. Speaking of which." He held up the slab. "I figured you might want to go over the results of the bloodwork and scans."

"Only if it's good news," I replied.

"Right." He turned around. "I'll come back later then."

"Wait!" I snapped. He paused. "Are you messing with me?"

"I don't know. Am I?"

"Come on, man. This isn't the topic to joke around about."

He turned around. "Your body doesn't want metal embedded in your skin. You don't need me to tell you that.

The restore sigil's knitting you back together and preventing rejection and infection. You already know that too."

"No news is good news on Earth," I said.

"I didn't say there was no news. We didn't know what would happen once you really started using the sigils. We have a little more data now."

"And?"

"What I can tell you is that the sooner you get that stuff out of your body, the better."

"So it's like we feared?"

"Not as bad as I feared, but yeah. The paralysis you experienced? The more often you go there, the more likely it'll become permanent. And even if it doesn't, there's a chance you'll lose a finger, a toe, a hand. Or maybe something will just go numb and you'll never get the feeling back."

"Not using sigiltech isn't an option right now."

"I get that. I'm not saying don't use it, and I'm not saying I know anything about what it's like to do the things you can do. But I do know that it's easy to be seduced by power. Next thing you know you're addicted to using sigils to do things you can do with your two hands, and then when the time comes to let it go, you can't help yourself even knowing what it might cost."

I nodded. "You're worried I won't be able to give it up."

"Aren't you?"

I resisted the temptation to say no right away, taking some time to consider the question. "No," I finally answered. "Keep was worried about me becoming addicted to the power too. But I didn't do this to become powerful. I did this to survive. I didn't come to the Spiral to get involved in a sci-fi Game of Thrones. I was just looking for a little adventure. Fun and excitement before I died. Instead, my friends are the ones dying. Along with too many innocent people. I don't know if the construct can be altered and left with just the restore sigil. If it can, I'll do it in a heartbeat."

He smiled. "Yeah, I figured you'd say something like that. I'm sorry your dream scenario turned into such a nightmare."

"I'm cancer free, and as long as the blue elf, the spiked blob, the Daft Punk wannabe, or the Karen and their minions don't get me, there's a good chance I'll have more peaceful excitement in my future."

"I hope so. If you get the chance, you definitely need to check out a Nebula Cruise."

"Nebula Cruise?"

Justus dropped the medical slab on the end of my bed, becoming much more animated. "It's been a dream of mine for a long time, but I don't think I'll ever see enough electro to pay for it. Do you like women?"

"Yes," I replied. "Human women, not aliens."

"A little limiting, but okay. Do you like exotic planets?"

"I definitely want to see some exotic planets."

"Perfect. Do you like rich food? And I mean real food, not assembler food."

"Oh yeah, you bet I do."

"Now we're talking. Do you—"

The door to the room opened and Meg barged in. "Captain," she said breathlessly, buzzing like a hummingbird. "Can you walk?"

"I haven't tried yet, but I think so," I replied. "How's the reactor install coming along?"

"It's progressing. Since you needed some extra downtime, Leo and I took the liberty of making some additional upgrades with the parts we found upstairs. You should try getting up. You could probably use the exercise."

"Upgrades?" I said. "What kind of upgrades?"

"That's not important right now. Why don't you try

getting up?" She looked like she was ready to jump out of her magboots.

I wasn't so daft that I didn't get that she wanted to show me something that would make me say *wow*. I couldn't help myself. "I think understanding what you're doing with my ship is pretty important. Especially since the reactor install was supposed to be done two days ago."

"I'm not saying it isn't important, Captain. The install will be finished in a few hours if you'll just get out of that damn bed and try walking!" She ended up shouting the last half in unrestrained excitement, mortified with herself after she did. "Sorry." She lowered her head, waiting for my rebuke.

I laughed instead. It felt good to have something to laugh about. "Justus, am I good to go?"

"You're asking me?" he replied.

"You are my doctor. Or at least the closest thing I have to one."

"And you're like Galaxy Man. You don't need me to tell you if you can stand up or not."

"Galaxy Man?"

"He's a B-movie superhero," Meg explained, rolling her eyes.

"Super speed, super strength, flight, even in space without a suit. Indestructible, immortal, impervious."

I was ready to roll my eyes too. "What's his weakness?"

"What do you mean?"

"He needs to have a weakness. If nothing can stop him, it's boring. You know, like Superman had kryptonite."

"Galaxy Man owns Superman. It's not boring."

"It's boring," Meg confirmed.

"You know what's boring?" Justus snapped back. "One weakness? So every plot has to do with getting a piece of green rock from somewhere and making a weapon out of it.

Totally contrived. At least Galaxy Man is honest about being overpowered."

"Which is boring," I reiterated.

"Boring," Meg parroted.

Justus shook his head. "Forget it, you two just don't understand. It's fine. What do you want us to see?"

"I'm not going to just tell you," Meg said. "Come on, Captain. You need to see it."

"Okay," I relented. "Justus, can you take this out?" I shook my arm, rattling the IV.

"Just don't pull," he answered. "You're liable to snap the needle off in your arm. Hold still." He leaned over me and removed the lines. When he did, a couple of drops of glowing blue blood oozed out, the light fading the moment air touched them.

"Thank you," I said. "Meg, help me up?" I held out my hand. Meg grabbed it and tugged, helping me slide off the chair. I was a little wobbly at first, but my legs managed to stay functional. After a few tentative steps, my strength began to return. Even so, Justus' warning remained fresh, and I concentrated more on the sensations from my nerves, feeling for any signs of tingling or numbness as I picked up speed to the door.

"Yes!" Meg exclaimed, rushing past me, her unbridled, childlike excitement returning. "I'm so glad you're feeling better, Captain."

"Not just because you want to show me something, I hope," I replied.

"Of course not." She moved in beside me and kissed me on the cheek. "Thank you for getting Leo and me away from Marsh. I should have said it before, when we were on *Starbright* but things were kind of crazy at the time."

"You're welcome," I replied as we left sickbay. Meg dashed ahead to the elevator, holding the door open while she waited for Justus and me to catch up.

"I think someone drank a little too much coffee," Justus remarked.

"I think she's adorable," I replied.

"Like *adorable*?" he asked suggestively. "Or just adorable."

"Adorable, like a puppy or a kid sister, even if she is older than me. She reminds me of my sis Sheri when she was nine."

"You do realize as the ship's engineer, all our lives are in her hands?"

"And Leo's," I added. "They haven't killed us yet."

"It's only been three days."

We boarded the elevator, Meg's infectious excitement piercing my otherwise reserved mental state. By the time we stopped on Deck Six, I couldn't wait to see what she had found.

CHAPTER 34

Stepping off the elevator, my attention immediately went to the reactor bolted into the deck a few feet away from the Star of Caprum's empty home. An octopus-like array of thick cables spread out from it in every direction before vanishing beneath the deck. The soft hum emanating from the reactor, along with a series of lights rapid-firing in a sequential pattern around its rim, indicated it was active.

"We're upgrading all of the primary conduits and wiring to handle higher output," Meg said. "You actually had a lot of spare cabling on board, though it wasn't rated as highly as what we wanted, so we separated out the strands and doubled the thickness. That took awhile, but I think it'll be worth it."

"What's the benefit?" I asked.

"Increased durability, especially against disruptor attack. The disruptor overloads the system which causes it to short out and the reactor and computer to reset. It'll be harder to overload this way."

"That's better than I expected," I said. "I thought you wanted to show me something?"

She laughed, her features animated. "I do. This way."

We went around the elevator shaft and through the hatch into the engine room, where the internal part of the main thrusters was visible. Leo sat on top of the left thruster, legs dangling over the side. He waved when he saw me.

"Captain! It's so good to see you mobile again."

"Thank you," I replied.

"Took you long enough to get here, Megaslowpoke."

"Why are you just sitting around?" she shot back. "Did you finish the cabling?"

"I thought we were waiting for the Captain before I did anything else."

She shook her head. "Can you get any more lazy?"

"You know I can, sis."

"Put your light on it so he can see."

"On it."

Leo stood on top of the thruster and activated a light banded around his head. Turning it upward, he illuminated a couple of scratches along the inside of the hull.

"There," Meg said. "What do you think?"

I stared at the mark. "I think one of you was careless and you scraped the inside of the sheet metal with something."

She sighed. "You aren't completely wrong. The only reason we found those was because Prince Leo the Reckless ended up chipping off the paint. But he didn't make the scratches. They were already there."

I did my best to cover up my disappointment at the discovery. "The Acheon used whatever scrap metal they had laying around to put the ship together. It doesn't surprise me that some of it was damaged. They probably painted over it to hide the scratches. I'm not sure what all the excitement is about."

"These aren't ordinary scratches," Meg replied, her frustration obvious. "They're sigil lines, like the ones on your chest."

I looked at the marks more carefully. "Just because there's a line in the metal, it doesn't make it sigiltech. Keep would have told me if he had put sigils on the hull." After saying the words, I realized I wasn't sure I believed them. Keep had kept a lot of things from me until he absolutely had to reveal them. The only reason he'd confessed to Omega Station was because he thought he could turn me into Galaxy Man. Besides, would it really be that much of a stretch? The elevator already worked some kind of unique sigiltech magic that didn't require an archon or a heavy power supply. Maybe that part of the tech remained lost to everyone except my sometimes mentor.

Maybe Meg was on to something.

"Captain," Leo said. "You should come up here and get a closer look. You can't see the whole thing from down there because the engine's in the way."

The steady flow of nutrients through my IV over the last few days had restored a good portion of the glowing vitality to my blood, but I looked to Justus with raised eyebrows as I pointed at the marks with an upturned hand for confirmation that I could exert myself that much. He shrugged. Like he had said, he couldn't judge how I felt well enough to tell me what I was or wasn't ready to do.

Not that I needed the construct to get to the top of the engine. I activated my magboots to scale the hand and footholds indented in the side of the housing, quickly joining Leo. Meg scampered up behind me.

"Look there," Leo said, pointing to the inside of the hull further down. "I already stripped more of the paint off so we could show you."

I followed his finger down the hull, and he dipped his head so the light on his headband made it easier to see.

Unlike with a scratch, the line curved as it neared the base of the deck before disappearing.

"If that's a sigil, it's a big one," I said.

"If that's a scratch, it's an awfully perfect curve," Meg replied. "I think it continues on Deck Five." She flinched when I glared at her in response to the statement. "Captain? What's wrong with Deck Five?"

I shook my head, annoyed with myself for the reaction. "It's okay. There's nothing wrong with it. Alter used to live there, that's all."

"Who's Alter?" Leo asked.

"She came with *Head Case*," I replied with a smile.

"I thought you were against slavery?" Meg replied, stiffening.

"Oh, she wasn't a servant or a slave. The ship was her home before it became a starship. She was an alien called an Aleal."

"A shapeshifter," Justus said.

"A lot more than that," I added.

"What happened to her?" Leo ventured.

"Killed by another Aleal who works for Sedaya."

"Oh, you mean Blorb?" Leo said. "You mentioned him back at the Junket."

"Yeah. I haven't gone to Deck Five since she died."

"I get it," Meg said. "It's okay. We can go check it out."

I shook my head. "No. There's no need. If these lines really are sigils and the hull is actually made of catalyst and not aluminum or tin, there has to be a sigibellum somewhere. I've been everywhere on this ship. If it was here, I would have seen it by now."

"You hadn't seen the etching," Leo said. "Maybe the sigibellum thing is hidden too. What does it look like?"

"A round platform with sigils etched into it, probably connected to the power supply with a pretty thick cable."

"How big is the platform?" Meg asked.

"The one I've seen was about ten feet in diameter. But I imagine it could be either larger or smaller."

"Once we finish with the reactor, maybe we can look for it," Leo suggested. "If we don't find anything, no harm done. If we do?" He smiled. "Maybe the next time that other sigil ship shows up we won't have to run away."

I stared at him. The thought of standing my ground against *Dominator* was incredibly appealing. "Okay, you can look for it, though I don't think you'll find anything. Finish getting the reactor fully online first. I want to be headed toward Melchior by the time I get hungry again."

"I don't think we can get it done in five minutes, Captain," Meg joked.

I grinned. "Smart mouth. Forget the upgrades. Forget the sigils. That's your priority, okay?"

"Aye, Captain," Leo said. "Your wish is our command."

I turned to climb down from the thruster.

"Captain," Meg said. "What about Deck Five?"

I knew she meant *what about giving us access to Deck Five?* For whatever reason, I processed the question with additional meaning. And then it struck me. "It can't be," I said, shaking my head and fighting to hold back a sudden burst of anxious excitement.

"What can't be?" Leo asked.

"The sand!" I cried, jumping off the engine. I *pushed* myself so I didn't land too harshly and sprinted for the elevator, leaving everyone in my dust.

"Sand?" I heard Leo say behind me. "What's that supposed to mean?"

CHAPTER 35

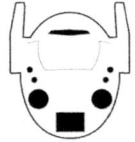

I stepped out of the elevator on Deck Five, heart racing, body shaking as I gazed across Alter's sand pile. Seeing it reminded me so much of her, and I froze in place, suddenly hesitant to disturb it. But why? Was I supposed to turn this entire deck into a shrine for her because she was gone? Leave it off limits and unused from now until what... forever. I knew she wouldn't have wanted that, especially if the sand held more secrets than I had ever guessed.

Perhaps one that could lead to defeating *Dominator* and Lyke. It may even hold the answer to defeating Sedaya and winning the rebellion.

Even so, I still didn't move, continuing to stare at the dune and the assortment of junk sticking out of the beige sea.

If there were a sigibellum buried under there, wouldn't Alter have known it was there? Why wouldn't she have said something? I couldn't believe she would stay quiet just because Keep asked her to do so. Maybe in the beginning, before we had gotten to know one another. But what about at the space dock when the sigils might have better protected us from the candy bomb? Or at any other time after that? She had seen the sigibellum on *Sashkur Starship One*. She knew what it looked like, so there was no excuse for her silence.

Unfortunately, I couldn't ask her. I also couldn't afford to make assumptions. If I did find the sigibellum down there, I would spend the rest of my life wondering why she didn't tell me about it.

But at least I would have a sigibellum, and a sigilship. I could live with that.

I breathed in deeply, activating the construct. Without any fanfare, I pushed against the sand, blowing a swath through it, dislodging anything that wasn't secured to the deck. Like dual sand storms, the sand hit the bulkheads on either side of me, dropping to the deck and piling up there, layer by layer.

A minute passed. And another as I cut the dune in front of me down from nearly six feet at its highest point to eight inches.

Seven inches. Six. The sand in front of me bled away.

Already excited, my excitement grew tenfold when the rounded side of a raised platform came into view, the sand sticking on it before flowing around it and away, revealing the prize I wanted so much to find.

"Jackpot!" I shouted, grinning from ear-to-ear as I ended the *push*. I hurried to the platform, stopping at the edge to examine the surface. The fractal pattern etched into the top matched the sigils I had seen on the *SS1*. Even seeing it, I could still hardly believe it. This was going to change everything.

If it worked.

Instantly nervous again, I stepped onto the platform and moved to the middle. I had seen Keep activate the one on the SS1 by putting his hand on it. I figured I should do the same. Lowering into a crouch, I reached down and placed my hand on the cold metal, closing my eyes as I imagined activating the sigibellum instead of my construct.

Warmth flowed from my chest, through my arm to my palm where a burning sensation and tingling in my fingertips confirmed something was happening. Opening my eyes, I celebrated silently when I saw the etched sigils on the sigibellum were glowing.

"Sedaya," I whispered. "Wherever you are, you are so fuc—"

A sharp crack rattled the deck, the warmth in my hand replaced by ice cold as the sigibellum went dark. The overhead lights flickered out, and the acrid smell of something burning hit my nose.

I started drifting away from the deck, artificial gravity offline as well. Thanks to my iridescent blood, I could still see well enough to navigate. I *pushed* myself toward the elevator, hoping the power would come back before I got there. It didn't.

"Idiot," I said out loud, mad at myself for my carelessness. I already knew using exotic catalyst required a big flow of power, and I had a feeling Keep never actually tested the sigibellum after the Acheon put it in. Of course, the million dollar question was where he had gotten it. From a sigilship, obviously. But how had it wound up on Demitrus? Had some unwitting salvager collected the remnants and delivered it to the junk world, trading the priceless artifact for a song?

Either way, activating the device had overloaded the system and probably knocked everything, including life support, offline. So much for leaving for Melchior within the hour.

I reached the elevator, which was supposed to have its own backup supply. Surprisingly, it was out of commission too. I had to physically pull the doors apart to gain access to the shaft. Looking down, I regretted that David hadn't included the *light* sigil in the construct because I really wanted to see what the shaft looked like when it reached Deck Three. I pictured it like a funnel, the entire cab shrinking as it passed through the sigils to the deck and expanding again when it returned to Four or higher. Fortunately I didn't need the cab and gravity to move up or down the shaft.

As I manually guided myself back to Deck Six, I couldn't help wondering what would happen if someone were to continually loop through the shaft in the same direction, growing smaller by half each time. Mathematically, I knew they would never disappear entirely, but could the power of sigiltech make that person as small as a single atom, or would they implode or something at some stop along the way?

I pulled open the elevator doors on Deck Six, turning my face aside as Leo's headlamp nearly blinded me. He stood in front of me with Meg and Justus, all three maglocked to the deck.

"Captain," Meg said, hands on her hips. "What did you do?"

"I found it," I replied. "The sigibellum. It's on Deck Five." I grimaced. "I might have tried to use it and accidentally blew the circuit."

"You didn't blow the circuit," Leo said. "You reversed the current through it. You're lucky the reactor failsafe kicked in or you would have blown us all to nanodust."

"What?" I said, confused. "I don't know all that much about electricity and wiring, but I'm pretty sure that's not how it's supposed to work."

"It isn't," Meg agreed. "The sigibellum must be booby-trapped or something. Maybe whoever put it there wanted to make sure only they could use it."

I nodded. "Keep would definitely do something like

that." My eyes flipped back and forth between the twins. "If you two know what's broken, why haven't you fixed it yet?"

"We needed to find you to make sure what you did wouldn't happen again," Meg answered.

"That makes sense. As long as I'm not touching the sigibellum, we should be good."

"I think it's better if we go down there to take a look first," Leo said. "At least one of us."

I still didn't really want them on Deck Five, but it was unavoidable at this point. "Okay. This way."

"You should have Asshole make some personal comm devices," Justus said. "It would make situations like this a lot easier to manage."

"My crew and I have comm devices implanted behind our ears. Well, except for Shaq but he was always with one of us. The crew members who created the comms are both dead. Maybe you could cut mine out and we can feed it to Asshole?"

Justus made a face. "I'd rather not. Anyway, if your crew members were smart they probably installed copy protections on the devices."

"Copy protections?"

He laughed. "Yeah. You think in a universe where things can be reassembled atom by atom there aren't safeguards built in so corporations can still make money?"

"I never really thought about it at all. Can we build Star Trek style communicators in an assembler?"

"What's Star Trek?" Leo asked.

"I'll explain it later," I replied. "But it's not that far off from our current reality minus the sigiltech and feudal system, plus communicators and teleporters."

"Sounds silly."

"The assembly rights have long expired on something

simple like that," Justus said. "We can pull instructions off the hypernet."

"In that case, you have a new mission once the power's back up."

"Sure."

"Meg, Leo, follow me."

CHAPTER 36

"Whoa," Leo said as we entered Deck Five. His head lamp swept across the deck, still hazy from the smoke. "Now I understand what you meant when you mentioned sand."

"That's a lot of sand," Meg added. "Why is it here?"

"Alter liked to hide in it when she was resting. It helped her feel safe."

"How did she breathe under there?" Leo questioned.

"She didn't need to breathe," I answered. "She wasn't human, remember?"

"Is that the sigibellum?" Meg said, walking forward ahead of Leo and me.

"Yes," I replied. "Don't ask me how to access the power to it from here. I have no idea."

Reaching the platform, she crouched down, running a hand along the outside. "I think the top comes off and the electronics are underneath." She dug her fingers into a seam I hadn't seen and lifted. Despite the lack of gravity, the lid didn't budge. "Something's holding it down," she said, looking back at me.

"There must be a latch," Leo said, joining his sister at the platform. They ran their hands around it together, feeling for a means to release the etched top of the sigibellum while visually inspecting the deck around it. "I can't find anything."

"Me either," Meg said, straightening up and looking around the room. "This is all kind of strange."

"What do you mean?" I asked.

"There's no view to the outside in here. No transparency. No screens. If you're trying to use sigiltech offensively, for example, how are you supposed to know what to target? It's literally like fighting blind."

I felt like an idiot for the second time in ten minutes. "You're right," I said. "That is strange. I'm sure Keep had a reason or a workaround."

"It doesn't matter if we can't get to the wiring to make sure it's clean," Leo said. "It's too dangerous to use, and nobody here wants to go boom."

"I guess that settles it then," Meg said. "As long as you don't use this thing, we can restore power, finish the install, and get underway."

I stared at the sigibellum. It couldn't be that cut and dry. "Wait a second. This is the tool of an archon. Maybe an archon needs to open it." Of course, an archon wouldn't open the device to look at its wiring before trying to use it. An archon would activate the platform. If the Star of Caprum were still installed there probably wouldn't have been a failsafe to trigger. Maybe I would have inadvertently made us all go boom. The idea sent a shiver down my spine.

"That sounds reasonable," Leo said. "Can you open it, Captain?"

"I can try."

I activated the construct and *pulled* on the lid, gently enough so as not to break it if anything was keeping it anchored down. It didn't surprise me when I met resistance. Something was definitely holding the top of the platform down. *Push* was the most common sigil, the easiest to use and master. If the test was to ensure whoever opened the top of the sigibellum was an archon, then maybe *pushing* on the platform would release it.

Pushing on the top of the sigibellum, I started softly, continually gaining intensity when the lid still refused to budge. It didn't take long before the catalyst that composed the platform began to groan in response to the pressure, threatening to shatter.

"Captain, whatever you're doing, I think you should stop," Leo said.

I didn't acknowledge the comment, adding more power to the sigil, pressing harder into the platform. I could see the center of it beginning to sag and buckle inward, losing its integrity.

"Captain," Meg cried. "Stop."

I didn't. I couldn't. I needed to get inside. I needed to get the sigibellum up and running so I could use it against Sedaya. I couldn't stand the thought of being so close to upgrading *Head Case* and not following through. Turning the ship into a sigilship would change everything.

I pushed harder, the etched fractals beginning to warp.

"Captain!" Meg screamed in warning.

I noticed Leo in my peripheral vision just before he grabbed me by the waist and dragged me to the deck, disrupting my focus. The *push* went with my concentration, and the sigibellum cracked again as the metal snapped back into place. Leo straddled over me, hands on my shoulders as I prepared to shove him off.

"What's wrong with you?" he said. "Are you trying to break it?"

I looked up at him, jogged out of my desperation by the takedown. Tears ran down the sides of my face as everything seemed to hit me all at once. "Damn you, Keep," I sobbed. "Why the hell didn't you tell me about sigils? Why the hell did you die?"

Leo slid off me, crouching beside me, his comforting hand pressing on my shoulder. I rolled away from him and up onto my knees, burying my face in my hands. Meg knelt down on the other side of me. "We're with you, Captain." I felt her hand thread gently into my hair at the back of my head. "We know what it's like to lose someone you care about," she added.

I closed my eyes, fighting to cool my frustration. The twins barely knew me, but they were doing their best to help. "I know you do," I said. Beginning to calm, I raised my head and sat back on my haunches. "If you want to help me..." I looked from one to the other. "...go fix the power and get us fully online. We've burned too much time already."

"Aye, Captain," Meg said. "Are you okay?"

"Yeah, I'm okay."

"You won't try to open it again and blow us all to bits, will you?" Leo asked.

"No. I promise. I just need a few minutes."

"Okay. We'll be just one level over your head. If you need anything, just bang on the overhead." He and Meg stood and headed for the elevator.

Focusing on my breathing, I shoved myself upright. I had already been prepared to make my rescue attempt without the sigibellum. Nothing had changed in that regard. But knowing it was right here and I couldn't use it sucked bigtime. I'd realized fate had it in for me back at Doc Haines' office, but this was next level cruel.

"I'm not letting you beat me," I said. "Do you hear me? You aren't going to beat me! I'm going to Melchior. I'm rescuing my crew and my best friend, and there's nothing you can do about it!" I was screaming by the time I finished, daring the universe to even try to stop me. A little crazy maybe. But it felt pretty damn good.

The lights flicked back on, my legs nearly buckling as gravity returned. I glanced over at the sigibellum, letting out a resigned sigh before returning to the elevator and riding it to Deck Four, headed for the flight deck.

Stearns occupied the pilot's seat when I arrived, taking his turn at the comms. I heard the now-familiar sound effects from *That Darn Cat* all the way from the rear of the flight deck, and when I reached the rebel, he practically jumped out of his skin.

"Captain!" he gasped, fumbling to pause the movie playing on the center console. "I...uh...this just came up when the power returned."

"I bet it did," I replied.

"Do you...uh...do you know what happened? To the power I mean?"

"Yes. We had a short in the reactor failsafe. Everything's fine now. I was just going to wait for Meg to give the go ahead for us to return to hyperspace. You're relieved of comms duty."

He glanced back at the movie, obviously disappointed he wouldn't be able to finish it right now. "Aye, Captain." He hopped to his feet. "I kept the seat warm for you."

"Thank you." I replaced him in the seat, my attention immediately attracted to the flashing comms light on the console.

"That just started flashing," Stearns said, face paling. "I swear."

I hadn't noticed the light on my approach to the pilot station, leaving me inclined to believe him. "Let's just try to pay more attention to the task at hand and less attention to that darn cat, okay? I know he's cute and mildly amusing, but we have work to do."

"Aye, Captain," he repeated. "It won't happen again."

"Dismissed."

Stearns dipped his head in lieu of a salute and left the flight deck. I secured myself in the seat and pulled on the flight helmet. The comms light continued blinking the entire time, though I couldn't begin to guess who it might be. Probably Lyke again, looking for another chance to gloat or threaten me.

Had the light been blinking before I accidentally killed the power? Or was the timing of my arrival on the flight deck just that perfect? I used the helmet's augmented reality system to answer the hail. "Who is this?" I said.

"Ben?"

A sharp chill raced through me at the sound of the caller's voice. "Gia?" I whispered, so shocked I could hardly breathe. "How? You…"

"I'm dead," she said, putting it out there as bluntly as possible. "I know. I must be since I'm self aware."

"Huh? What does that mean? How am I talking to you right now? Or is this really Blorb?"

"It's not Blorb, Ben. I promise. Though I do expect you to kill that slime for what he did to me."

I sat back in my seat, wondering if all of this was a dream. Maybe I was still in sickbay, in a coma from using too much chaos energy. Or maybe I had died back on Omega Station, and I was actually in Hell. "I'm so confused."

"It's not as confusing as you think," Gia said. "Take a few deep breaths and I'll explain."

"Okay," I replied, doing as she said. What did I have to lose?

"Are you ready?" she asked once I had a chance to calm down.

"I think so."

"Gia, the living organism is dead, killed by Blorb on Omega Station while trying to save her friends, including you. She left you a message on the neural link before she died. Did you get it?"

"I got it."

"Good. So you aren't suffering from overwhelming feelings of guilt?"

"No. I probably haven't thought of you as much as I should have, to be honest."

"That's all right. I'm sure you've been busy."

"So if you aren't Gia the living organism, *the* Gia. Then who or what are you?"

"Well, as you know I'm a legend, and legends can never die, right?"

"I'm pretty sure that's meant to be a figure of speech."

"In this case, it's reality. The neural link contained an expanded hidden and encrypted datastore that held a duplicate of all of my memories, which were periodically copied to servers buried deep inside my castle whenever the link had hypernet access. The storage continued up until the moment my heart stopped and I went braindead from blood loss. But when you reactivated the link, not only were the rest of the memories transmitted but the device also recognized the power signature had changed and assumed that meant I was dead. Thus, virtual Gia was born. As Avelus would say, badabing badaboom."

"So you're Meta-Gia now? An AI?" I asked, smiling as everything started making sense again, and grateful that I wasn't in a coma. Or Hell.

"Exactly. I've actually existed for quite some time as organic Gia's understudy, but the complete personality and memory transfer wasn't made until the bell tolled. The same thing would have happened if that assassin had killed me while we were having dinner, although I think that circumstance would have been a little more awkward all the way around."

"But Blorb killed you, which means Sedaya knows

you're dead. He'll know that this you isn't the real you. He'll move to take your planet."

"Which is why we still need to stop him from stealing the Hegemony. Which is why I contacted you, at no small risk to myself. Sedaya has no chance of ever reaching the servers I'm stored on in person, but a well-placed explosive like Archie's candy bomb would probably be enough to take me offline for good."

"You died before Blorb shared that bit of news," I said. "Sedaya already has control over the Hegemony. Blorb ate the Empress before it ate Alter."

"What? Well, that's not what I wanted to hear. You'd better get a move on then, Ben. I'm glad you're still alive, by the way. How *did* you make it out of there?"

I was ready to believe I was talking to a virtual Gia. I wasn't ready to trust her completely. Not until I at least talked to Justus and confirmed what she claimed was even possible with the technology in the Spiral. "That's not important right now. I saw something on the news about you introducing an all new show?"

"Yes. It's going to be totally cotton candy. You should definitely come and see it once you aren't a wanted fugitive."

"If you aren't real, how are you going to perform?"

"You don't need to be real to perform. In fact, the whole theme of the show and my next album is going to be about pushing the boundaries of reality. Organic Gia had to find time to create new music. But I can just build songs by merging the existing catalog with keywords. If that's not the most cotton candy thing ever, I don't know what is."

I could probably think of a few million other things that were better. The last thing the universe needed was an algorithm creating awful music seeded by other awful music.

"You do know Matt and I had convinced you to stop saying cotton candy, right?" I asked.

"Sorry, it's built into the base personality algorithm. She never had a chance to delete it."

"Great. I'm glad you contacted me, really. But considering it was at no small risk, I hope that means you have something I can use. To make it worthwhile for both of us."

"Always right to the point. Respect. Yes, I do have something for you. I know where Matt is."

"So do I. Melchior."

"Who told you that?"

"It doesn't matter."

"Well, you aren't going to like this, but whoever told you that is wrong. Matt and the others aren't on Melchior."

"How do you know?"

"I'm a supercomputer."

"And?"

"And I spent years building an algorithm to track Sedaya's ship movements."

"Except *Dominator* is unregistered and can use sigiltech to transit."

Her moment's hesitation almost gave me a chance to gloat over stumping her. "I see. Well, that explains a lot."

"Like what?"

"Like how *Dominator* is crossing from one system to another so quickly. When a ship like that shows up anywhere there are other eyeballs to see it, people start talking. And Windfall Station isn't the only place it's been spotted. I should have thought of that, but I didn't think it was possible."

"It isn't possible without the Star of Caprum. Which potentially gives *Dominator* a major edge. Has it been seen near Atlas? It would have to go there to drop off Blorb."

"No. I doubt Lyke moved the ship into visual range if Blorb is also the Empress. If Lyke can transit, she might have teleported Blorb back into the palace to avoid suspicion."

"Avoid suspicion? Blorb has masqueraded as Alter for two weeks, while the Empress was where? Just gone?"

"While the Empress was privately mourning the kidnapping of her son. All of her audiences were canceled, remember?"

"You don't think—"

"That they expected us to show up at the palace? No, but I do think they seized the opportunity."

"Let's cut to the chase," I said. "If Matt isn't on Melchior, then where is he and how am I supposed to trust anything you say?"

"You blamed me on Omega Station," she replied. "You didn't trust me then and I still died trying to save you. Do you want to make the same mistake twice?"

"No, but this is important."

"I know how important it is. Blorb killed my parents, remember? Sedaya sent it to murder them. I'm on your side, Ben."

I hesitated, struggling to have faith in anyone after what had happened with Alter and Blorb. But even if this Gia wasn't the real Gia, she was still right. She had been there for me even after I had accused her of betraying us. And even if Blorb had taken her persona, virtual Gia knew about the message on the neural link that the real Gia had composed after the Aleal had already left her for dead. I couldn't guarantee this wasn't another trick, but I had to put my faith somewhere.

"Okay," I decided. "Where to?"

CHAPTER 37

I called an all-hands immediately following the finalized installation of the cold fusion reactor, before making the jump to hyperspace. As usual, I asked everyone on board to gather in the lounge on Deck Three. Unlike my normal MO for all-hands meetings, I arrived first, assembling a half dozen pizzas and some beer for the occasion.

Of course, Ixitat was the first of the crew to enter the lounge, practically sneaking up on me in unintended silence, scaring the crap out of me when I turned and came face-to-chelicerae with her for the second time.

"Crap!" I shouted, jumping back. "Ixitat, I think I need to get you a bell."

"Yesss," she clacked in laughter before shifting in each direction, looking around the room.

"Wherever is most comfortable for you is fine," I said, assuming she was searching for a place to sit. "Can I get you something to eat or drink? I don't know what your species likes."

"Eatsss anythingsss alive," she replied.

"I'm afraid the assembler can't make living things," I

said. "And we don't have any rats on board that I know about."

"Isss okay. I'm fedsss." She moved behind me and settled near the piano, tucking her legs underneath her body.

Kat and the rest of his unit arrived next, all of them sweaty in their workout clothes. "Captain," he said. "Kat Litter reporting."

"Kat Litter?" I laughed. "Is that new?"

Kat smiled back at me. "Since we're informal here, we figured we needed an alternate unit designation under Team Hondo."

"It was my idea," Stearns said.

"We voted on the name," Ki said.

"Yeah, but my idea won."

"I like it," I said, glancing at Narayan, who sported a large bruise on his cheek. "What happened to you?"

"O'Neill didn't pull her kick enough," he replied. "It's nothing."

I looked at O'Neill. "I'm impressed you can kick that high."

"She can go higher," Narayan added.

Kat Litter took up standing positions around the lounge, looking every bit the military unit by standing at parade rest. Meg and Leo filed in next, their coveralls coated in grease and smelling like metal and sweat.

"Nice work on the reactor," I said to them. "Thank you for getting it done."

"You're welcome," Meg said. "Sorry we didn't have a chance to get cleaned up. We were running some extra diagnostics, just to make sure we don't encounter any hiccups."

"Better safe and stinky," Kat said.

"Agreed," I added. "Just don't sit anywhere you'll leave a stain. There's pizza and beer for anyone who wants it."

"Pizza?" Leo said. "What's that?"

"You've never had pizza?" I replied.

He walked over to the boxes and looked down at the pies. "Oh, it's like flatbread."

"It's nothing like flatbread," I replied, shaking my head. "This is so much better. That one's pepperoni. That one's chicken with barbecue sauce. And my personal favorite, garbage pizza. It's got a little bit of everything on it."

"You eat something you call garbage?" Meg asked.

"Don't knock it until you try it."

Leo grabbed a slice of the garbage, sliding it onto his plate and stepping away from the boxes while Meg went over to try the garbage too. Kat and the others took that as their prompt to help themselves too, picking out slices and pouring beers.

"Mmmm," Leo said, having just taken his first bite. "Yeah, this is good."

"It's not better than flatbread," Meg said.

"Yes it is," Leo countered.

"No, it isn't," she argued.

"What? How can you even say that?" He took another huge bite, exaggerating his enjoyment for Meg and drawing laughter from Stearns and Ki.

"Where's Justus," I asked, glancing at the time. Ten minutes late already, when Meg and Leo hadn't even stolen a few minutes to shower and change.

Running footsteps answered my question. "I'm here," Justus said, bounding into the lounge and nearly tripping down the steps. He held a small open box with quarter-sized badges piled inside. "I had Asshole make the badges like you wanted, but then I needed to modify one of them so Ixitat could wear it." He reached into the box, lifting one off the top. It had an elastic band around it which he held up to Ixitat. "You can wrap this around one of your pedipalps. At least, that's the idea."

Ixitat moved forward, lifting one of her forelegs and reaching out for the badge. I watched in fascination as her tarsal claws bent like fingers, pressing together to create enough pressure to hold the badge. Using her other foreleg, she agilely attached it to her left feeler, then used her chelicerae to tap it on and off.

"Worksssss," she said.

"Great," Justus replied. He handed me the next comms badge.

I smiled when I realized it resembled the outline of *Head Case*. "Nice design." A small pin on the back allowed me to stick it to my shirt. Tapping it, I nodded at the activation sound, which reminded me of Star Trek too. "Great work, Justus."

"I think it came out well," he agreed. "I had searched the hypernet archives for the sound. It's identical to the comms on the original colony ship."

"Cool." I tapped it on and off a few more times as Justus circled the lounge, handing out the badges. Once we were all equipped, I moved to the front of the room. "First, I want to thank you all for being here. After what happened to me on Omega Station, I was convinced I would die there alone and forgotten, my friends left in peril, the Hegemony destined to fall to Duke Sedaya's schemes. I managed to survive, in no small part thanks to Duchess Dryka's aid. Justus, Kat, and the rest of the Litter. I'm grateful to you for helping me get this far."

"We're grateful to you for standing up to Sedaya," Justus said. "We had no idea how deep his treachery went. Now that we do, maybe we can convince others to fight back."

"And we've enjoyed training with you, Captain," Kat added. "And being part of your crew."

"You don't need to thank us," Meg said. "Leo and I are grateful to you for getting us away from Windfall. Especially since you were willing to buy out our contracts. I don't know how much you might have spent, but I'm sure Marsh wouldn't have made it cheap."

"I'm glad we ran into each other," I said.

"Thanksss you," Ixitat said. "Freesss. Happyssss." She bowed to me while clacking and chittering.

"Are you going to stay with us a while, then?" I asked. "Because I can drop you off somewhere."

"Stayssss," she answered.

"The reactor is running smoothly," Leo said. "All of the diagnostics look great. Not to sound arrogant, but the upgraded systems are all operating perfectly."

"Does that mean we're headed to Melchior now?" Justus asked.

"We're not going to Melchior," I replied. "That was the next thing on my agenda."

"Not Melchior? I thought you wanted to rescue your crew? Are we going after Prince Hiro first instead?"

"We're still rescuing my crew. But they aren't on Melchior."

"What makes you say that?"

"I had a conversation with a digital version of Gia. It's her virtual self who's preparing a new show on her planet, though I'm still not sure how that's supposed to work. She's also keeping an eye on Sedaya. She told me she tracked *Dominator* to Kirillia, where she believes Matt and the others were transferred to another ship. She wasn't sure where that ship was going, so we need to go to Kirillia to find out."

"A virtual Gia?" Kat said, smiling. "I've heard some of the wealthiest in the Spiral have digital backups of themselves, but those were just rumors. I guess it's true. If there's anyone who should have a virtual backup, it's her."

"You do know Kiriliia is in Sedaya's territory, right?" Justus said.

"I looked at the star map already, yeah," I replied. "That's why I called this meeting. It's going to be dangerous to head anywhere Sedaya already controls. If anyone wants off this ride, this is your chance to speak up."

"We're under orders to stick with you, Captain," Kat said. "And like I just said, we enjoy being part of your crew."

"We're definitely not leaving," Meg said. "Though it feels nice to have a choice in the matter."

"Staysss," Ixitat repeated.

"Thank you all again," I said. "It didn't feel right to me to make a unilateral decision."

"Kirillia," Leo said, looking thoughtful. "That sounds so familiar. Meg, did Katana ever do a hop race from there?"

"Not that I remember," she replied.

"Damn. I know I've heard the planet name somewhere before. More than once." He smacked the side of his head with his palm. "Come on, Leo. What is it?"

"Gia thinks they were put on another ship," Justus said. "Did she have any idea at all where it might be going? Can we definitively rule out Melchior? I mean, that is where Sedaya sends the people he really wants to have a bad time. Maybe the closest transportation was orbiting Kirillia."

"She couldn't rule it out completely," I replied.

"Melchior's nowhere near Kirillia," Kat said. "I don't think it's likely. Besides, if *Dominator* can teleport, then why bother dropping them off anywhere that isn't their final destination?"

"It's risky to use sigiltech to transit somewhere you've never seen," I replied. "Maybe Lyke's never been wherever Sedaya sent them. That's what we need to go to Kirillia to find out."

"Kirillia," Leo said again. "I feel like it's right on the edge of my brain." He looked at the television beside me. "Does that have hypernet access?"

"It does," I replied. "Hold on." I didn't see the remote. Digging into the sides of the couch cushions, I found it without too much effort and passed it to him.

He turned on the CRT. I expected him to search for *Kirillia*, which is what I should have already done. Instead, he ran a search for something called *Kill Spree*.

"What is that?" I asked.

"Entertainment for sickos," Meg said. "Why did you even type that in?"

"Hold on, I'm looking for something." He selected the first result. An informational page similar to Wikipedia, it was all text with an option to have the information read aloud. It seemed kind of primitive at first glance, but the link used some kind of embedded AI to determine the best medium to present the information in for a specific user. Leo scrolled through it quickly, stopping maybe a third of the way down. "There." He ran up to the screen and tapped on it, leaving a greasy smudge. "Sorry," he said, pulling his hand away.

I glanced at the text above the smudge. Apparently, contestants on Kill Spree were famously delivered to a staging area on Kirillia where they would train for a week or two before participating in the game.

"So Kill Spree is what? A game show?"

"A disgusting game show," Meg said. "Produced for the worst part of society. It should be illegal, but somehow Sedaya convinced the Empress to let him keep it."

"Wait, I've heard of that," Justus said. "They collect the most violent criminals they can find and offer them a chance out of their sentence. All they have to do is be the last one standing."

"That's right," Leo said. "The whole thing is broadcast, tracked by drones and edited by AI to put together a compelling stream in real time. They use a virtual host to narrate. Her fans are more rabid than Gia's. Fortunately, she doesn't have nearly as many of them."

"You're right," I said to Meg. "It is disgusting. I assume there's a lot of gambling involved with picking winners."

"And losers, and injuries, and anything else you can think of to bet on," Leo said.

"How do you even know about Kill Spree?" Meg asked, turning to her twin.

His face flushed, body stiffening. "Uh…I…uh…I may have watched it once or twice."

"Seriously?" Meg said. "How could you?"

"I was trying to make friends with Klath. I watched it so I could talk to him about it. He loved it."

"You don't need friends like that, Leo."

"I know. I'm sorry." He shrugged. "I can't unsee it. And it actually came in handy right now."

"If I were Sedaya and I wanted to do bad things to your crew, I'd stick them on Kill Spree," Kat said.

"Me too," I replied, feeling sick. "As much as I hate to admit it. Tell me more about this show. They have a staging area on Kirillia. How does it work?"

"All I know is that they cycle through a group of uninhabited planets whose locations are kept secret. All of the equipment is shipped in with the prisoners. They drop in, dump the contestants at different areas within a ten mile radius of one another, and let nature take its course. The last man standing is picked up, brought back to Kirillia, and presumably set free."

"Last man standing," I repeated. "One winner?"

"Yeah."

"Which means even if Matt, Druck, Quasar and Shaq were to all somehow make it to the end, they would need to fight one another. What happens if they refuse?"

"The drones are armed. The producers can deal with runaways and campers remotely."

"Campers?" Justus asked.

"Contestants who try to hide to wait it out. The drones only allow them four hours of stationary time max."

My fists and jaw clenched, my anger with Sedaya increasing exponentially. Melchior wasn't enough for him. Using my best friend and my crew as slave labor wasn't enough. Instead, he had decided to use them as fodder for some twisted show that shouldn't even exist.

"How can we be sure that's what Sedaya intends to do with your crew?" Meg asked. "It could be a coincidence."

"I doubt it's a coincidence," I said. "But we can hope."

"Captain," Leo said, pointing at the television screen. "I just brought up the promo for the next installment."

I turned my attention to the screen. The woman filling it was unnaturally attractive, her flawless porcelain skin contrasted by thick dark hair, large violet eyes and full red lips, perfect white teeth beaming out at the camera. She wore pink and white military fatigues fitted tight against her slender yet buxom frame, like an anime come to life.

"That's Sprite," Leo said. "The host of Kill Spree." He tapped the controls to play the promo.

"Hello again, Spreedlings," Sprite said, her mannerisms as if she had taken a page out of Gia's playbook. "I'm sure you know, the next edition of Kill Spree launches next week. And what an ultra special edition it is. I don't want to give too much away. Spoiiiiilllerrrrsss! But will share a couple of tasty tidbits to tide you over to the premier. First off, we'll be introducing an all new location. That's right, as of next week we'll be adding an eighth planet to our rotation, and this one is going to be the toughest, most challenging field any of our contestants have ever encountered. I guarantee, if they don't kill one another, the environment will kill them first." Her high-pitch laughter sent shockwaves of anxious anger through me.

"This is bad," I said.

"We have our next batch of contestants in our training facility as we speak, learning the ropes of how best to survive and win on Kill Spree. And I have to say, this group is some of the most experienced and deadly killers in the Spiral, gathered from all over the Quads. We've put together a little preview of some of the personalities we'll be following, but we've got some other surprises lined up you won't want to miss. Of course, you'll have to tune in to get all the action as it unfolds. In the meantime, check out some of the faces you'll be seeing get obliterated."

She was replaced on screen by a shot of a weight room, where a huge, muscular hulk sat at one of the benches, curling hundred pound weights. A scar ran across his cheek, his eye an inhuman red beam. It seemed they had captured Kano from Mortal Kombat.

The frame froze, a stamp dropping on top of the image, followed by text which Sprite read aloud in the background.

COLONEL MOFFAT COIL

Former member of the Silvanian Special Forces. Convicted of murdering his entire platoon after they accused him of raping three of the women under his command. Volunteered to appear on Kill Spree for the fun of it.

FAVORITE WEAPON: Explosives.

That was followed by a rapid-fire clip of Coil in training, beating the crap out of a few of the other contestants and breaking the neck of one during a sparring match and laughing about it afterward.

"Leo, turn that off," Meg said. "It's horrible."

"Wait," I said, trying to look beyond the action to the faces in the crowd, searching for my crew.

The stream switched to a freeze frame of a fit woman in an orange prison jumpsuit.

EMERALD JONES. THE BUTCHER OF MIDAS

A mass murderer with over sixty confirmed victims,

including her very own sister and four of the six Planetary Defense agents sent to apprehend her. A master of weapon improvisation and a former member of the Advanced Research Collective, a highly-regarded think tank dedicated to the advancement of technology in support of the greater human good.

FAVORITE WEAPON: Everything and anything I can get my hands on. And also my hands.

The promo followed the same process, showing clips of her in training. Like before, I scanned the other prisoners around her, searching for Matt or the others without luck.

"Captain," Meg said. "The reactor's ready. We should stop wasting time watching this garbage and get underway."

"Yeah," I replied. "I think you're right. Leo, turn it —wait!"

The video froze again, this time on a black screen. Larger text stamped down top of it.

TOP SECRET: SPECIAL CONTESTANT. FOR YOUR EYES ONLY.

The black screen faded away, Matt's mugshot from Persephon replacing it.

MATTHEW SWANSON. EARTHIAN.

Murdered three law enforcement officers. Escaped from Persephon Penal Station in a murderous rampage along with three others. Convicted of attempted murder of Empress Li'an. Former top ten, Royal Guard's Most Wanted list.

FAVORITE WEAPON: Unknown.

"Shit," I cursed, heart pounding so powerfully it threatened to burst out of my chest as my hardened gaze swept across the others. "We're going to Kirillia. We're going to find out where Kill Spree is being filmed, and we're going to put a stop to it and save my crew. Any questions?" I didn't give any of them time to actually ask anything, suddenly desperate to return to the flight deck and get us into hyperspace.

Leo stopped the stream as I turned toward the hallway and froze, my heart finding a new gear when I realized someone was leaning against the wall in the corridor just outside the lounge.

It couldn't be.

"Hey kid," Keep said, straightening up as the largest grin I'd ever seen on him cut across his face. "Looks like you're planning a rescue. Count me in, with bells on. Badabing badaboom!"

———

Thank you so much for reading Eight Ball! For more information on the next book, please visit mrforbes.com/starshipforsale7.

OTHER BOOKS BY M.R FORBES

**Want more M.R. Forbes? Of course you do!
View my complete catalog here**
mrforbes.com/books
Or on Amazon:
mrforbes.com/amazon

Forgotten (The Forgotten)
mrforbes.com/theforgotten
Complete series box set:
mrforbes.com/theforgottentrilogy

Some things are better off FORGOTTEN.

Sheriff Hayden Duke was born on the Pilgrim, and he expects to die on the Pilgrim, like his father, and his father before him.

That's the way things are on a generation starship centuries from home. He's never questioned it. Never thought about it. And why bother? Access points to the ship's controls are sealed, the systems that guide her automated and out of reach. It isn't perfect, but he has all he needs to be content.

Until a malfunction forces his wife to the edge of the habitable zone to inspect the damage.

Until she contacts him, breathless and terrified, to tell him she found a body, and it doesn't belong to anyone on board.

Until he arrives at the scene and discovers both his wife and the body are gone.

The only clue? A bloody handprint beneath a hatch that hasn't opened in hundreds of years.

Until now.

Earth Unknown (Forgotten Earth)
mrforbes.com/earthunknown

Centurion Space Force pilot Nathan Stacker didn't expect to return home to find his wife dead. He didn't expect the murderer to look just like him, and he definitely didn't expect to be the one to take the blame.

But his wife had control of a powerful secret. A secret that stretches across the light years between two worlds and could lead to the end of both.

Now that secret is in Nathan's hands, and he's about to make the most desperate evasive maneuver of his life -- stealing a starship and setting a course for Earth.

He thinks he'll be safe there.

He's wrong. Very wrong.

Earth is nothing like what he expected. Not even close. What he doesn't know is not only likely to kill him, it's eager to kill him, and even if it doesn't?

The Sheriff will.

Deliverance (Forgotten Colony)
mrforbes.com/deliverance
Complete series box set:

The war is over. Earth is lost. Running is the only option.

It may already be too late.

Caleb is a former Marine Raider and commander of the Vultures, a search and rescue team that's spent the last two years pulling high-value targets out of alien-ravaged cities and shipping them off-world.

When his new orders call for him to join forty-thousand survivors aboard the last starship out, he thinks his days of fighting are over. The Deliverance represents a fresh start and a chance to leave the war behind for good.

Except the war won't be as easy to escape as he thought.

And the colony will need a man like Caleb more than he ever imagined...

Starship Eternal (War Eternal)
mrforbes.com/starshipeternal
Complete series box set:
mrforbes.com/wareternalcomplete

A lost starship...

A dire warning from futures past...

A desperate search for salvation…

Captain Mitchell "Ares" Williams is a Space Marine and the hero of the Battle for Liberty, whose Shot Heard 'Round the Universe saved the planet from a nearly unstoppable war machine. He's handsome, charismatic, and the perfect poster boy to help the military drive enlistment. Pulled from the war and thrown into the spotlight, he's as efficient at charming the media and bedding beautiful celebrities as he was at shooting down enemy starfighters.

After an assassination attempt leaves Mitchell critically wounded, he begins to suffer from strange hallucinations that carry a chilling and oddly familiar warning:

They are coming. Find the Goliath or humankind will be destroyed.

Convinced that the visions are a side-effect of his injuries, he tries to ignore them, only to learn that he may not be as crazy as he thinks. The enemy is real and closer than he imagined, and they'll do whatever it takes to prevent him from rediscovering the centuries lost starship.

Narrowly escaping capture, out of time and out of air, Mitchell lands at the mercy of the Riggers - a ragtag crew of former commandos who patrol the lawless outer reaches of the galaxy. Guided by a captain with a reputation for cold-blooded murder, they're dangerous, immoral, and possibly insane.

They may also be humanity's last hope for survival in a war that has raged beyond eternity.

Man of War (Rebellion)
mrforbes.com/manofwar
Complete series box set:
mrforbes.com/rebellion-web

In the year 2280, an alien fleet attacked the Earth.

Their weapons were unstoppable, their defenses unbreakable.

Our technology was inferior, our militaries overwhelmed.

Only one starship escaped before civilization fell.

Earth was lost.

It was never forgotten.

Fifty-two years have passed.

A message from home has been received.

The time to fight for what is ours has come.

Welcome to the rebellion.

Hell's Rejects (Chaos of the Covenant)

mrforbes.com/hellsrejects

The most powerful starships ever constructed are gone. Thousands are dead. A fleet is in ruins. The attackers are unknown. The orders are clear: *Recover the ships. Bury the bastards who stole them.*

Lieutenant Abigail Cage never expected to find herself in Hell. As a Highly Specialized Operational Combatant, she was one of the most respected Marines in the military. Now she's doing hard labor on the most miserable planet in the universe.

Not for long.

The Earth Republic is looking for the most dangerous individuals it can control. The best of the worst, and Abbey happens to be one of them. The deal is simple: *Bring back the starships, earn your freedom. Try to run, you die.* It's a suicide mission, but she has nothing to lose.

The only problem? There's a new threat in the galaxy. One with a power unlike anything anyone has ever seen. One that's been waiting for this moment for a very, very, long time. And they want Abbey, too.

Be careful what you wish for.

They say Hell hath no fury like a woman scorned. They have no idea.

ABOUT THE AUTHOR

M.R. Forbes is the mind behind a growing number of Amazon best-selling science fiction series. He currently resides with his family and friends on the west cost of the United States, including a cat who thinks she's a dog and a dog who thinks she's a cat.

He maintains a true appreciation for his readers and is always happy to hear from them.

To learn more about M.R. Forbes or just say hello:

Visit my website:
mrforbes.com

Send me an e-mail:
michael@mrforbes.com

Check out my Facebook page:
facebook.com/mrforbes.author

Join my Facebook fan group:
facebook.com/groups/mrforbes

Follow me on Instagram:
instagram.com/mrforbes_author

Find me on Goodreads:
goodreads.com/mrforbes

Follow me on Bookbub:
bookbub.com/authors/m-r-forbes

Printed in Great Britain
by Amazon